Irving Place Editions

Also by John Lauricella

2094 [forthcoming]

The Pornographer's Apprentice [pending]

Home Games: Essays on Baseball Fiction [1999]

Hunting Old Sammie

(The Terrorist Next Door)

a novel by

John Lauricella

Irving Place Editions

This book is published in this format exclusively by
Irving Place Editions.

Copyright © 2013 John Lauricella
All Rights Reserved. Except for brief quotations used for exemplary purposes in critical articles or reviews, no part of this book may be reproduced or used for any purpose whatsoever without written permission from the author, who may be queried on such matters through the publisher of this edition.

An earlier version of the first chapter appeared in *Stone Canoe: A Journal of Arts, Literature, and Social Commentary*, Number 6 (January 2012).

Hunting Old Sammie is a work of fiction. Names, places, incidents, and events not obviously belonging to the historical record are the author's inventions. Characters depicted in the narrative are not intended to represent, either by implication or explicit statement, human beings, living or dead. Words and deeds ascribed to said characters do not purport to be transcriptions from life and should not be construed as direct renderings of actual occurrences. Superficial similarities are convenient only to making what is fictive seem plausible; supposed or perceived resemblances are, in light of everything else, trivial.

Cover photography by Leah Rose
Cover concept and design by John Lauricella
Interior design by John Lauricella

ISBN: 978-0-615-77990-4
ISBN-10: 0615779905
Printed and bound on demand in the United States of America.

Hunting Old Sammie is the first publication of Irving Place Editions.
Suspend Your Disbelief—*Read On!*
www.irvingplaceeditions.com

First Edition
Second Printing, August 2013

This book is for my wife, Risa;

my son, Daniel;

my daughter, Julia:

without you, nothing.

We pause in terror before the human deed:
The cloud of annihilation, the concentration of death,
The cruelly casual way of each to each.
But in the stillness of this hour
We find our way from darkness into light.

>	Rosh Hashanah Morning Service
>	*The Gates of Repentance*

Hunting Old Sammie

Featherbed silence of summer night and still Armand Terranova cannot sleep. Anything can happen. One-and-a-half million tons of plate glass and steel have fallen from a cloudless sky. A windstorm of ash and dust has hurtled through the streets.

Liberty. Greenwich. Albany. Thames.

Armand pictures his house's doors, front, back, and side. He knows the dead-bolts are locked because he has locked them, yet these seem flimsy enough to fail. Ditto the sash latches of the windows. And if they fail and a ruffian enters, a roughneck, a tough, a berserker, a murderer in a mask, only Armand will stand between it and his family.

Tree-broken moonlight throws cold shadows on the walls. He lifts the sheet and swings his legs clear, stands with the delicacy of a man about to attempt the high-wire. Leah craves sleep, loves it better than food or money. Armored in spandex, she lies on her stomach with the sheet at her feet. No nighties anymore, no lacy scanties. It's like sleeping with a triathlete.

Men and women stumbled through the debris fog. Ashed-over, gray as ghosts.

He slips around the bed and out the doorway, turns right into his home office, and from a place only he knows retrieves the key. Slides it into the cylinder and in half a turn unlocks the rack. Armand lifts the gun down. Pumping the mechanism, he feels compressed air fill the chamber. He crosses the landing into his son's bedroom and from its big window surveys sidewalk and street, the sparse yard shaded by an ancient maple, the nightblue sky that seems to hang, billboard-like, between the great tree's branches and the limitless surround of interstellar space under which their home lies naked.

A woman in a business suit—blue? black? pearl gray?—stepped through a window. Her hair flew up as she started to fall, arms spread in empty air a quarter mile above the streets.

Washington. Cortlandt. Vesey. Church.

A cat pads up the driveway, right on cue. A big male with orange-and-white fly-away fur, the oldest, largest, and ugliest of the next-door menagerie. Armand sees it often, knows it well, hates it just-because. It prowls the midnight, no doubt headed for Armand's patio, whose flagstones it and the others smugly foul. There are by Armand's count eleven cats in all, *eleven,* and Armand, despite having considered filing a complaint with Animal Control, has until now done nothing about it.

The window being open, all that remains is to lift the screen. Which he does. The cat pauses. Like a doomed president in an open car, it is exposed on the asphalt. Armand sights down the barrel, imagines yellow eyes in his crosshairs, and holds his breath. He can kill it; steady his hands, evenly squeeze, fire a BB into its brain. Kill it outright or wound it grievously so that his neighbor would have no choice but to have the animal euthanized.

Is Armand willing to start a war over catshit? He asks himself this question with his finger on the trigger. Is he? With two children in the house and his neighbor evidently a man with nothing to lose? A conglomeration of freebooting cats, three mangy dogs. Plenty of potential targets, yes, but what, all together, are they worth? Whereas Armand has everything.

The cat skulks off. Armand knows he has missed his chance. He isn't sharpshooter enough, the gun is not accurate enough, to hit a moving target in the near-dark. He squeezes the trigger and an air-release *pop* sends a BB invisibly into the night. He hears it tick off the asphalt, he can't tell just where. Anyway, the cat is gone.

Armand lowers the screen. He nudges the window down halfway, for the air has cooled. Alessandro is deeply asleep; Armand does not even hear his breathing. He slips from the bedroom and returns the gun to its rack, reaching up to set it on the pegs. He secures the lock and returns the key to its secret small place, then silently descends the stairs.

His next-door neighbor, he does not know the man's name, is more or less Armand's age. Lives with his mother. Has a brown beard, a gray-streaked ponytail, wears a bandana on his head. Collects cats, cultivates a garden. Seems to feel most comfortable in blue jeans, sometimes denim overalls, worn at knees and seat. To Armand, he is Jethro. Guessing, Armand would say Jethro wrecks a scale at 300 pounds. He is not sure what this weight might mean. Perhaps it and the hair and hippie headwear are mere signs of a misfit but even at that, how can Armand know how Jethro might respond when he, a neighbor recently arrived, suggests his cats be donated to the SPCA pending adoption?

Crossing his kitchen, Armand lectures himself on the triviality of catshit. Through the back door's sectioned glass his eyes find the orange-and-white on the patio, now licking its paws, now leaping on the cushions of Leah's awning'd swing and stretching out. How about a saucepan of cold water, a door stealthily opened, a calm approach, a surprise behind his back? That's legal—isn't it? Chasing off a cat with a bolt of cold water? It can't hurt the cat, however much it hates getting wet. And isn't that the point? For the cat to hate it and stay away?

People crawled under cars to shelter from free-falling concrete and plummeting steel. A firefighter, at least one, was killed by a falling man.

Armand doesn't do it. Not that he wouldn't love it. But he isn't sure. The cat might attack him. It has claws, God knows, and once the water is gone, what would Armand have? A saucepan? Could he fend off an angry cat with a saucepan? He is an ordinary guy, an ex-analyst, not an expert of self-defense. And someone might see. You never know who is insomniac and peering from windows. Also, he's weary, having worked all week on the house, not just in the yard but atop the roof, specifically the porch roof, onto which he crept with a six-inch steel blade fixed to a four-foot wooden shaft to scrape emerald-green moss off asphalt shingles. That job took nearly an hour and hit Armand like a workout of sit-ups and knee-bends. Leaning back so as not to fall off the roof, pushing forward to force the blade through leather-tough moss. It grows back, the moss. The maple's huge canopy keeps the roof in perpetual shadow.

The tree is at least a century old. It dwarfs the bungalow, which it would crush if its fall-line happened to go up-slope rather than down. Armand has contemplated the architectural puzzle of a deer blind amid the maple's stout limbs, now fortified by two braided steel cables whose installation cost him three hundred dollars. Not to ambush the starveling deer that infest the surrounding hills and invade residential blocks to devour juniper and hosta and luscious mountain laurel (although now he has thought of it, that's not a bad idea), but to fire a blue dart of low-velocity BB into the brain of every trespassing cat that empties its bowels and bladder on Armand's grounds.

He might scamper upstairs right now and get the gun. A level shot at close range: all he has to do is open the door noiselessly and the cat is as good as plugged. A little blood on the cushions, a yowl to prickle the hair on his forearms and he'd be rid of it. Sure, there are others. But he has to start somewhere.

Actually, for Armand it started with the house. Now it never ends. He expected that a six-month, basement-to-roof renovation, once done, would allow him and Leah and the kids to settle in. Feel at home. Relax. But no. The old driveway had to be ripped out and a new bed excavated and fresh gravel laid, all to the tune of $5500. Then Leah wanted a patio out the back, where the so-called grass was always dying on the so-called lawn. The patio-building process was remarkably similar to the one that installed the driveway (excavation; gravel), and soon they had a flagstone expanse as large as a dance floor. Then the main sewer line had to be rooted-out and the gutters cleaned of leaf-muck, and finally the rotting porch steps had to be demolished and new steps carpentered with twin railings, as per code.

And then Armand began to notice dark brown, almost black fecal pellets on fresh treads of new wood, as well as along the base of his foundation. He heard raucous couplings or sudden fights under his bedroom window, which made his lost sleep ever more elusive. Now the new grass he has been at pains to cultivate in the maple's perfect shade is burned brown by cat urine. Other spots are torn up, gouged and shredded. Injury added to insult: the cats do it on purpose, from the spite of their malicious hearts, as payback for the coyote urine Armand lays along a perimeter to ward them off. It doesn't work, not completely and never for long. Witness the cat on Leah's swing, stretched out for a nap.

Who knew cats liked to dig? The damage they inflict on the grass cannot really be called digging, in the dog sense of the word. It's more like tearing, ripping, rending, as if these punky felines are devouring an antelope in their dreams.

Armand stops watching and turns away. The cat would kill him if it could. He is sure all cats hate him. He hisses them off his porch, his grass, his driveway, the brick path and flagstone patio that all together have cost more than 8Gs, not counting the wooden table and six chairs and matching bench seat and swing-with-awning Leah wanted, plus a large umbrella and its wrought-iron base they agreed they should have. Now cats lounge on the patio as if Armand has laid the stones just for them, in particular that big orange-and-white with its jaundiced eyes and fly-away fur, obviously male, who makes free with Armand's grounds in front of Armand's face, and whom Armand, returning from Ithaca Paint with new brushes and fresh rollers and additional gallons of Benjamin Moore exterior latex, finds lying by the back door as if expecting Armand to let him in.

Not on his life. Not on its life. Not on your life, her life, their lives, all 99 of them. Armand hasn't prematurely retired and moved his family 200 miles north and west to steward the local fauna. He has come here—returned, actually, he and Leah—to escape the crowds and taxes and manic consumption of everything from gasoline to sushi that afflicts people who work too many hours and have too much money and live too close to each other while remaining strangers half-recognized on commuting trains. Fifteen years as a petroleum industry analyst were five years too many, which he toughed-out because the money was too good to give up. A steady paycheck and twice-a-year bonuses added up to much more than he makes investing on his own. But Leah, God love her, has a job that provides in-coming cash and health insurance.

Armand climbs the stairs. Really, he has nothing to be upset about. He should not pay attention to his neighbor's pets. But it is annoying to be beset by catshit when he himself does not own a cat. It seems unnecessary: a simple problem whose solution should also be simple. Except he hasn't found it yet.

On the landing, Armand stands in the low glow of a nightlight and looks at his face in the big mirror bolted to the wall. His life amazes him: how it has changed, how he has changed it. When he was working, Armand felt rich—except that he had to keep working. He would never go back to the grinding hours, the prospectuses and annual reports, all hammered out in boilerplate and more than half, he suspected then and is convinced now, deft spin and bullshit. He is happy not to have to monitor the news, to be free to ignore, say, an oilfield in Saudi Arabia that has fallen below its expected production two years running, or a pipeline in Iraq that has been sabotaged, again. It used to be his bread and butter to know about such events the moment they happened. Now he concerns himself with home maintenance and humdrum chores, native wildlife, other people's domesticated animals. Strange: a man once savvy about currency exchange and interest rates, global trade imbalances, economic "dark matter" and how these interacted to affect the petroleum industry, now cares where a cat takes a piss.

He knows how it happened. Looking into the mirror, Armand can travel back without trying—back to the clement September morning when distant threats came home to roost.

He was at his desk in the mid-town office at 8:46:40 and heard a soft boom. A big, far-off sound that lasted a long time. Screens flickered, consoles lit up. First reports sounded incredible, as if someone were floating an outrageously stupid joke. Then CNN switched live to downtown and minutes later everyone was watching what television could show, or would show, of human figures crowding windows of the North Tower, trapped on upper floors above the stricken segment, from which black smoke roiled; and human figures walking into open sky and falling nine hundred, twelve hundred, thirteen hundred feet to the concrete plaza.

The smoke was dense and black. It poured from blown windows, billowed and spread and seemed each minute to grow more fierce, as if it were a living thing.

Moments later a scream rent the sky and television showed a silver jet sharply banking, aluminum skin strangely dark in the clear morning light. Everyone shouted a second before its wedge-like shape smashed into the South Tower and became an orange-red fireball amid a tremendous explosion of glass and steel.

People reached for cell phones. Networks flooded, connections failed. Land lines tied up. For hours, what felt like hours, communications froze. Television showed the Towers from various angles. Above, helicopters uselessly circled. For the first time in his life, he hopes for the last, Armand saw human beings wholly desperate, purely desperate, desperate unto death. Men and women trapped 100 stories above the streets waved white towels in an appeal no one could answer because no rescue was possible.

Armand knew people who did not get out. Other analysts, colleagues with whom he might check a fact or piece of news in careful conversations, lest a scrap of proprietary intelligence slip loose. On September 11 they became news, part of its awful proximity, and everything changed.

People started looking for exits. Armand dug in and defied them. *I shit down the throats of terrorists* he growled each morning in his then-bathroom mirror, lit much more brightly than the mirror on the second-floor landing of his rebuilt home almost three years later. He meant it, felt it; wished he, forty-plus-year-old Armand Terranova, could strap on body armor and parachute into

Afghanistan and with a rifle and his bare hands bring red, white, and blue, star-spangled payback to Islamic heroes hiding in caves. And when that job was done, hunt down others in their camps and mosques, their shared apartments in Hamburg, safe houses in Karachi, Istanbul, Yemen—and Los Angeles, he soon learned, and San Diego, and Paterson, New Jersey. Never mind that it was beyond his strength, never mind that he had no training. Armand dreamt of catching bin Laden cornered in a cave and killing him like a rat, then bringing his head back to Manhattan on a pike.

In his last six working months Armand played the good soldier. With everyone else, he endured super-sensitized metal detectors and empty-pockets, pat-down searches every day. The markets' downturn he tried to ride out, queasy with doubt. Then they made the break and moved to Ithaca, where the grasping greed isn't close to what afflicts the New York megalopolis, despite college kids roaring uphill and down in silver BMWs and gold SUVs the size of bedrooms. Most of them, Armand knows, come from families that live in places just like the one he and his family have fled.

He blinks and the mirror's images disappear. He turns and, passing though the doorway next to Alessandro's, ghosts into Julietta's bedroom. His daughter sleeps in the same well of unconsciousness into which Leah and Alessandro also fall. Julietta lies on her side, head tilted slightly back and up, as if she has dropped off while staring at the sconce fixed to the lavender wall beside her bed. Armand painted her bedroom himself, as well as Alessandro's (light blue walls, night-blue ceiling; luminous plastic stars ticky-tacked to the inner sky so that Alex can imagine himself in space), as well as his and Leah's own, also the bathrooms and his home office and Leah's office off the new kitchen and the kitchen itself, also the dining and living rooms—in short, every wall and ceiling and inch of trim, and all the doors, too. He and Leah are all-in, they have replaced or remade everything that wasn't the thing they wanted, to the point that Armand cannot look at any wall or ceiling, not even the refinished floors, without thinking of all it took to get it to look as it does, be what it is. The tear-down of cracked plaster ceilings, the installation of sheetrock, the screws that hold the sheetrock in place countersunk and spackled; the taping of seams, the spackling of tape and surface flaws, the patient sanding-smooth and the fine white dust such sanding creates; the sizing and priming; the first coat of paint; the second.

Corkscrew willow. Light cocoa. Mocha cream.

Pulling nails from window trim and filling the holes; extracting screws from the same trim and filling those holes; and sanding, always the sanding: to level excess wood fill, to remove alligator'd paint, to clean a vertical surface neglected forty years. Then the priming. Then the painting. One coat for base, a second for coverage, a third for luster. Leah picked the colors.

Skysail blue. Arizona tan. Autumn wheat. Travertine.

Armand stands at the casement, cranked open a hand's-breadth. Again he hears it from the run-down house next door, an old-lady cackle that explodes in a cough. It is the smoker's hack he hears through his bathroom window, which also faces the Cape Cod. Armand has never seen the mother's face, he does not know the son's name. He is taller than Armand, maybe six feet, but his weight shortens him. He never looks at Armand, never nods, waves, or says hello, as if one of them is invisible.

Tube light strobes behind lace curtains of a ground-floor window. Armand cannot see who stares at television in the heart of night. Likely the old lady, up at all hours, while Jethro retreats to his room with a tube of his own. He lowers the sound. Mother mustn't know. What does he think Mother thinks? A man of thirty-five, forty, it is difficult to tell his age, living with his mother: not a man's life.

Armand checks the upstairs windows. All seem dark. He can't tell if the liquid sheen is soft interior light bleeding through thin shades or a reflection of the milky moon. It troubles him that an unmarried recluse lives next door, in a bedraggled house whose rear windows face his daughter's bedroom, because whoever Jethro is, a sad shy guy whom women turn wordless or something sinister, a man's desire must express itself. Armand has heard repeatedly that the suicide teams were young unmarried men. At a CU symposium on the first anniversary of 9/11, the talking heads made the point again and Armand thought of his neighbor.

Jethro seems to be jobless and seldom to leave his house. He does not bother to walk his dogs, just goads them into the small park across the street or gives them the freedom of Armand's yard. If he seemed normal in any way, Armand would knock on his door and invite him outside for a man-to-man about the difference between a neighbor's lawn and a vacant lot, between curbing your dogs and allowing them to shit on your neighbor's porch steps, about the option of litter boxes in one's cellar to service the excretory needs of one's prowling cats, and *what-say we have those felines fixed, 'ay Jethro?* At this point, Armand does not trust himself to remain civil. Besides, Jethro might come to the door with a shotgun in his fist.

Y'all talkin' 'bout mah cats? What y'all got to say? Huh? Huh?

Let it go. Maybe Jethro is nutso and odds are he's armed. It's only catshit and dogshit, dumb animals pissing new grass to death and not, Armand thinks, looking at his daughter, his baby who is almost seven, a cause for war. Especially not when your daughter's eyelids are electric with dreams, and her dreams are secrets you can never share, and the meaning of her life will unfold so far in the future you cannot live long enough to learn it. Julietta's dark hair is glossy and straight and smells like apples. Armand kneels beside her and holds his head close. Her eyelashes are long and delicately curved in a way people a hundred years ago would have described as buggy whips, a phrase no one uses anymore because no one understands. In this way knowledge is lost. Armand does not use the phrase despite thinking it always when he sees his daughter. Nor does he describe Julietta's tender skin as custard, or her round, dark eyes as pools. He knows everyone has heard it, that no one would listen or care, that they are indifferent to his beloveds and would ridicule the language he uses to cherish them.

He stands at his daughter's window and stares down at his neighbor's shabby house. The world is deadly. Killers conspire in a Michigan mosque, in Dearborn, if Armand is to believe what television tells him, plotting to detonate a dirty bomb on Fifth Avenue at lunch hour, and all he has to protect Julietta and Alessandro and Leah and himself are a shovel and a hammer, a pick-axe bought at a barn sale, a garden spade from the hardware store downtown and chiefly used to remove scat and dung and sundry excrement from the vicinity of his windows. There is the BB-gun, yes, which might serve to chase off shit-happy cats but is less than useless when killers appear.

It galls him, *gall* being another word he does not find much in print and precisely the word Armand believes best describes his mixed feeling of resentment and fear. It is one thing to lie low and hope the enemy misses you in pursuit of larger targets. But when a man gets shit on and shit on and shit on, he cannot help turning fierce.

Standing beside his daughter as she sleeps in the peace of an ordinary night, Armand understands. He cannot attack his neighbor. He doubts a conversation is possible, assumes that broaching the subject will cause an argument, maybe a fistfight. Most galling of all, Armand cannot even superficially wound even one of the cats, which the law protects as well as humans and in some circumstances treats better.

On September 11, human beings fell from extraordinary heights. One, two ... eight, ten, sixty, two hundred—how many jumped? They jumped alone or together, men and women holding hands, holding tightly, all accelerating in awful descent, aware of what was happening to them and about to happen.

Like small bombs, their bodies hit the plaza.

In a quiet way that provokes no response, Armand will fight. He is determined to live the life he has imagined in the house he has bought with the money he has earned. The house he and his family have made their home. A life that does not include shoveling shit.

Soul-lonely days of stay-at-home plant Luke Robideau in Dad's old chair. Watching satellite news via flatscreen, he wonders for the hundredth time how nineteen freaking Saudis got on those planes. Luke doesn't fly, can't stand to, what with the tight seats and bad air and narrow cabin, but he figures someone should have noticed. He's no genius but commonsense says people will try anything, so look out.

He hears Mother in the kitchen, sneaking up on lunch. Drawers slide out and rattle back, plates knock on the table. The refrigerator door, open five minutes while Mother hunts, sucks shut, rubber strip kissing the metal. She's dear to him but Mother's fiddling gets on his nerves. Every day is a task he meets by being mindful of the shocks and surprises, the whole bad ninety miles of never-thoughts and not-enoughs and who-would-have-believeds, the long bereavement of early death.

Luke touches a button and the picture flips. A beef-fed face recites price-to-earnings ratios as quoted in selected quarterly reports. Below the face, a gold-on-red paisley necktie asserts itself against a crisp white shirt. The NASDAQ crawl underscores this portrait, white hieroglyphs on an electric blue ribbon. The face says new housing starts are up and 30-year mortgage rates remain historically low. Consumer confidence is strong.

"News to me," Luke says.

"What's that? I couldn't hear."

"Nothing, Mother," throwing his voice toward the kitchen.

"All right," like a sigh.

He hears sounds of unwrapping. Butcher's paper, aluminum foil, a slipping-free of sheer plastic.

INS knew they were in the country, overstaying their visas. FBI was aware that some of them were living in Florida and learning to pilot major planes. Luke isn't sure if Atta or Jarrah or Shehhi made the TIPOFF list or if the passports they had faked masked their identities better than the beards they no longer wore. Years ago, a CIA analyst had named the method. Suicide terrorists turning passenger jets into guided missiles. Which, Luke figures, does not make the guy clairvoyant—kamikazes did something similar—but does show he was paying attention. Except no one connected the dots. No one imagined a plan that featured nineteen freaking Arabs filling one side of an equation that erased 3000 lives. To Luke it is obvious and mystifying—a paradox after-the-fact commentators repeat and repeat. Leaked intelligence, unsubstantiated claims. Web-spread rumors, details anonymously sourced: Hanjour, al Mihdhar, and Moqed were flagged by CAPPS when they checked in for flight 77. CAPPS picked out Atta in Portland, before he connected to Logan International; his baggage was held off the plane, loaded once he was on board. At Dulles, Mihdhar and Moqed twice tripped metal detectors; they were wanded and waved through. The 9/11 Commission report is due soon. Nineteen days of hearings, testimony from 160 witnesses. Luke plans a cover-to-cover reading and thorough study. To understand that day and the years that led to it. To learn how these people came to hate us.

He considers it his work, his real work. To keep tabs, develop knowledge and insight. Sitting at the flatscreen, ears open, eyes peeled, Luke has curried the equivalent of a Master's degree in multiple disciplines. Bin Laden in 1998: "We believe that the worst thieves in the world today and the worst terrorists are the Americans. Nothing could stop you except perhaps retaliation in kind. We do not have to differentiate between military or civilian. As far as we are concerned, they are all targets." *Game on,* Luke thinks, *and the gloves come off.* Bin Laden in 2002: "It is saddening to tell you that you are the worst civilization witnessed by the history of mankind."

The worst? Really? Well, we make a lot of mistakes.

The Government grants visas to just about anyone, or used to, if they're students, and doesn't, or didn't, bother to track people who go underground. Living in the margins. Luke knows something about that. Buying groceries with traveler's checks. Drawing cash from banks in the United Arab Emirates through ATMs in New Jersey, Las Vegas, Miami FLA. Knowing only each other. Pretending to be what they are not. Then the Prince of Eternal Resentment says *Boo!* and jihadists commandeer jets out of Boston, out of Newark, out of Dulles International in broad daylight. A warm, bright September morning whose clarity became obscene. Luke saw it on television. Not on the flatscreen, which they didn't have; on a 27-inch General Electric they watched for fifteen years, then trashed. Not that it would have looked different. It never could have looked like anything other than what it was. One jet into the North Tower, a second into the South. Maximum spectacle.

It can't happen. He watched the second plane bank sharply, then knife into the column of steel and glass, disappear, become a fireball that filled the space where the plane should be. Smoke stained the sky of lower Manhattan, soot-black, dense, hanging heavily amidst the buildings. Luke, numb in front of the tube, staring, lips moving, thought, *It isn't possible. It's a mistake.* He tried to make sense of volcanic fireball and roiling smoke, the crippled Towers, carnage in the air, mayhem in the streets. Men in white shirts, still wearing ties, women in gray or blue business suits, leapt through broken windows 100 stories above the plaza. Helicopters circled overhead. Luke wondered how FDNY could put the fires out and with another part of his mind understood it could not be done. He knew the Towers would fall, that they would have to, that the ruined sections could not support the sections above; and at the same time resisted this thought, hoped or tried to believe the fires would stop and the calamity end. That the final horror would stay a dream, a haunting.

Nothing so large can fall. Then the letting-go. Nauseous certainty of the irreversible. What no one could halt or change. The top stories slammed down and smashed through and crumbled, beginning a cascade of concrete and steel and, yes, human beings, live persons who quickly and horribly weren't, who couldn't, who never had a chance, crashing out of a sky that two hours before had been so serene and clear and infinitely blue that Luke wondered if it had been made just for them, perfectly for them, the better to rapture their souls to heaven.

8:46:40. 9:03:11. The South Tower collapsed at 9:58:59 and in ten seconds became a tomb inside a mountain of rubble. The North Tower fell at 10:28:25. Two thousand, nine hundred and seventy-three persons died. 2973. Among whom were 343 New York City firefighters; 37 members of the Port Authority Police Department; 23 officers of the NYPD.

Luke knows it all, the numbers, the names. Working the night shift, he has time to learn. Special Reports and Select Committees, exclusive interviews and shoot-from-the-hip talk shows, people in smooth clothes opining, hair freshly clipped. He reads magazines, newspapers, sure, but not tabloids because tabloids purvey fictions to frighten the bejesus out of people, who seem to like a good scare as long as the bearded stranger, eyes lit with martyr's lust, stays in his cave an ocean and a continent away.

Bin Laden: "The Nation of Martyrdom desires death more than you desire life."

The Net trolls up stuff print media ignore. Luke has a serious interest in backdoor scuttlebutt, innuendo, whatever is hinted or implied. He is suspicious of a lot that crosses his screen. Because who put it there, and why? Maybe half of it gets corroborated. Such as the hijackers being mostly Saudi nationals. Hani Hanjour. Satam al Suqami. Majed Moqed. Names impossible to pronounce. Ahmed al Haznawi. The three al Shehris: Luke still hasn't gotten it straight if they were brothers or cousins or members of a tribe, or just born in the same godforsaken village half-buried in the sand. Ditto the al Ghamdis, three of them, too. And a pair of al Hazmis, Nawaf and Salem. Saudis all. And our sitting president and his old man before him, and his thieving brother, too, are cousin-cozy with the House of Saud. Oh, it has come out since, cable news has done exposés and people have written books, but no one seems to care. Luke himself has no special knowledge, primo inside info not being in the habit of walking the streets of dear, dirty Ithaca, and he doesn't really believe George Senior or Dubya or ol' Jeb is truly up to something evil. But what does it mean, all that hand-holding with sheiks in white robes, bejeweled daggers aslant in their sashes? Those shit-eating smiles the Bush Boys wear can't just be about their hobnobbing with a bunch of do-nothing Princes who, if God hadn't been so profligate and perverse as to put an ocean of oil under their otherwise worthless land, would still be living in tents, picking fleas off camels. But there it is. Texas oilmen and Saudi oligarchs look into each other's eyes and see a brother, oil being thicker than blood and a lot more valuable. Suicide bombers? We have an endless supply. U.S. Armed Forces personnel, ditto. Regular Americans, among whom Luke counts himself, wave flags while a couple thousand mothers' sons, likely more by the time it ends, if it ends, die in Iraq. Sons mostly and daughters, too, Luke's lately noticed, nothing being sacred and no one's life of consequence because regular folks are expendable. When push comes to shove, of course we are. Especially now, with millions of hard-working smart Indians and genius Chinese and who knows who else not just willing but eager to do your job for a tenth of your salary. So be grateful you can buy bread and milk and have some cash for that Super Shopper six-pack when you swing by at nine miles per gallon in your fat-ass SUV, yellow ribbon magnet stuck on its tailgate, *Support Our Troops* in fancy type.

An electric buzz lifts Luke's eyes from the flatscreen to the window. Through a cloud of pollen dust and Mother's lace curtain stained amber, he sees his neighbor in face-mask respirator and plastic goggles and insulated earmuffs, standing almost at the top of a ladder that is too short for the purpose, sanding the underside of wood-slat eaves. Luke does not know his name, does not want to know, has never said so much as "Good morning" to the man, who strikes him as charmed by more luck than anyone deserves and ungrateful besides. Something in his face rubs Luke the wrong way. The total effect of pressed-shut lips and notched brow and glaring eyes suggest he is permanently pissed-off. He isn't ethnic, exactly. Luke's neighbor is not black, or rather African-American, as they say at CU, not Chinese or otherwise Asian, not, Luke thinks, Hispanic, although the guy's flesh tone is a couple shades darker than Luke's own. It's the skin, ditto the large nose and middling stature and rolling, peasant's walk that clue Luke to the fact that this guy is not American in the authentic sense of Luke himself.

Luke's ancestors came from famous European countries when the North American continent was pure wilderness, ancient forests and crystal springs, ruled by bear and cougar, which those ancestors fought to the death with knife and musket, or maybe it was a blunderbuss, even as they built houses and cleared land and planted fields with wheat and rye, potatoes and turnips, carrots and rutabaga and spinach and so on, not to mention raising all manner of cows and goats and chickens. Horses to plow and haul and carry. Pigs for bacon. And also laid roads, raised cities, framed government and wrote law. And constructed from granite and marble and white limestone the churches and statehouses and meetings halls that represented their aspirations for this new land, this experiment in democracy, which was to appear to the world as a shining city on a hill. Something like that, if Luke remembers correctly. And signed their names to the Declaration of Independence, which was like signing their own death warrants, should General George and his yeoman army lose the war. For want of a shoe a horse was lost and so forth, and colonial soldiers going shoeless at Valley Forge, then fighting blood-tough and gritty and not quitting and so coming through. And later signed treaties with the Indians, who as it turned out were a bitch to move off land they could not seem to appreciate no longer belonged to them, if it ever had. Hard, bad, rough work, you bet it was, and a lot of solid, God-fearing people died doing it. Of whom Luke Robideau is a descendant, and proud.

Bin Laden: "We call you to Islam. We call you to all of this that you may be freed from that which you have become caught up in; that you may be freed from the deceptive lies that you are a great nation, that your leaders spread amongst you to conceal from you the despicable state you have reached."

Luke knows nothing about his no-account neighbor but he has him pegged: a Johnny-come-lately spawn of feckless peasants who showed up after the hard work was finished and the local wars won and proceeded to connive a living off the fat of the land, taking their ease in the sweat of other people's, real Americans', Luke's ancestors' brows. At the moment he looks like a giant mutant anteater, what with the strap-on respirator and clunky goggles and outsized earmuffs. The sander whirs, rasping off sun-baked paint that explodes into shards. A cloud of fine particulate matter billows from under the eave.

At least he isn't an Arab. That would be too much after what those jelly-eaters did, if a dervish in a turban whirled down on Cooper Circle and did a devil's dance on the old bungalow's worn-out roof, which he, the dervish, plucked from under Luke's nose as boldly as you please. Usurpation. Luke knows all about it, having not only attended the university whose campus begins just five blocks away, but having graduated from it, too. Double-majored in history and political science, which together tell him it is grounds for war, usurpation, so that if a raghead really had moved into the bungalow, Luke would have to do something about it and have his neighbors do the same, although he does not speak to them as a rule, just so the Islamist next door, who is not actually there, is clear about the main point.

One nation, under God. Despite what university malcontents would have you believe, this is still a Christian country.

Bin Laden: "Be aware that you will lose this Crusade Bush began, just like the other previous Crusades in which you were humiliated by the hands of the Mujahideen, fleeing to your home in great silence and disgrace."

Be grateful it isn't that. It's just a Johnny-come-lately with a shark's fin nose and blacked-in eyes and stormy brow, almost simian, Luke thinks, and an annoyingly pretty wife, a blonde if you can believe it, and two noisy kids. Luke has noticed the wife, mostly on hot afternoons when she passes his window in those clingy tops she wears. The children he mainly hears: the little boy, who is older and seems disturbed, being noisier than the smaller girl, who seems to have just finished her first year of school and who looks nothing like her mother while being at the same time a completely beautiful child. Luke notices them every time they open their mouths to scream dialogue parroted from what he guesses are TV cartoons. It isn't as bad as some foreigner snapping up the old lady's bungalow but it is bad enough. Real Americans should have staked their claim. Then Luke would not have to sit in Dad's old chair, eyes straying from flatscreen to window and brain thinking, *You asshole.*

The old lady, he figures, had no choice. What with the bungalow being near-derelict (peeling eaves the least of it), she couldn't pick and choose. Luke knows a thing or two about that house, having done fix-its in trade for no complaints when Rex and Speckles and Barney and the cats visited her yard. Not that there was anything wrong with it, such excretions being organic and the old lady not picnicking or rolling naked in the grass. So dust to dust. But now this Johnny-come-lately lays down stinking cat and dog repellant from a five-gallon plastic drum. Coyote piss, Luke figures, sprayed on the front walk and along the foundation, where he's found turds beneath his windows and nigh upon his porch. Rex and Speckles and Barney and the cats, warned off, wait for rain. They do not, cannot understand that the old lady is gone, salted away in a senior community high on South Hill, and that the old dispensation has ended. After the repellant washes away they go about their business. Luke sees no reason to retrain them and anyway enjoys watching his neighbor stalk straight-backed and fuming to the garage for his spade. He has developed a technique: gentle the tip underneath the shit, shift it, lift it, flip it into the andromeda and rhododendrons and carousel mountain laurel Luke has been at pains to grow. *It's organic!* he wants to shout from the comfort of Dad's old chair, invisible behind the screen. But no, his policy is not to speak to neighbors, not even the blonde whose jelly donuts he's noticed, you bet, because the more you speak the more they know and think they know and the more you start to know them, if you listen back, and the greater the knowing the more likely the impositions, favors asked and granted. Luke does not care to live that way. To each his own, is his motto. And every man for himself.

Cheeky proto-whores undulate on the flatscreen. Luke stares. His guess is these girls had flat stomachs and slim hips before they ever stepped on a treadmill. Tapered legs, asses beyond description or compare. Twin bubbles. Heart-shaped, sort of. Meaning, like a valentine. It is nothing to him. Luke knows no one with such a figure, has no expectation, no hope. To him, every commercial is another taunt about something else he will never have.

Bin Laden: "You are a nation that exploits women like consumer products or advertising tools calling upon consumers to purchase them."

Outside, just beyond the property line, his neighbor is sanding lead dust into his own face. No rocket scientist here, ladies and gentlemen, but give him credit for the goggles and respirator. The bungalow itself, its neglected condition and dire needs, are not his fault. The old lady lived in it forty-eight years and raised four kids who were almost Luke's friends while they were all in school. With her husband teaching English on South Hill, major renovation was not in the cards. Luke helped them hide the cracked ceilings by stapling acoustic tiles to furring strips he first nailed to the plaster. Twenty years ago, it was, about the time Freddie, their idiot eldest son, glued a green plastic carpet, Luke guesses you could call it, to the kitchen floor. The rest they tolerated, then ignored: paint turned to chalk on sun-baked stucco, peeling eaves, heaved walls, a sagging center beam that barely supported bowed floors.

Then the old lady sold out. A month after she decamped, a crew showed up and the Great Demolition began. Knob-and-tube wiring, lead-pipe heating, galvanized steel plumbing, all ripped out with the acoustic tiles and furring strips and walnut veneer paneling and plywood partitions, and piled in the backyard in a reeking tangle of rust and must and fray. The crew tore off the old roof before raising new dormers on both sides the whole length of the house, then laid down fresh plywood covered by an ice and water shield and new architectural shingles whose gray, Luke noticed, watching from his bedroom window, was hued to imitate slate. He kept an eye on the comings and goings, noted dozens of empty boxes set out for recycling, was first surprised and eventually depressed by the early-morning arrival of carpenters for six months, an electrician's van that appeared daily for seven straight weeks, the mason who custom-mixed fresh stucco to cover new walls.

And now, Luke figures, the cash spigot has tapped out and the Johnny-come-lately has to do the painting himself. Which means it will be awhile before the bungalow greets the world with a fresh face. Which means Luke, who has given up trying to keep their Cape in trim, will have many opportunities to watch his neighbor struggle on the dwarf ladder and try to power-wash engrimed stucco while chalked paint flies like yellow confetti into his face and hair. Also the tedious fun of watching him trying to get exterior latex to adhere evenly to rough stucco, always more difficult than anyone thinks. Anyone except Luke, who has done his share as a per diem house-painter.

"But I won't help him," he mumbles at the flatscreen. "No sir. Not even if he paid me."

Satellite news tells him al Qaida thrives. Expelled from Afghanistan, dispersed throughout northern Africa and the Eurasian landmass, it has implanted sleeper cells in every Western country. A shrouded figure speaks from an unknown location inside Pakistan, among unreachable heights of ancient mountains. *Al Qaida depends absolutely on Muslim anger directed toward the United States.* The man is almost invisible; only his black eyes show. The words of his language, so incomprehensible to Luke he does not know even its name, are repeated in English by a translator, not identified. *Without recruits al Qaida cannot exist. Our intent is to fight as holy warriors and die as martyrs. In this respect, the infidel Bush has assisted al Qaida greatly. New recruits have never been more plentiful since the American aggression began. We look forward with great joy to bringing jihad, God willing, to Americans in their homes.*

The tape ends and the shrouded spokesman flashes off. Who knows if it isn't Old Sammie himself?

"Just you try," Luke says. No passel of ragheads, crossed bandoliers on their chests and Kalashnikovs in their fists, is going to do shit to the American citizenry because the American citizenry, as every idiot knows and anyone with half a brain could tell you, is armed. To the teeth. Luke himself has a .44-caliber handgun in addition to a Cold War-vintage shotgun, made right in town at old Ithaca Gun, and a deer rifle with telescopic sight. Plenty of ammo, which he continues to double-stock. Old Boy Scout Luke knows it is a matter of being prepared, and so we have the simple business of a sniper's nest in the attic. To build it was nothing, toil of an afternoon. Sandbags from Agway he filled himself, cardboard boxes for shadow. Luke settles in when spirits move him and from the nest's small window reconnoiters the street, his neighbor's front walk, the side-yard they almost share. For an hour on either side of dawn, rifle at the ready, he waits for the ragheads to bring it on. As a shootist he is almost Marksman-level. The rifle scope makes him lethal from a hundred yards. So is Luke frightened of Islamists massing on Ithaca Commons and swarming up East Hill to lay siege to his hearth and home? He is not. When you come down to it, his asshole neighbor is a bigger threat. Sanding lead dust into the air. An airborne carcinogen that a wrong-way breeze could carry right through Luke's screen, into Luke's home where Luke and his elderly mother could not help but inhale it. Worse than second-hand smoke, which Luke read about on a Web site and afterwards quit smoking and made Mother quit, too. And her having loved her cigs all her life. That wasn't easy. Doing the right thing generally isn't. But it is finished now and they are better off, despite the short-range headaches and extra appetite and trouble with sleep.

"Luke! Lunch's on!"

Which he was going to say, aroma of grilled cheese having crept in from the kitchen. Sliced tomato melted between slabs of yellow American. Whatever Mother cooks Luke smells, wherever he is in the house, even upstairs with the door shut. Nothing to complain about, pervasive food-scent, after so many years it sponges into the walls, and that way he knows when Mother—

"Luke! Come an' get it hot!"

Atmosphere of home. The domestic surround. He pushes himself up from Dad's old chair. The flatscreen he leaves, first running the volume up a dozen hash-marks so they can hear it while they eat. The news repeats itself, or rather the news shows repeat their coverage. That suits Luke fine. He is on the lookout. He is not about to be blindsided as they were in the Towers. Almost three years ago, and Old Sammie is still on the lam in Tora Bora or God knows where. Not on Luke's watch, he wouldn't. Luke would have made Special Ops go in and go in and go in until they dragged that bastard out by his crapulous beard. Summary execution on national television. Hanged, drawn, and quartered. You bet. Three thousand lives. Three thousand human beings who should be alive, who would be living, having their lives in the greatest country God ever invented, now not alive nor living nor having. Gone, lost and gone, gone completely. Obliterated.

It is possible to erase a human presence from the world. It is possible to reduce monuments of the American Way to smoking ruins.

The land of the free. The home of the brave.

How dare they. How dare these no-account ragheads, chronic complainers, history's losers, pretending in their sneaking, puny way to tear down our fabulous civilization. Not if Luke has anything to say about it. He is on the job. His eyes are wide open and his mind is on fire. He is not going to miss a thing.

Asshole.

First morning free of school and Alessandro Terranova, just turned ten, tumbles from blankets at 6:45 and pads over hardwood to his parents' room. Their shut door, the early hour, the fact that his parents are asleep do not stop Alex from pushing inside. He knows only that it is morning, school is out, the sun up, that he himself is up and hungry, bladder tight with pee, mind impatient to be about the business of cartoons and video games, a trip to Pyramid Mall to scout new releases and recent issues, then a burger with fries or pizza if he prefers, followed by a visit to Target to inspect the toys. His father will take him, Alex figures, his mother not having learned to drive. So it's high time dad got out of bed.

He scoots around to his father's side, old floorboards creaking at every step. Half asleep, Armand hears; fights to stay under; hopes Alex will notice, take pity, let him be. But no. Alex has no idea of pity or that a small portion would help his father and so stands at bedside and pokes Armand's shoulder six-seven-eight-nine times, "Dad? Dad? You want to know something? How to defeat the Grievous Troll on level eight? Dad? Come on, I want you to listen." Armand does not want to listen. He loves his son but does not want to hear, to know, to think. Not now. He wants to be unconscious, at peace and ease. Alessandro is merciless. "Dad, you know what? You empty the gasoline from the tanks on your hydrofoil into the Black Moat then hold the diamond shard so the sun shines through it onto the Map of Lost Oracles, then when the Map catches fire you throw it into the moat and you know what happens? Whooosh! Crispy deep-fried Troll. It's so cool, c'mon, you have to see."

Still in fingertip contact with sleep, Armand cannot quite make out what his son is saying, its significance to life in this world. Process: his brain cannot process Alex's report, does not want to. Won't, not before coffee. Refuses. He mumbles, "That's great, Alex. Go back to bed."

"I'm hungry, I want breakfast, I want to play *Fiends of Sodom*. But first I gotta pee!"

Alessandro darts around the bed and into his parents' bathroom. The floor complains loudly and now Armand can't deny it: he's awake. Leah stirs, too. When Alex flings up the toilet seat and looses a torrent of held-in urine, she sits up and says, "Goddamnit."

It is her favorite word these days. She says it more and more, Armand has noticed, not exactly blaming her, what with Alex's rapid-fire verbal assaults and faraway-fantasy strafings. Yet somehow, he feels scolded, as if that and this and everything else were his fault. Leah seems to think so; to think that his efforts to smooth things over are nothing compared to all that wrinkles the fabric of existence. Armand believes she shouldn't mind so much. *Aplomb* is the word he's reaching for, although no one uses it these days. Sure, it's irritating to be jolted from sleep by the plastic crack of a toilet lid and a stream of blasted pee, but look, Armand figures, on the bright side. Such as, it wasn't a bomb that woke her. It wasn't an air-strike or mortar round or small-arms fire, as it might have been were they living in, say, Iraq or, more plausibly, Israel—in the Occupied Territories, let's imagine, because what would a forty-year-old American Jewish woman with a flair for clothes be doing in Iraq at the present time, or ever?

Leah picks up the digital clock and holds its glowing display close to her myopic eyes. "God*damn*it," and sets the clock down as if she means to embed it in her nightstand's walnut top.

Armand, lying on his back, eyes closed, hopes she will roll toward him and touch him, yes, *there*. It's futile, with Alex in the bathroom and any second out, and would be even if the boy were still asleep or he and his sister were out of the house entirely, although God only knows where in that case they would be. It is obvious to Armand that Leah liked him more before they had kids, and even that is almost nothing compared to how she liked him before they were married. He is absolutely certain, despite having done nothing so crass as keep count, that they had sex more often when he worked on Wall Street and they lived in Westchester—in Ossining, as a matter of embarrassing fact, which Armand was sure never to mention around brokers and salesmen. These men pulled down millions and lived in Bronxville mansions, on Scarsdale estates, in Park Avenue penthouses with private elevators opening on marble foyers. Had they known that Armand, scraping along on 300K, was living in a 3-2 A-frame on the edge of a slum in a town with a prison, they might have had him fired.

Alessandro lets the toilet seat drop, flushes, hoists his pajama bottoms, and bounds into the bedroom. He clambers onto the bed, heedless of where he plants hands and feet, careless of the fleshy places his knees and elbows poke. Leah curls up, arms covering her head. "Alex, be careful!" she cries as the giggling boy launches himself at his father. He lands on Armand's chest, "Daadee!" half-mimicking some cartoon and partially in pursuit, Armand is sure, of the next thing he must have. Right now. Because without it he cannot live.

"God, Alex, you're heavy," Armand says, breath knocked half out of him. His eyes are still closed "When did you get so big?"

"It's getting-up time," Alessandro declares. "Today is the day."

"What day?"

"The release date."

"What are we talking about?"

"*Daa*-add. The new XBOX game. *Hunting Old Sammie.*"

Armand opens his eyes. He looks at his son looking at him. The boy's eyes are only inches away. "You're kidding."

"It's the newest best game. You hunt down terrorists and kill them." Lifting his voice, *"Deploy teams of Black Berets into the ancient mountains of Tora Bora. Track implacable terrorists to their cavernous lairs. Rain withering fire down on the homicidal masterminds who planned the horror of September eleven, two-thousand-and-one.'"* The kid's memory is canny.

Armand lifts Alex off his chest and sits up. "Who invented it?"

"I'm telling you, dad. It's an XBOX game."

"We can get it today?"

"No," Leah says. "Absolutely not. The last thing he needs is another violent video game."

"Mahhuum!"

"How bad can it be?" says Armand.

"How would you know? A minute ago you hadn't heard of it."

"And you had?"

"I saw a promo. Helicopter gunships with giant machine guns. Soldiers with flamethrowers, turning bearded men into candles."

"Sounds great."

"Armand, really. How old are you?"

"I don't see what my age has to do with it."

"Dad, it's totally cool. 'Uncover mountain strongholds with thermal imaging technology. Call in air-strikes by F-16s. Destroy terrorist cells with laser weaponry. Wage pitched battles against mujahideen. Capture bin Laden alive or kill him on the spot. March down Fifth Avenue with jihadists' heads on pikes. Make the world safe for democracy.'"

Safe for Dick Cheney's profits, Armand thinks, knowing all about it from his former life, but says nothing. It's pretty much impossible to explain the complexity of how things work within the greater systemic dysfunction. Instead, he asks the one question that matters.

"How much does it cost?"

Alessandro's mouth minces sideways. He holds up fingers, then realizes he needs more than two hands.

Armand can see the kid doesn't want to say. "C'mon. 'Fess up."

Alex sighs. "A one with two zeros."

"One hundred dollars."

Alex's eyes slide away. Rapid nods, face averted. "Yeah."

"For a video game, Alex."

"Yhep."

"No way."

"*Daa*-add! It's the greatest game ever!" The boy is beginning to whine.

"Don't whine," Armand tells him.

"On TV it's awesome. The army guys are flaming a cave and when the terror guys try to escape, they shoot them."

"Neat."

"Their turbans are on fire."

"Even better."

"Armand," Leah says.

"Dad," says Alessandro.

He will not admit it but Armand is hooked. It would be deeply satisfying in the second-most intimate way imaginable to kill al Qaida terrorists holed up along the Afghanistan-Pakistan border—something the actual U.S. military cannot or will not completely do. But a hundred bucks. It isn't really the money, although living on interest income Armand has become more frugal. He can boost the C-note but what message would it send? Hunting virtual terrorists in cyberspace is all well and good. But plunking down $100 for a toy seems irresponsible and possibly wrong in a country where tens of thousands are homeless and millions have no health insurance and children continue, incredibly, to go hungry. Fifty million Americans live in poverty and he's looking to play games.

The thing is, Armand doesn't know people who are poor. He has always lived in a place where everyone has a house and no one suffers from treatable illness, much less dies, and all the little children and the big ones, too, have clothes and food and parents. He and Leah are aware, they read the papers and watch the news, they know people are destitute, billions of people all over the world, and that their lives are skimpy and dangerous, and they are hungry and cold or wet or too hot and terribly, terribly thirsty; that the land around them is dying, is nothing but sand and rock and flimsy tents, or is flooded by surging rivers and awash in fecal waste, or is poisoned or sanctioned or landmined or bombed; and that the human beings shunted to such places own nothing except their bodies and sometimes not even that, and have nothing to enjoy or love, not even dreams, and can care for nothing except the food they do not have and cannot get, and that their days are meaningless, their hours worthless, and they themselves are doomed, doomed. Alessandro, just turned ten, and Julietta, six-going-on-seven and currently asleep, have no clue.

Alex studies him, brown eyes brimful of hope.

"Let's think about it," Armand says. "A hundred dollars is a lot for a toy."

"It's not a toy, it's a game. The coolest game in the history of the world."

"It'll still be cool a year from now when they halve the price."

"By then they'll all be gone."

Armand laughs. "Nothing is ever really all gone, Alex. If they sell out, they'll make more."

Alex frowns. "What if it's a limited edition?"

"Limited to, oh, a billion copies? Alex, trust me: you have nothing to worry about. Worse case scenario is we have to wait until kids get bored and start trading-in. Then we buy a pre-owned copy for twenty bucks."

Armand knows he's right. He has analyzed market dynamics in economic structures large and small. What gives him pause is randomness: irruptions of chance, error, luck, the unpredictable and serendipitous. These cause slippage in the otherwise-dependable meshing of supply and demand. The problem shapes itself as a question as simple as it is hypothetical: Will anyone care about hunting a virtual bin Laden after the real one is finally caught? Patriotic ire, to say nothing of blood-lust, is a queer duck. The cyberdesigners responsible for *Hunting Osama* seem to expect continuing futility in the search for the terrorist chieftain. And if Armand buys the game before U.S. Special Forces, Black Berets or Navy SEALS or Army Rangers or whoever they turn out to be, snare Old Sammie, is he rooting for the wrong side?

"No," Leah says again. Half her face is pressed into her pillow. "No more violent video games."

"But mom, all video games are violent."

"No more video games, then. Go outside and play baseball."

"Baseball?" Alessandro makes a face.

"Or read a book."

"Ooowwww! I hate reading books! I hate stupid boring baseball! You know I'm no good at sports."

Yes. Armand has shied whiffle balls at Alex that the boy has flailed at and widely missed, not even a loud foul, over and over. It surprises him, this absence of hand-eye coordination. Armand himself is, or rather was, a minor athlete. Nothing serious, not close to scholarship material, but able to hit behind the runner or turn on an inside fastball and rifle it down the line, none of which means a thing to Alessandro or Julietta, and of course Leah cannot be expected to know or care. It's ironic, he thinks, although maybe not; he hasn't played baseball since before they met. After he dies, hopefully not sooner than sixty or seventy, let's say seventy-five years from now, his family will find the scrapbooks and read his schoolboy baseball clippings. They will realize he wasn't just a dad his whole life, or a sloppy amateur house-painter and all-thumbs repairman, following his stint in the vineyards of high finance.

A flash: these thoughts flash and vanish. Leah flounces out of bed with a sigh and a grimace. Seven a.m. and already exasperated.

Start of another day.

B rilliant sunshine of summer morning reminds Leah Goldman of the state of her dismay. Here she is walking toward another paycheck while her husband continues his vanishing act. Armand wears rags, takes forever to paint a radiator, a window frame, a bit of trim. He lives off investments, makes no effort, shows no interest, and (despite disappearing) is getting fat.

Leah herself is peaking. Just forty and twice a mother, she is in the best shape of her life. Her health is good, her shoes are new, her shoulder-length hair, color of sandalwood, is flipped under just so. Her polysilk eggshell blouse and linen skirt, its blue a match for the limitless sky, show her figure, which draws looks wherever she goes. Heads incline, eyes smile. Conversations, such as they are, pause. Leah sees them looking and smiles back, guessing it is a matter of time.

Turning a corner in Collegetown, she spills out her go-mug. Coffee streams in a twisted black ribbon into a sewer. Armand's homebrew nauseates her. The coffee bar is dimly lit and at eight o'clock almost empty. Leah has the barista fill her up with Kona, to which she adds a splash of cream. Sugar she forgoes. She can't taste the first sip, Armand's diesel roast having sent her tongue into shock, and anyway the Kona is too hot. While it cools Leah walks, dialing up the music in her ears. She follows a footpath that runs through a tunnel of oaks. Beneath the trees the air is cool. Leah stops; sips; is careful not to dribble onto her blouse. How would it look if the Dean wandered in and she was wearing stains? What would Max think if he dropped by to suggest lunch? Not that Max is snappy in his washed-up cotton and grimy pants. But a man wants the woman he's with, even just a friend, to look good.

Across the footbridge she goes, cataract rushing in the gorge two hundred feet beneath her. Leah crosses into sunlight and climbs a flight of concrete steps to the Engineering Quad. *Boogie Oogie Oogie* lifts her almost dancing up the stairs. From the Quad she can see her office window recessed amongst the red and black bricks of Sage Hall. To Leah it is just alumni affairs but by most measures her job is one of the best on campus. In Manhattan her salary would buy next-to-nothing but in Ithaca it covers them. Best of all, she is freed from full-time mommyhood.

The air is warm and Main Campus desolate on this cloudless morning of late June. Classes are in recess, the students are gone, Reunion is done. There is nothing to worry about, no upcoming events or alumni visits, nothing at all. Still, Leah frets. Her brow tightens as she checks her watch, wondering who might be keeping tabs, how much they notice, whether they care. It is eight-fifteen; she isn't close to being late—whatever that might mean for someone on salary rather than the clock. Can she relax? Well, she can try. And so she bends her steps toward the patio of the Statler Hotel, where she can sit in a teak chair at a table shaded by an umbrella and, given twenty minutes alone, enjoy her coffee.

Leah on the loose. *Got to Give It Up* on her iPod. A touch of perspiration on her neck and the top of her chest. Crossing the Engineering Quad, she realizes working makes her happy. Her job is not the most interesting proposition in the history of creative thought and colleagues often frustrate her, but all in all she likes it. Having an office to go to, people to see, conversations to initiate and follow-up, contacts to make, plans to put in play. All the email she has to answer isn't the best fun but that can't be helped. When she thinks about it, Leah sees it is satisfying to be able to give people what they need.

One thing is certain: she likes it better than mothering. Spooning out puréed peas, changing crapped diapers, laundering puke-crusted bibs and onesies. It was making her stupid. Very gratifying, yes of course, to love her babies and see them grow. *How big is the baby? Soooo big!* But Leah felt she was wasting herself. It did not seem to matter because of Armand, his job, the money it brought in. Except it did matter. But nothing might have changed if the planes had not gone into the Towers.

Leah stands on the corner and waits for the light. There's no traffic, she could cross against the red except Campus Security has a way of appearing from nowhere to write zealous tickets. The air smells fresh, sweetly-scented, what with a light breeze and flowering trees, until a **TCAT** swings by. Leah covers her mouth and nose and hurries across on the green. Veering to avoid bus fumes, she thinks, *Forget it,* and heads directly to Sage. She enters through the front door, climbs two flights, and strides toward her office over a tightly-woven carpet the color of wheat. She turns off the iPod, removes the earphones and shoves the works into her bag. The lights are bright, the air-conditioning frigid. Everything smells clean. Surfaces that are meant to shine, shine. Lacquered woodwork and latex'd walls are spotless. Things are good. Life is. It is working out, their escape from the rat-race and relocation to this college town. They rebuilt an old house, she has her job, their kids are in school. Only Armand struggles. It isn't good for him, this business of staying home with chores and errands. A business of no-business, of not doing business. Because what is he? Instead of an answer, Leah thinks of a blank.

It isn't just about money, although she wishes he were bringing some in. It's that Armand-Jobless is pretty dull. While she wakes early for a video-guided aerobics and tri-cord workout, Armand snoozes. Leah walks the half-mile from their house to Sage Hall, works eight hours and walks the half-mile home, and Armand—does what? Drifts. Putters. He has been painting the house for two months and isn't half-done, which means he does not paint every day. It isn't possible; no one could be that slow. And let's see: he complains: about grass that dies soon after it germinates; about the plastic, glass, and cardboard he carries in bins from the shady side of the bungalow to the front curb; about the damp basement and groundwater seepage through rotting concrete; about the dust that covers their floors, the dirt and *schmutz* and gummy smears that mar the kitchen hardwood, kids' grimy fingerprints on new walls. Also about traffic on Route 13; the weather in every season; the crowds at Wymans, where housewives kibitz at the deli counter and chew samples without moving their carts, solely for the purpose of pissing him off. Ditto cackling bluehairs slower than hour hands who won't yield right-of-way.

Leah unlocks her door and pushes inside. She sets the doorstop with her foot as a photoelectric motion detector switches on the overhead lights. It isn't just about energy-saving, Leah suspects, the detector. Well, here she is, at her desk, fit and ready, alert, on-the-job. She sets down the go-mug and on her keyboard taps a key. Her monitor wakes up and Leah scans her screen. Maximized, her email window reveals the top twenty of eighty new messages.

She does not understand it. All Armand has to do is walk string-straight aisles of linoleum polished as smooth as glass and snap up packages of pasta, cans of crushed tomatoes, some chicken, some fish, napkins when needed and so on, from shelves on which all good things are displayed, and place them in a cart, which, let's not forget, has wheels; then stand on line a few minutes, ogling the cover girls while the checker scans bar codes and puts everything, flank steak and red potatoes, organic peanut butter and milk and whole wheat bread, into reusable canvas bags. Which have handles. And set the bags, now loaded with food that keeps them alive, into the cart again, so that all Armand has to do, after swiping their AmEx Gold Card through the touch-screen/scanner and signing his name with the electro-sensor pen, is push the cart out of the store and across the parking lot to the car, pop the easy-lift hatch and transfer the bags from cart to car, shut the hatch, return the cart, get into the car, turn the key, start the engine, and drive, drive, drive, all the way home. Where, yes, he has to carry the groceries from driveway to door. If it's raining, yes, he gets wet, they do not have an attached garage, the house is antique and the neighborhood old, both built before people had cars and even today, *even in America,* as Armand himself likes to remind her, *you can't have everything.* Because there are limits, despite what people like to think. But come on. Once the bags are in the kitchen all Armand has to do is unload and stow the food. Boxed and canned and packaged non-perishables in the pantry, which is just inside their back entrance (and how convenient is that?), milk, etc., in the fridge. Is this a problem? Is this a strain? The way he carries on, the big baby, anyone would think she was telling him to hunt dinner with a bow and arrow after plowing the north forty behind an ox.

    Leah scrolls. Most of her email comes from alumni, who ding her day and night. Events in distant cities. Personal visits at their offices or at home. *When-is-this? Who-is-that? Why-aren't-you-doing-this-other?* Some email is from staff, her nominal colleagues. Leah reads these last, having learned they are often needless. A handful of messages kite in from faculty. Her computer chimes and a fresh message pops up with Lunch today in the Subject line. In the window below, Max has typed, The usual? ME.

Leah clicks Reply. *Carriage House @ 12:30. See you. -L* ☺. The fancy font is her latest grace note. She clicks Send.

Max, known to the students at Sage Hall as Professor Obermann, is thirty-two, married with a young daughter and a baby pending. A year from the end of his appointment, Max is unlikely to win tenure. The problem has been his reluctance to commit to paper his insights on the science of marketing in a global economy. Leah knows all about it because Max tells her. He isn't a writer, he says; has never claimed to be; does not want to be; is not interested. He is a professor of marketing economics. Why do they insist he write? Well, he knows why; it's the academic gig. Publish or perish. So he and Rachel and Rebecca and the new baby, when it comes, are likely to be packing house and leaving town to start over, maybe at another university, maybe in private industry. Consulting, even, although he is short on credentials for that. To all of which Leah nods, thinking less of Max, who at these moments is right in front of her and talking, talking, and more of her husband, who had a job Max might kill for. Which he, Armand, quit.

Less interesting. Piggy goes to market, piggy comes home. Piggy paints the house, cuts the grass, vacuums carpets, dusts shelves, mops floors. In summer grills steak. In winter waits for her to get home and, as she is walking through the door, asks, "What are we having for dinner?"

Leah works. Despite Armand's economies, they need steady income. There are dividends, there is interest on investment, there are Treasury Notes, Precious Metals Funds, Exchange-Traded

Funds, Bond Funds, Index Funds. For the optimists in our audience, there is Social Security. To Leah it is crazy to rely on financial instruments whose payouts are suppositional at best. Money: what you cannot afford to take on faith. If oil soars and the dollar tanks, where will they be? Where will anyone be? Fifty million jobs, hers included, might disappear. Precious Metals and 30-Year Treasuries will be all they'll have, the latter just about worthless. And owning stock in gold mining companies is not the same as owing gold. And if they did own gold, how would they convert a shiny Double Eagle worth 35,000 of the old dollars into bread?

She tells herself it can't happen. *Cannot.* She is worrying about nothing. It is America, not some dodgy Third World jerkwater with illiterate natives and toilet-paper currency. The United States. We won the war, we lead the world. Never in human history have so many people been so prosperous, owned so much, lived without fear of hunger or scarcity. And why? Because we work. Hard. We earn. As Leah does, every day. As Armand used to.

She answers email, fields a dozen calls, and when she looks up sees it is quarter-past twelve. She'll have to hustle. Max might be late, anyway, afflicted as he is with the time-blindness of an academician in summer. It is quite a gig, being faculty: a six-figure salary and three months paid, plus term breaks, a travel budget for conferences, regular sabbaticals and what have you. Leah wishes she had thought of it. If she had known how plummy it could be, she would have made it her business to cobble together some research and if she had placed three or four articles, who knows? She might be the one in line for tenure, knocking down $170,000 a year to teach a few classes and grade multiple-choice tests, plus a tidy consulting practice on the side.

As it is she's mired in alumni affairs for a measly 70Gs. And Armand earns nothing.

Before she leaves Leah starts her screensaver. She knows she is supposed to put the computer to sleep or shut it down, CU official policy being to Go Green and employees encouraged to conserve, but the rigmarole of waking up and logging-in gets in the way—is a *rigor on morale,* she realizes just this second. The image is a white-sand beach somewhere in the south Pacific, Tahiti or Fiji or the Maldives or Marquesas, maybe Polynesia, and a single palm tree, its trunk looking both rigid and a-sway—like a penis, Leah cannot help thinking—as it extends toward a cloudless, sapphire sky.

When you have just ten minutes, the walk to Carriage House is brisk. Leah hurries as well as she can, heels clicking on concrete, headed downhill, *Tell Me Something Good* in her ears. Running is not an option. It isn't just the heels. Her bra, a lacy pink thing to match her panties, does not provide sports-support and the jostling hurts.

The restaurant has, indeed, been built inside an old carriage house. Leah has always found its décor of manual typewriters and wrought-iron, glass-topped tables a bit befuddling. The overall look is heavy-beamed and sort of polished-rustic, as if a farm outbuilding has been gentrified. Oddest of all is the black baby grand piano standing on a platform in the center of the room. As far as Leah knows, no one plays it. The line is a dozen long when she arrives and most of the tables are taken. Luckily, Max is third and knows what he wants, Leah knows, because they always get the same thing. She sidles to him around close-set tables, careful not to bump, conscious of her hips, of the skirt that hugs them. Max sees her coming and smiles. Leah, too, is smiling. It is her signature trait, a big, open, bright smile that makes anyone who receives it feel loved.

When she gets close enough to say, "I made it," as if she has jetted over on short notice from France, Max says, "Hello," and leans in and kisses her. On the cheek. Friendly, it does not have to mean anything. Except he has never done it before.

They order personal pizzas, one apiece, and claim a table. Max repositions the alphabetical placard that the waitress will use to link them to their food. The black plastic 6x8 rectangle bears the letter "b" in typewriter font.

"'Beauty,'" Max says, reading the definition of the word under the letter, "'a formal quality, either sensual or apprehended, the perception of which is specially pleasing for reasons that are often ineffable and generally vary with the beholder; a person or thing possessing this quality.'" He has never done that before, either, read the placard aloud, although Leah has noticed him looking.

"Who made that up, I wonder?" she says.

"Cribbed," says Max. "Sounds like the *OED*. No one who works here could've come up with it."

Leah looks at him as she looks at her children, mainly Alex, when they are insisting on an especially obnoxious lie. "Max. How can you say such a thing?"

He laughs. "Are you kidding? Look around. Take notes. Test on Friday."

He is very certain, Max is, about what he thinks and knows, which in his own estimation is everything. Leah finds it trying; Armand, she realizes, is much the same. That is not, however, why Max seems familiar and certainly does not account for their getting along as if they have known each other since childhood. It is, Leah believes, the shared heritage of being Jewish. Well, almost shared: Max is descended of German Jews and retains their sense, evidently inborn, of being superior not only to other Jews but to everyone. Leah also is Ashkenazi but her antecedents are Russian,

Polish, Lithuanian, and Austrian—a mixture that, when she recited it, put a crimp in Max's brow and a sniffle in his nose—something he learned from his parents, she guesses.

Leah and Max have been lunching together at least once a week for two years. Leah knows their professional relationship, which includes Max's giving Faculty Talks to alumni about marketing theory, became personal long ago. But Max is married and knows she is, too, and has a daughter who is three and a baby on the way. Max is younger than Leah, although his hair, drought-brown and thin enough for his scalp to show on those rare occasions when he drops his head, makes him look her age. His wife, younger than Leah by ten years, also is Jewish. Leah has decided she dislikes Rachel, but that's another story

And Armand? Well, Armand is not a Jew. Does not pretend to be, has never mentioned converting. It used to bother Leah, his non-Jewishness, but she set it aside because he was not seriously religious in any organized way. His having been born and raised in the Catholic Church presented no obstacle to their establishing Judaism as their home religion. When she is honest with herself, Leah mentally acknowledges that she wanted Armand to convert— that she still does, although she has stopped dropping hints. Persistent and gentle, easy to deny, these little goads used to take several subtle forms. Such as mentioning the ancient community of Sephardic Jews that has lived in Rome since the age of Empire— longer, even—and might not it be possible that Armand is a descendant of this tribe? Given his general antipathy to and ongoing estrangement from the Holy Roman Catholic and Apostolic Church, it certainly seems possible. No one has traced the family history back that far, which is probably impossible, anyway, after centuries of decay and carelessness and barbarian invasions, fires and floods and famines and plagues, all of which feature irretrievable losses of unique records, especially when these are on paper, or parchment. As if to make matters that hardly could be worse, worse. As far as anyone knows, Armand's family, that is, the Terranova side, comes from Salina, a tiny Aeolian Island in the vicinity of Sicily. Southern Italian with a vengeance. It is a miracle they made it to America at all. In all likelihood, Armand's ancient ancestors were illiterate, superstitious fishermen. Praying to the Madonna. Weeping at Mass.

Has she mentioned any of this to Max? Leah can imagine the look on his face. Which would sour further if she added that Armand's grandparents on his mother's side were born in Italy—Naples and Florence, she thinks it was—and came to America in steerage, at best. His maternal grandfather, Leah is pretty certain she remembers Armand saying, was a stowaway—that is, an illegal immigrant at a time when these were called WOPs.

No, she definitely has never said a word about it.

However: when she thinks of Armand in this way, he seems not so different from a Jew. A child of diaspora. Fled starvation for the Land of Plenty. Then again, compared to Leah's ancestors, Armand's folks had it easy. Leah's people were axed by Cossacks in Old Mother Russia, ghettoized throughout the Austro-Hungarian Empire, murdered by Nazis wherever they were found, and otherwise persecuted for millennia in every country of Europe—including, sadly, Italy, although Leah never mentions that, either.

Still. To Leah it seems not implausible that a family adventuresome enough to cross an ocean to start life over in a foreign land might well be descended from a Jew who sometime left Rome and traveled south down the Italian peninsula and, eventually, made a short Mediterranean crossing to a small island, where he believed and hoped he would prosper and live in peace. Which might be when he converted. Or she. Which is to be counted against him, or her, because this ancestor's conversion has made Armand less Jewish than he might have been. Then again, without conversion, why would this ancestor have left Rome, the most cosmopolitan city of early Christendom, to take up life on an island so small it almost does not exist and, as far as Leah can tell, lacks adequate economic opportunities? What are commonly called jobs. To live there as a Jew, conspicuous among his neighbors? To Leah it seems unlikely. So, no: this ancestor once a Jew turned Christian for reasons of his own, of her own—possibly, it suddenly occurs to her, to marry; and for other reasons impossible now to know, quit Rome by its southern gate or in any event wended his way southward; then, after incidents and accidents impossible to reconstruct, washed up on a shore of Salina; where, after centuries of living and dying through countless defeats and disappointments, a great-to-the-X-power grandson of this original Sephardim risked everything to cross an ocean; and in America met—who knows?—his distant, also-ex-Jewish tenth cousin twenty-eight times removed, who had similarly abandoned her village and household gods in search of the fulfilled promise of city streets paved with gold. Thereby making Armand possible.

Leah's thoughts used to run along these lines pretty often. When she and Armand became engaged and then were newly-married, she imagined his Sephardic heritage into a certainty. It made her like him more. Now she wonders why she cared. How can it matter, if one of Armand's ancestors was Jewish more than 2000 years ago? Armand isn't Jewish now. As she is. As Max and Rachel are. And the children.

Waiting on their pizzas, she and Max talk shop. Professional-level gossip. Leah is careful about what she says; Max, she assumes, does the same. Max is certain that insufficient publications, plus a heavy percentage of negative student reviews, will scotch his chances of getting tenure. It's the old story, according to Max, of students blaming the teacher for their own ineptitudes, to say nothing of their resentment about needing correction, except now the situation is worse because everyone not silver-plattered an A is disgruntled. And this in the face of a re-grade policy that Max has to explain twice before Leah believes he isn't joking. It seems that any student dissatisfied with his grade on a paper or project (exams are exempt) can fill-in a form that states the terms of this dissatisfaction and a rationale for having the professor evaluate said paper or project a second time. The student submits said form with the original project or paper without any correction or emendation or revision, another thing Leah cannot believe. At that point, the professor is obliged to grade the paper or project again.

"As you know," Max says, "the customer is always right."

"And students rail at the university for being paternalistic."

"Not business students. They love paternalism. It's capitalism's safety net, except when it hinders rational markets. Then, it's interference."

"The infantilization of Generation X. Or is it Y?"

"It's everyone under thirty. They expect to become effortlessly rich—automatically, I mean, as if by birthright. If it doesn't happen, it's your fault."

"But re-grades on demand. What a cave-in. The School is pandering to these kids."

"They're not even kids. These are not eighteen-year-olds learning to do college-level work. They are people in their mid–twenties. They've been in the workforce an average of four years and ought to know better."

"What it says is, they're not serious students."

Max laughs. "Of course they're not serious students. They're businesspeople looking for connections. I tell them at the beginning of term, I even put it on the syllabus"—Max's voice slides into Herr Doctor Professor register—"*Submitting a request for re-grade does not guarantee a higher grade. Understand that the original grade can go down.* Up front and in writing. But who reads a syllabus? The syllabus is not on the exam. Why waste time, why make an effort? The ones who submit for re-grading work I went easy on first time, I nail. That B they were so indignant about turns into a C. You should see the look on their faces. As if they've been made to swallow dogshit."

"Max, please." Leah holds up her hand. It is a small hand with short fingers, almost like a child's. "We're about to eat."

"Can't you compartmentalize?"

Leah shuts her eyes then slowly opens them. "So. Do they then apply for a second re-grade?"

"Mercifully, no—only because it isn't permitted. One re-grade per item. A few truly shameless ones complain to the Dean."

"He backs you up, I hope."

Max shrugs. "More or less. He tells them it's my course and I'm responsible for conducting it, grades included. Sometime later, he and I have a private conversation in which he asks if I know what I'm doing."

"How encouraging," Leah says. "How supportive. It's nice to have a vote of confidence. And you tell him … ?"

"… that these dolts should never have been admitted and will be lucky to graduate."

Leah winces and mock-slaps her forehead. Pantomime of incredulity and dread. Doesn't need to say, *Oy vey!* "Max, I'm thinking those are not the words of a man looking for tenure."

"Oh, I want tenure, all right. Rachel's going to have the baby in six weeks. It's no time to be looking for a job."

"Surely they'll renew you until you find a suitable position."

"Don't bet on it. Once they vote thumbs-down, they want you gone."

"When is the vote?"

"Last of September."

Leah stares at him. "Let me get this straight. The faculty is going to tell you a month into term whether or not you're tenured and if it's a no they expect you to teach until May with a happy heart?"

"Leah, Leah." Max is pure supercilious rue. "No one gives a damn about anyone's heart. It's business."

"It's inhuman."

"They let you appeal. If they vote me down and I subsequently publish something and get better evaluations for the fall term, I can re-apply for another vote in the spring."

"Sort of like a re-grade," says Leah.

Max blinks. "Well, yes. Except in my case there would be new material to consider."

"I'm kidding, Max."

"Oh. Sure."

The pizzas come and they eat.

After they've finished and split the check and squabbled about the tip and stood to leave, Max leans toward her. Leah stops him.

"What are we doing?" she says.

"What are we doing?" says Max. His expression is so out of character that Leah moves past him and through the door. On the sidewalk, she does not exactly wait for him and does not run away, either. A minute later Max emerges, still not looking himself.

"I didn't mean anything."

"I think you meant something. Not that there's a law against it. Only why now, is what I'm wondering." They are standing fifty feet from Carriage House. New concrete underfoot, old cobblestones paving the road. Cars pass in both directions along Stewart Avenue. No way will he try to kiss her out here. Anyone might see. Leah isn't sure how many people noticed the hello-kiss. All strangers, anyway, who won't bother to remember. A kiss between friends. A man kissing a woman of whom he is fond. A woman fond of him. Not a big deal, when you think of it. Not an occasion to think twice. Neither law nor custom says you shouldn't or can't. A perfunctory kiss on the cheek. But out here, on a sunny June afternoon, after an obvious lunch date or what will look like a date in the hanky-panky sense of the word to anyone who happens to drive by as Max's lips are touching her face, they would be asking to be misunderstood.

"All right, so I'll say it. You are completely charming and I love that we're friends. I love talking with you. I look forward to having lunch with you. Our conversations are always a pleasure."

How long has Leah waited to hear these words? How keenly has she wished Armand would say them? She listens with a lump in her throat and, surprise, surprise, a more intimate disturbance elsewhere that will make for a clingy afternoon. She has not thought of Max Obermann in this way before this moment. Not that she was aware of. And isn't sure she wants to think of him this way now. Her response, however, is unmistakable.

"I'm glad," she says. "I'm happy we're friends."

They smile at each other, then walk in the direction of Sage Hall. They do not touch. Max holds his hands in his pockets. Leah has her purse to grab. After they cross the Stewart Avenue bridge and turn right up lower Campus Road, Max says, "I don't want to give you a wrong idea. I love Rachel. And I haven't forgotten, by the way, that we're having a baby."

Leah, by the way, hasn't forgotten, either.

"I'm not proposing something crazy," he says.

"What are you proposing?"

"Oh—nothing, really. Just that we continue having lunch and being... being..."

"Friends, Max. The word you are looking for is *friends.*" Always, it comes to this. Try to have a simple friendship with a man and he, whoever he is, eventually gets around to the other. Not that Leah hasn't thought of it before and isn't flattered by it now. But he is the one who brings it up—drops it on the table, so-to-speak, so that now there will always be this other thought between them.

Goddamnit. The cotton is warm and damp between her legs. Is it possible that she might do something crazy? She, with Max Obermann?

"Look, I'm not talking about, you know, leaving Rachel or anything like that, just that it's not unusual for two people who spend sort-of significant time together, having the kind of conversations we've had, to, you know, start to feel, well... a bit intimate. And then certain thoughts pop up."

"In a manner of speaking," Leah says, and they laugh. "Max, you're making me nervous. I had no idea you felt this way."

"Neither did I, actually. But you agree it's not unusual."

"It's not unusual. I've thought for a long time that you can't get everything you need from one person."

"That's what I mean." With an effort, he says, "How is Armand, by the way?"

Leah shrugs. "Armand's always pretty much the same."

"Meaning?"

"Meaning he's Armand. Angry and unhappy."

"What's he got to be angry and unhappy about? Retired at—how old is he?"

"Forty-three."

"And a made man! Has you for his wife. Two smart, good-looking kids. A nice house, good health. What's not to like?"

"Who knows?" Should she tell him? Does their intimacy, conversational and otherwise, allow it? Welcome it? Expect it? If Leah reveals that she and Armand are seldom intimate and that she submits without enthusiasm, will Max think she is agreeing to his idea? She says, "Right now he's busy being angry about painting the house, which would not be necessary if he would hire housepainters. But no. Actually, I think he likes being angry. It makes him feel alive."

"How's he treat you?"

Ah, now she remembers. They are halfway up the slope, within sight of the Law School. They will skirt it on their right and continue up Campus Road to Sage Hall, which they share five days a week for eight hours a day, although they do not spend more than ten minutes consecutively in the same room alone, always with the door open. But that is not what Leah remembers or what she is thinking of now. "Armand treats me fine," she says, "when he remembers I'm not the cause of his anger."

"I hope so. Not to mention the fact you work. You bring in money."

Leah nods. "Armand loves me. He loves me regardless."

Crossing the intersection of Campus Road and College Avenue, they approach the restricted lot of Sage Hall, where Max parks his silver Audi A6 and from which Leah, were she to drive to work, if she knew how to drive, would be towed. A prince of the academic world: Max is. Leah and all other support staff are civil servants in comparison. But what it, the proximity of the Sage lot, means to Leah is that this line of conversation must end. She stops walking. Does not quite turn to Max. Or turns halfway, discreet, and does not look at him. She says, "I enjoy talking to you. I enjoy your take on the world. Certainly, I'm fond of you." She should stop there. Already she might have said too much. But isn't it right and fair that she tell Max as much as she knows? "It is, however, troublesome. And disruptive. And embarrassing."

"How is it embarrassing?"

Leah smiles. "Max. I'm forty. I've got eight years on you."

Max shrugs. "And?"

"Oh, come on. Rachel's—what—thirty?"

"Rachel's twenty-nine and almost eight months gone. As big as a barn and you know what that means."

Yes, Leah knows, having twice achieved barn-like dimensions herself and over the past two years having nearly killed herself with exercise. Armand rolls over, away from the light she purposely turns on, for another hour's sleep. Or maybe he is faking until she leaves the room. The way he carries on about not enough sex, you would think he was going to die—and now Leah understands what Max has been trying to say. That they play on the side. Pretend to be great friends, just friends, go out of their way to make their great just-friendship generally known, to the point of openly joking about their Secret Love Affair. And then to have that affair. No jealousy, no melodrama, no scuttled marriages and abandoned families. Just playtime, pure and simple. Rachel is a good three months at best from her next episode of sexual intercourse, depending on the baby's delivery and her post-partum mood, and in the meantime Max has to take it somewhere. Why not to Leah, his great female friend? No doubt he has sensed her coolness toward Armand and figures she is lonely. Unsatisfied. What would Max say, Leah wonders, if she let him in on a little secret of her own, namely, that she dislikes being touched? Is his confidence so huge that it would prompt him to boast, *That's your husband's fault. I'll give you the best time between your legs you've ever imagined.*

What would she do then?

What should she say now?

Leah says, "It's a good thing your wife doesn't hear you talking about her."

Max waves this away. "Oh, she knows. She says it herself. She's even hinted, you know, that she wouldn't blame me if I got some on the side. She doesn't come out and say it, of course."

Of course. Leah does not believe him. When she was pregnant, both times she was pregnant, she wanted Armand right beside her, to the point of wishing he could take a leave of absence from his job. Weight gain and chronic nausea had cancelled her awareness of her husband's needs. The notion that she might have granted tacit permission for him to satisfy himself with a stand-in—a lie-in?—is absurd.

Leah strides toward Sage Hall. She is ready for this conversation to end. She has had enough of Max Obermann for one day. All in all, lunch has been a bit too interesting.

They enter through the door at parking-lot level and climb two flights to her office. Max does not try to kiss her before continuing to the faculty wing. He says, "I'll ping you," meaning another email.

Leah enters her office and shuts the door. The overhead lights twinkle on. It offends B-School culture, the shut office door, not that there's a rule about it, but as a matter of personal preference and especially right now, Leah wants privacy.

Her computer animates at a touch. And there it is in her Inbox among a dozen new messages: a note from Armand, to say he has called her three times in hope of a lunch date and has gotten nothing but voicemail. *Where are you?* he wants to know, and Leah wonders if his facetiousness is just uncanny or whether early retirement has given him ESP; *out with your boyfriend?*

"Oh boy," Leah says, right out loud, as if someone might be watching, and maybe listening, too. She clicks Reply.

You're funny. Right now I'm so busy I wouldn't look up if Brad Pitt and George Clooney offered to take turns. Sorry about lunch. Love, L. ☺. She clicks Send.

A minute later her computer chimes. Leah clicks, reads. *That's right now. It's the rest of the day I wonder about.*

And below that,

Take turns? You naughty, naughty girl. Love, Armand.

Yes. Love Armand. Try to, naughty girl.

Luke Robideau quarters his hamburger and stares as blood and liquefied fat pool on his plate. Sides of broccoli and beans heaped in bowls are easier for Luke to ignore, easier for Mother to notice he isn't eating them. Or rather, not eating the broccoli, which he hates, even pan-fried in butter and salt à la Mother's Way. The beans appeal, baked in molasses and brown sugar, but his bottom line is and always will be nothing beats a burger and most things get in the way.

"You don't miss the bun?" says Mother.

Luke forks a quarter of the oversized patty into his mouth. Mother is seventy-five. Her hair is bunned so tightly the tension looks enough to peel back her scalp. She has fixed him three meals a day all his life and until two years ago made grocery runs herself. It brings Luke down to see her old, in one of those cotton dresses. House dress, it used to be called. Mother launders her five every week, irons them and also, Luke thinks, applies a little starch. The problem is patterns, this one especially, bright print of marigolds and daffodils and tulips too much for Luke's eyes. Matt and John bear him out, that this dress has too much going on, is too ambitious for its purpose. Even Cindy agrees, although they visit so seldom Luke is sure they cannot appreciate the full effect.

"No, Mother."

"Not the ketchup? The cheese?"

"Maybe the cheese." He lifts his glass and drinks off the water. Mother begins to exert herself in ways that, eventually, will raise her from her chair. Luke holds up his hand. "It saves money. Vermont cheddar is pushing twelve dollars a pound."

"A scandal. I never thought I'd live to see the day."

"Everything costs, Mother." Luke gets up and opens the refrigerator, refills his glass with ice water and sets it on the table, then refills the pitcher at the kitchen tap. He replaces the pitcher, shuts the refrigerator door, sits.

Mother sighs. Luke knows her thought, having often heard it spoken. Matters of cash flow, shortfalls of funds, send her mind along a well-traveled channel toward a familiar end. He says nothing, having learned that nothing helps except lies too obvious to be believed.

She says, "I'll ask Matty this time. Just for some nicer foods."

"Please don't do that, Mother." Luke's expected reply—his line, delivered on-cue. "Matt does plenty already. John and Cindy, too." His siblings carry them month-to-month, as Luke and Mother well know. Because it is not mainly a question of cheese or toilet paper but of larger necessities; such as, *How do we pay the property tax?* Also there is gas & electric. And they cannot avoid the school tax despite the fact Luke finished at Ithaca High more than twenty years ago. The cost of living a decent life has left them behind. Post-9/11 trends are driving up values all over town. New people are buying old houses with City money, bidding against each other and paying over the ask. The locals are closed out. Luke has seen a textbook example from the proximity of one lot over, of downstate stupid money running headlong into upstate greed. When the old lady told Mother what she had sold for and Mother told Luke, his first reaction was fear. Not only because the purchase price would raise their assessment, which had already spiked forty percent in two years, but because Mother might want to sell, too.

Luke does not want to sell. Selling means Matt and John and Cindy divvy up the profit as recompense for fifteen years of checks, then draw straws to decide who gets Mother, loser take all. And Luke? What becomes of the six-foot, 290-pound baby brother, with his cats and dogs and night-shift job, his distrust of strangers, really of every human being outside his family?

"I know, I know," Mother says, startling him. For a second he thinks she reads his thoughts. "My children are good to me and I am lucky to have them."

Some of them. Luke fills his mouth with a quarter of hamburger and chews.

"Who could believe your father would die and leave so little?" A major theme. Mother circles it always, touches it on schedule. Luke could set his watch if he had one. Summing her legacy from a husband who died too soon.

It hurts Luke to remember his father. Fifteen years feels like so many days. Dad at fifty-eight was trim and strong, never a smoker, a moderate tippler of lively spirits and, everyone assumed, headed for a long, slow reckoning. One day he turned up early, home right after class. Said it was nothing, a touch of drowsiness, head too heavy to sit at his desk. So he had clocked off early and here he was, hunting a nap, just to close his eyes for an hour, *so please Luke turn down the television, all right?*

All right. Luke had noticed his father's face, how gray it seemed, eye sockets dark, eyes sunken. He does not remember if he was worried as he sat on the couch and watched cheering throngs of

East Germans knocking chunks of concrete out of the Berlin Wall. They pounded it with sledgehammers until the concrete cracked and broke and fell away. *A historic event,* the CNN anchor pronounced it, as if Luke didn't know a watershed moment when he saw it. As if he had been to school for nothing. November 9 it was, 1989. A big day for Germans, really for everybody, although most could not say how. Luke knew, knows, will not forget. 11/9/89: a numerical sequence that pins one day amid countless days that make up the past. The day his mother told him (needlessly: he smells food two rooms away) that dinner was ready *so please go upstairs and wake your father.*

Dad? Dad? Dinner's on. Touching his father's shoulder. A slight shake. *Dad?*

He does not want to remember. It is the thing he lives with. What nothing can change. It was maybe a minute before Luke realized his father wasn't breathing. Eyes closed, lips slightly parted. It was his first denial, he believes, his insistent effort to wake a dead man.

Dad.

A moment; another. How long does a moment last? How long until Luke understood? Until he accepted what it was? His father might have passed while Luke was climbing the stairs. A peaceful drifting-off, half-asleep. Or semi-conscious of the final, brokenhearted throb. It is something Luke cannot know, something *else* he cannot know, and maybe it does not matter except it might, Luke thinks, help him answer a question that does matter very much to him: Why, after fifteen years, is he still sad?

On television the Wall fell. It had stood between East and West all of Luke's life and now it was gone. He sat on the sofa thinking he was watching a major event. And it was: one for the history books. But for Luke, a greater event happened soundlessly in an upstairs bedroom. Today, the absence of the Berlin Wall is commonplace. For Luke, his father's absence is always remarkable. He tries not to think about the disparity between before and after, how *now* becomes *then* and so much can change. Thinking does not help. When he knew his father was gone, Luke felt flooded with his own worthlessness. That his father could die so easily, in privacy and quiet without the sky's having to fall, the moon's having to wander, told Luke he was naked in a world that cared nothing for him and was indifferent to whether he, too, lived or died.

He cannot stop Mother, compelled to rehash his father's death. Luke listens, it is the least he can do, the most meaningful kindness in his power. Why else does he live with her? Aside from matters of practical economy, which rule out a place of his own that is not a double-wide in the trailer park behind Wymans. It is said that you cannot hide from your problems. Luke hears it on television, reads it in magazines. That you must face reality, take steps, make changes, move mountains. Turn the page. He himself has learned that talking about the past, feeling sorrow as he felt it then, when he was twenty-three and had had so little of his own life, is no help in putting anything behind. Maybe it works for some people. It does not work for Luke. Dad's brown eyes stare at him whenever Luke closes his own. Dad's dry lips and the cold, immobile weight of his body haunt his son, to say nothing of the bed Luke cannot look at and in which, incredibly, Mother continues to sleep.

She is still talking. Luke reminds himself it is purely her due. He eats the third quarter of hamburger and some beans. The broccoli he flips with his fork, torturing it as the cats do mice. He is looking for a crown soaked with butter, coated with salt. Waxy stalks, acid-tinged florets. A hint of urine. Mother does not admonish him for playing with his food. On the other hand, Luke is not playing. He is containing hazardous materials, WMDs of skillet and saucepan.

"Who would believe these prices?" Mother says to him, to herself, to no one. "Your father's Social Security is nothing." As if his father might be listening, out among the stars.

Luke nods, then shakes his head. It would be a neat trick to do both at once. "It covers basic costs. We can't expect it to do more." He holds the glass in his large hand and drinks off half the water. He wipes his fingers on his shirt.

"But to live on. It's not enough. Not nearly."

"Yes, Mother." They worry this topic, a bug bite that won't quit. Scratch until it bleeds, wait for it to scab over, then pick the scab. How many times have they said exactly these lines, felt precisely this dread? Anxiety of pinched living. How many more times must they run the gauntlet of Who-would-have-thought and No-one-could-have-guessed before she understands there is nothing he can do?

Luke says, "I don't believe Social Security is meant to be a retirement plan."

"Yes, yes." She waves his comment away as if her gesture will cast the spell that saves them. "So your father said. You and your brothers got used bicycles all those years. Cindy's, of course, he bought new. Just one telephone in the house. And vacations in the car. I didn't argue. He was the man and was supposed to know. We had a budget and not a dollar left, I can tell you, by the time the next check came. We did without plenty. Never thought about champagne on New Year's, much less caviar, much less dinner out. I would have liked that, wearing fine clothes, dining at a hotel or a smart restaurant, listening to music and seeing people, everyone done up to the nines. But no. *Amateur night,* he called it. As if people had to be card-carrying members of something or other to have a good time. Well, I thought, at least we'll have a nest egg.

There'll be that. Then he dies, and after all those years living like misers I find pennies."

Luke stares at her, amazed. She has not strung together so many sentences in fifteen years. Not even on the telephone with Cindy does she speak so. The last time he heard anything like a rant from her, he was a teenager intent on some destructive piece of mischief. And she has eaten her dinner, every scrap, broccoli included.

"I'm sorry, Mother." Luke forks the last of the hamburger into his mouth, chews and swallows. "I'm sure Dad didn't expect it."

"Oh I know, I know. We're lucky he had life insurance."

Lukes skewers a broccoli stalk. He can't stand its waxy look or rotten-grass smell but here goes, and with the fork also piled with beans shovels it into his mouth. He chews quickly, trying to swallow before taste sets in. "What I mean," he says, wiping the tang off his lips, "is that Dad must have thought he had time to save, and that the savings would earn interest, so when he reached sixty-five—"

"Luke, I understand, I do. But he never saw sixty and we could have lived a little better in the meantime."

"And now you wouldn't have a pot to piss in." It's stunning, her illogic. "As things stand, you'll pay off the house in another year."

"Well, there's no use arguing. I am referring to quality of life. But what's done is done."

Yes. And any subject that does not submit to Mother's discontent she dismisses. How is it possible to think they ought to have spent the money his father was salting away now that the yield on that money has turned out to be inadequate? Mother's fuzziness makes for maddening conversations. Most of the time Luke feels they do not speak the same language.

Unsurprisingly, they resolve nothing, reach no verdict, agree on no plan. He himself is certain Dad played smart by saving what he could while putting Luke though college, and Matt and John and Cindy before him, while carrying a mortgage and paying taxes and day-in, day-out operating costs all on an academic salary. Almost: back then, faculty kids paid just twenty-five percent of full tuition, and Luke and his siblings took loans to meet the balance. The costs of room and board they covered by having work-in-aid campus jobs. Also, Dad came into some money when grandma Annie, whom they called Snowflake, died. Not to take credit from the old man, who in Luke's mind is nothing short of a hero. But no one does it alone. Everyone gets help, some more than others, some almost none, some from strange unexpected sources. Luke is not ashamed to take money from his brothers and sister while he, frankly underemployed, superintends the family manse, currently Mother's house and to another way of thinking a mutual investment. Call him a caretaker, chronically out-of-pocket and on the family dole, and call the Cape his collateral. During almost forty years of Robideau ownership the house has been altered and added-to and generally improved. The front steps have been rebuilt and the windows replaced, the attic has been extra-insulated and the chimney re-pointed. The cellar, it's true, is basically what it was in 1910, with exposed knob-and-tube wiring and an earthen floor. But they do not use the cellar for much and Dad always said that money spent on a cellar was money buried without a map. Besides, it's dry; the floor doesn't become muddy every time it rains. It is actually a curiosity of sorts, the earthen floor, modern houses being all sealed concrete and florescent lights. In the current market the Robideau Cape is worth upwards of $200,000, maybe something better when you consider the landscaping, all of which Luke has done himself, including a Zen garden secluded on three sides by privet hedges, with wood-slat meditation bench and reflecting pool, the latter ringed with eight smooth stones, all white, aligned with a compass.

Luke checks the kitchen clock, a clunky wooden thing with Roman numerals and a round face, hanging from the soffit above the sink. Possibly hand-carved, it came, he thinks, from Maine, where Mother bought it maybe on her honeymoon more than fifty years ago. He seems to remember her having said so. "Time to watch the news," he says, carrying his plate to the sink. He leaves the broccoli in case Mother's food guilt forces her to Saran-wrap the stalks and leave them in the refrigerator to sour. The other bowl he rinses and racks with his plate in the dishwasher. Says, "Thank-you for dinner, Mother," and on his way to the flatscreen, hears, "You're welcome, dear."

Two hundred thousand dollars. Two-ten. Two-twenty-seven, five hundred and fifty. Those stones took time to gather, all of a size, nearly the same shade of white. Luke sits in Dad's old chair and sparks up the flatscreen. The remote control is nine inches long, gunmetal-gray. A small earth-station aimed at the sky above South Hill uplinks them to the satellite, which feeds-in WGN from Chicago, TBS from Atlanta, local affiliates of national broadcast networks in Los Angeles and New York, MSNBC and CSPAN and CNN from wherever they are. These are the chief sources of Luke's news, the outlets that brought him the spectacle of 9/11. The Towers stood just four driving hours south and east from the spot in which he sits, call it four-and-a-half with traffic, and sat that Tuesday morning when regular programming was interrupted and incredible pictures appeared. Luke watched it live and watched it again when they replayed it and replayed it all that day and the next, one jet then another, then the blackened wreckage at the Pentagon, finally the remnants of a fuselage smoking in a Pennsylvania field. He was here when the Towers fell, in Dad's old chair with green-and-gold plaid upholstery and wide wooden arms to hold a glass of beer, a mug of coffee; and also later, when CNN ran a videotape, shot amid crags of barren mountains, of Osama bin Laden in headdress and robes, Kalashnikov slung on a shoulder, wooden staff clasped in one hand as if Satan were a shepherd, long black beard as kinky as pubic hair, thanking God in a gentle, controlled voice for America's fear and promising greater atrocities to come. Old Sammie himself, standing no one knew where, unscathed and serene, presaging airliners falling from the skies, blood on the walls, bodies piled in the streets.

There having been no al Qaida attack inside the United States in the almost-three years since, Luke has concluded Islamist fundamentalists have a different understanding of "soon."

On television, he sees a young Korean man begging for his life. Two hooded figures, another pair of courageous Islamic knights-errant, stand behind him, bright knives crossed on their chests.

I don't want to die! I don't want to die! Please, please, do what they ask!

Nausea laps at Luke's throat. There is something final here, a sense that is desperate and knowing. The Korean's name is Kim Sun Il. His executioners have not dressed him in an orange jumpsuit of the sort other victims have been made to wear. They have let him keep his clothes, as if to suggest that this young man, a translator if Luke has heard right, isn't doomed.

I don't want to die!

The poor guy is wailing. His face is panicked, eyes rolling. Luke wonders if Kim Sun Il knows satellite networks are showing this videotape all over America and Europe and Asia. Have his ballsy executioners told Kim Sun Il that militant Islamists also watch and puff out their collective chests at another proof of Muslim might?

"Of course you don't want to die," Luke whispers; thinking *Three thousand people incinerated and crushed on 9/11 didn't want to die, either. Nor deserved to any more than you. Ditto 900-some American troops ambushed and blindsided and sneak-attacked since last spring. Also the independent contractors murdered and burned, their charred corpses strung up on trestles in Fallujah, as thanks for trying to put that rotten country back together. Not to mention Iraqi civilians killed accidentally or on purpose by truck bombs in Baghdad or small-arms assaults on American checkpoints and convoys. Not to mention the others, who and how many only God knows, whose names and stories never get on television. Not to mention the thousands or maybe millions of people who are going to die before it ends, if it ends.*

Islamist militants. Baathist hardcores. He shouldn't watch the news, it gets him worked up. South Korea is not going to cancel its deployment of additional troops. Luke knows this as perfectly as if he were sitting in the president's office in Seoul. And Kim Sun Il, who looks young enough to be a student, is going to have his head cut off.

Old Sammie's been hidin'.

Mother walks into the room, sees what Luke is watching, and walks out. He wonders how much she spares herself, trying not to notice.

"It's about time," she calls from the kitchen.

Luke presses the button marked INFO. Together with some text and peripheral graphics, a digital clock appears in the upper right corner of the flatscreen. 7:43. He'll have to hustle to punch-in on time. He should get a watch. The last one stopped after four months (a month after its limited warranty expired) and Luke has not convinced himself to spend for another. Besides, clocks exist almost everywhere he goes. It is the one thing he knows he can get whenever he needs it, and for free: the correct time.

He pops off the news and says, "Thank-you, Mother," despite being none too happy. Almost forty years old, a CU graduate with honors, and how does he spend his life? Is he making a difference, setting a tone, affecting the hearts and minds of his fellow Americans? As a matter of fact, no. What he is doing, Mr. Genius PoliSci major, is working the overnight shift. Floor maintenance. In plain English: mopping. Every night, he sweeps and cleans. Twice a week, four times in winter, he polishes. The big challenge is 3000 square feet of ceramic tile in Produce and 3200 square feet of it in Market Square. The latter, really more of a rectangle, is decorated to imply a village market, vaguely European and thoroughly faux, where customers harvest meat and fish and delicatessen. The twelve-inch-square, gold-taupe tiles that pave its promenade are filthy by the time Luke arrives. Ditto the tile in Produce. It requires a different cleanser, what with the grout, than the sleek, seamless linoleum that covers the rest of the 80,000-square foot interior. Four nights a week, Luke and a man who says his name is Dave, just Dave, haul out two heavy, dual-disk rotary scrubbers, fill the twin canisters with hot water and a secret emulsifier that Wymans has formulated especially for ceramic tile (and on which it holds patents), and set to work. When they finish, they drain the canisters, fill them with water and detergent and do the linoleum. By the time they finish the pet food aisle the natural foods section is dry. On polishing nights, they go back with the buffer to raise a shine. On off-nights, another crew does the same job more or less the same way without, Luke believes, getting quite the same result.

A nothing job. A chore. Most of what Luke does is a chore. But he makes a paycheck and is allowed to take home no-longer-fresh vegetables on a daily basis. And he has medical insurance, which he figures sooner or later to need. *It could be worse.* He could be unemployed and on welfare. Or denied welfare because he is able-bodied and not quite middle-aged—how could he think anyone would hand him a check? He could be a Fort Pendleton jarhead in Iraq, a government contractor or Halliburton drone shoveling shit in Baghdad, or Nadja, or Mosel, or Ramadi, or Kurkuc. He could be sitting handcuffed in a windowless room, wearing an orange jumpsuit, guessing the time.

Thinking this way changes nothing but it does help to balance his anger. He and Mother have to watch every dollar with an intensity of concern that would seem superstitious to a person who has never come up short. Not enough money, without John's checks, to pay the property tax. Plain hamburger on a plate—but then, they are lucky to have hamburger, which is beef and much more expensive than, say, pinto beans. So he should be grateful. Count his blessings. He should. He is an American, after all, and isn't that what being American is all about? Blessings? Luke has no wife, no girlfriend, but at least he does not live alone, not yet. Except it is pathetic, how he and Mother have been left to themselves in the old house with too many animals that are never enough to replace what is missing.

Old car with rust mothing its wheel wells. Fat swaddling his waist, padding his arms and chest. Thighs tight inside his overalls. Gray-flecked beard he has no occasion to shave, gray-streaked ponytail he has no reason to barber. Derelict garage behind the Cape Cod, sagging walls and three large holes in its roof that invite raccoons to come and go. He thinks bats might hang in there, yellow eyes blind and beady in the night. Scraped-down shingles on the back of the Cape that he is afraid to paint because the improved appearance will bump up their assessment. Things have gotten out of hand. Spruce up your house with a fresh paint-job, put on a new roof, have your porch steps rebuilt, and the assessor's office sniffs it out. Here they come with a kink in their brows, a twist to their lips.

Doing a little home improvement, are we?

Then tack-on another twenty thousand, inking numbers onto forms pinched to their fucking clipboards. Which raises your property tax. Which already you cannot afford.

It would make Luke scream, were he a man given to screaming, or weep, if he were a woman. But Luke Robideau has his pride and so he goes about his business. He tries to forget that he and Mother are being priced out of their family home. They have lived here almost forty years, the only home he has known. He cuts his grass, tends his ornamental shrubs and native trees, shows up for work more or less on time and works until his shift is done. He keeps tabs via satellite news on dangers that surround him and those fomenting overseas, and tries not to look too closely but notices nevertheless that his Johnny-come-lately neighbor has not only a blonde wife with prime-time casabas, plus two cute kids, plus a red Mercedes-Benz, plus a full head of black hair and no problem with his weight, but also a hell of a lot of free time, most of which he is using lately to scour off leaded paint and brush primer onto old wood and power-clean peeling stucco and paint it all with high-quality Benjamin Moore exterior latex, until the old lady's 90-year-old bungalow looks better than new, its Johnny-come-lately asshole owner obviously not concerned about property tax.

Who is this guy? How did he get so lucky? Luke hates him and the hatred feels right. The invisible line that divides their respective yards seems like a perfect symbol.

Luke shrugs into his windbreaker, pockets his keys. He says, "I'll be back around six," although he knows Mother knows. Luke is steady, as steady as the wind that carries Arctic air out of Canada and down the long length of their local Finger Lake, as regular as the cloud-cover that makes their town one of the grayest places in the contiguous forty-eight. Luke has worked the overnight fifteen years, a surprise casualty of his father's endless nap.

His mother, needlessly: "Be careful."

Tracking cats across the midnight, Armand breaks from the window and goes for the phone. It takes him three seconds to move through Alessandro's bedroom and across the landing to the master. Just inside the door, a cordless unit lies on the rush-woven seat of an antique chair. Leah's idea. A decorative touch she learned from a magazine. Give your home a rustic patina; create lived-in textures of the shabby-genteel. Armand lifts the handset on the second ring and thumbs the oval button marked TALK. He holds it to his ear, hears ghost-air of an open line, then a smoker's cough.

"Hello?" he says. "Hello?" Armand hears a mouth working on itself, tongue slow along the gums, tremor of soft palate. He is about to click off when an elderly voice, cigarette-hoarse, hisses into his ear.

"Dirty Jew. Kike bastard."

"Who's that?" Armand hisses back. He wants to bark the words, let this Nazi know he is not to be fucked with, but he's standing right beside sleeping Leah. He slips through the doorway and into his office, shuts the door behind him, phone still in his hand, venom sizzling into his ear.

"You stole that house. A sweet, clean old lady. Stole it. A filthy piker. A dirty Jew."

Armand thumbs TALK and lays the handset on his desk. A teleflame. It's his first and has come from close by. The Neighborhood. Someone who knew the old lady. Whose home their home used to be. Also: a woman. It sounded as if she were calling from the next room. A ragged voice. Crackly consonants, vowels cloudy, unless he means congested. Nothing smooth or flowing, no bell tones, although her accusation came through loud and clear. Stole the house, did he? Ripped-off a kind old lady. Salt of the earth, and he fleeced her. Picked her clean. And why? Well, of course: he's greedy, and a Jew.

A hate crime. Here he is, forty-three years old, mostly happily married, two healthy kids, blessed, absolutely blessed in every way that matters, prematurely retired maybe but minding his own business, tending his garden, as the saying goes, although it's more accurate to say painting his house, and out of nowhere he finds himself harassed. At least harassed. That voice, its insults, make him feel at-risk. Vulnerable in his own home, unsafe his skin. Which makes him, Armand figures, a victim. Set aside the fact that Armand is not Jewish. Technically, the hate-monger has fired wide. So: a near-victim. Except that Armand, born and schooled Catholic, might as well be Jewish in every sense but the strictly religious because Leah is Jewish, which means Alessandro and Julietta are Jews. Armand himself is not embraced by Jewish Law, as he is well aware, marriage being a mere convention compared to motherhood. Which means he is odd man out and destined, if the old myths are true, to be divided from his family in the Great Hereafter. Still, in the here & now he is a virtual Jew. How can this Nazi know that? What kind of evil eye inspires such a guess?

He picks up the handset. Is he really going to dial 911? The call is finished. The telephone has not rung again. Hate crime it may be but as an emergency Armand doubts it qualifies. Except it could become one. Easily could something like this escalate. Easily. Armand holds the handset, undecided at first then feeling he is better off not filing a complaint. Not yet. It might be a one-off: some crazy old witch took a few too many nips of the Irish Cream or Amaretto and found nothing on television to equal her spite. And so dialed, and so said the ugliest things her fuddled brain could conjure. How does a mind form, a tongue speak such words? And why, always, does religious hatred boil down to who is Jewish and who is not?

Armand has parsed it, his *de facto* Jewishness, with an immigrant's care. During times of peak paranoia he has mentally run through a dozen dire scenarios featuring right-wing evangelicals marking for internment or deportation or worse Jews who refuse to accept Christ as their personal savior. In such a predicament, Armand will protect Leah and Alex and Julietta. Their fate is his own. Set aside that he would probably be powerless to save them. Set aside the coward's dodge he could use to save himself. Then again, there is no guarantee that fanatics would spare him, no matter how many Hail Marys and Apostles' Creeds he might recite, especially if those righteous Christian soldiers judged him on the evidence of his circumcised penis. Whichever way you cut it, no pun intended, there is nothing heroic about Armand, who kept clear on September 11 and has effectively retreated to what the government might consider a secure location. He does not think of himself as brave. Never has. It is a matter of love. A husband's love. A father's. So even if he is not Jewish by race or creed, Armand is nominally Jewish in the face of anti-Semitic rage, or resentment, or whatever it is that has impelled whoever it was to ring his phone in the dead middle of the night and accuse him of robbing an old lady blind.

He switches off the ringer before he returns the handset to its cradle. He tries to forget the call, makes an effort to think of better things. Statue-still in bedroom darkness, Armand looks at his wife. Leah sleeps on her stomach, sheeted from the waist down, her ass a bubble under the fabric. Just a bra tonight, Armand notes, no shirt or chemise or nightgown. Fancy lingerie is a pleasure of the past. He thinks he can unclasp it, the bra, without waking her. If she turns in her sleep or just shifts a little, he might slip one strap or both off her shoulder or shoulders and uncover her breast, or breasts. That would be sweet because Leah's breasts, well … but what is the point of thinking about something, two somethings, that he can't see and she won't let him touch? In the long run and even short-term his sneakily getting her half-naked will not help. The last time he woke her with a hard-on Leah hit him. Slapped him, actually, in distress maybe more than anger, Armand thinks or hopes, because between sex and sleep, Leah picks the Zs every time. *Every time.* So what is the point of getting enthused?

Armand drops his boxers, pulls his tee-shirt over his head. Why is he doing this? Why is he standing bare-assed beside the bed in which his wife sleeps, moving now to the door and shutting it? What is he up to, manipulating his penis in the dark? He can't just do it on her, hot spatter clingy across her back without a sound. Or rather he could do it, thinks so, but damn well better not. Also: standing. Can he do it standing? Has he ever? It troubles him to realize he isn't sure—that he cannot remember having achieved orgasm on two feet and also cannot definitely say no, he hasn't. Does it matter? Is it just something else Armand has failed to keep track of? But never mind; the question is: Does he want to now? Can he make it? Does he dare to try? Goo will drool off his hand onto the pathetic floor. He'll never be able to clean it in the dark. Even if he mostly gets it, say with toilet paper, there will be residue, a film, and if it's sticky and even if it isn't, Leah will notice, she might. What if she suddenly wakes up and catches him, ah, red-handed?

Strange, unsavory man.

It goes away. Just sort-of dwindles down-and-out and slips from his grasp. Literally. Also actually. His own touch has started to fail him. It isn't exciting anymore, is more effort than pleasure. Now Leah, she is pleasure: her touch, how she feels, her look and scent. But Leah takes effort, too. If Armand had to sum it up, say if someone put a gun to his head and threatened to blow it off unless he came clean, he would say Leah is not interested. Not in him. Not in sex. Not in sex with him. Love him still she might, it is not impossible. But want him? No. Much less crave him. On no day, at no time, under no set of circumstances or conditions. Oh, why? Better to ask, Why not? *Pourquoi pas,* lonely soldier? Well, a dozen married years might explain it. Because Armand does not look like George Clooney or Jude Law or Brad Pitt. He does not come close. By no stretch of a generous imagination or blur of myopic eyes does he belong even to the lesser universe of male magnetism that occupies the existential plane two or three levels below the universe in which chuckling Hollywood studs mount starlets and Centerfolds. Charisma: Armand lacks charisma, might be the least charismatic man in America. At least America. Compared to ClooneyLawPitt he is invisible. And it is Clooney Leah prefers, has said so many times. Armand does not keep count but guesses it is more than "sometimes" and shy of "often." Luckily, she has never met him. If Gorgeous George showed up in Ithaca, Armand would be wearing the horns. Leah would light out without a second thought or a good-bye kiss. Weepy farewells to the children.

Mommy will visit you, baby. Don't bet on it, kiddo. Once Clooney sweeps her off her feet mommy will forget you exist. Can you blame her? Really, seriously blame her? Life is short and your beautiful self lives just a moment in this vale of tears. Who wouldn't grab her fantasy by the lapels if the fantasy came knocking? Pull him inside, falling toward the bed. *Life is once-around.* Isn't that what they say? What someone says? *Enjoy the ride.*

Cats prowl, fouling his grass. Right now Armand doesn't care. He is philosophical for the nonce, also tired, not that he has done much today. It is more the not-sleeping. Short rest. They say it of a pitcher who takes the mound a day or two sooner than his usual start: he's pitching on short rest. Of fathers and mothers, husbands and wives they say, *Tough it out.* Or *No one said life would be easy.* Nowadays, their local holier-than-thou bleeding hearts would nail him with, "Got it tough, have you? How about living in a cage for three years at Guantánamo Bay?" That also makes Armand tired. The burning issues and desperate plights. The acute crises and ongoing situations. Chronic abuses of human dignity. Catastrophes of suffering in every direction. He is supposed to care about it, all of it, he knows he is, because the country is at war. As if anything he can do would change that.

He walks around the bed and lies face-up on the top-sheet. His dick is nothing, a rag, a soft sea-creature with one blind eye, washed up and drowning in the air. Leah doesn't care, does not want it, isn't interested. Unless she has a boyfriend. George Clooney is not coming to Ithaca because what would a guy like that want with a crummy, run-down town like this when all of southern California is his playground, but it would not take a miracle for some joker who looks like Clooney's kid brother to materialize. Leah might meet him anywhere. At work, on the Commons, in one of those overrated, pain-in-the-ass restaurants that plague the locals with pretentious entrées they never prepare quite right. Nothing to it. How can Armand know how she spends her day? Leah easily could be screwing some guy, especially if George Junior has a downtown apartment or a house in Cayuga Heights. Discreet neighbors mind their own business. Most of them work, anyway, so who's around to notice? Attached garage for clandestine comings and goings. Especially comings. Anyway it isn't spywork, espionage of state secrets photographed or stolen, national security imperiled, lives at risk. It is a simple matter of consenting adults. Armand would never know. *Un cornuto.* It would explain her uninterest, if she were getting it elsewhere, and good. And that would be bad. Bad for him, bad for them. Bad for Alex and Julietta. It is better he not know, better Armand never know, assuming something is going on of which it is worth being ignorant, because if he knew, he would have to kill her. Leah. Oh, he would kill George Jr., too. That goes without saying and would not even be difficult, in the sense of giving Armand what some people call pause, because Armand would want to kill him. And if you want to kill a man, it is easy to do.

Leah would be tough. Armand loves Leah. He might not be able to do it except that he'd have to. What choice would there be? What other action could he take? Paste on a smile and offer his blessing? Ponder the frailties flesh is heir to? Regard a poaching stud's porking his wife with serenity and detachment?

No. No. And no. Armand is not a Philosopher-King, he is not a Buddhist priest. So, no, sorry. Or rather no, not sorry. Angry. Very angry. Terribly angry, monstrously angry. Insanely angry. That's it: Plead insanity. A crime of passion, committed on provocation. An insult not to be borne. He would have to catch them at it, sex-wet and naked, Leah on her back with legs outflung, hands kneading the brute's ass-cheeks while he, the brute, pistons in and out. Cries of pleasure rattling the glass. That is the instant to blast Georgie-Boy's head off.

Why does he think these things? He seems compelled, but why? Armand turns on his side and tries to sleep, to will himself unconscious. Why can't he just nod off with a smile and wake up eight hours later feeling great? But no, no, he cannot let it go, cannot let anything go, his mind will not allow it. It drives on and on, as if his brain is the thing that wants to kill him. Not Leah, not George Jr., whoever he is. Not Jethro and his nasty cats. Not even Old Sammie and his henchmen. Armand's brain is trying to kill Armand. Or rather, his mind. His thoughts. The mental images his thoughts assume to make themselves noticed. Armand cannot help thinking how a shotgun would turn the trick on Georgie-Boy, nicely-nicely. Armand does not have a shotgun but knows where he can get one. The big new sporting goods store at Pyramid Mall sells firearms. Dan's, he thinks it's called. Or Dick's. A nice, ah, touch, if the store is called Dick's. Where better to buy a weapon to kill a freelancing penis? Which is maybe redundant, because isn't a lance penis-like? What is usually called a phallic symbol? Freelance = Penis on the Prowl = Cock on the Make = Dick Set Free. At Dick's, rifles and shotguns stand in racks. Revolvers and automatics are locked behind glass. The Great State of New York requires three peer references for a handgun permit and Armand does not have peers enough for one. So, a shotgun. Pump-action, multiple-load magazine. At close range he couldn't miss.

But Leah: that would be tough, even *in flagrante delicto*. Blood on the walls, a headless corpse in the bed. Offal of its voided bowels. Well, who's fault is that? It wasn't Armand's idea that she fuck the nuts off some cherry-picking celebrity look-alike. Leah is the one. Very independent; always has been. What is Armand supposed to do? Writhe on humiliation's rack for the rest of his nights and days? Relive the eye-widening sight of enflamed genitals sliding in and out and together and apart and up and down and side to side with frantic, churning, grunting fuck-lust, while the brute groans and Leah yelps and he, Armand Terranova, cuckold, schlemiel, glums alone in a corner, trembling, weeping, pulling his noodle?

Hell, no. He'll kill her first.

Except it might run its course. Then Leah could maybe forget it. And they could go on with their lives.

Such generosity. What a prince, to choke down macho pride for the sake of his family. Two innocent children. Alessandro and Julietta do not know the first thing about how people lie and cheat, how they murder each other's souls. A class act: Armand is, if he does say so himself. Or doesn't say so, just thinks it.

Sighing toward sleep. *So complicated,* he thinks, swooning down, down, through indigo depths of fall. How complicated it has become, this business of being Armand.

Come morning he is out bright & early with ladder and paint, best brush in a pocket, 5-in-1 tool in hand. Armand intends three hours' work before the heat sets in. He hears the clanky deadbolt and Leah's shoes on the porch, then the noise of the door shutting behind her. She minces down the porch steps in a yellow-and-white seersucker skirt, narrow stripes, and snug double-knit yellow blouse. Yellow high-heels, which cinches it. As if her chest doesn't attract enough attention. Armand wants to peel off her clothes and press his face into her babysoft flesh but Leah has not welcomed such acting-out since before Alessandro was born.

"What are you up to today?" she asks him, as if he might be headed to Disneyland, or a burlesque club.

"Painting," he says, "this eave," pointing. "Until it gets too hot."

Leah's smile is not happy. "We can afford house-painters."

"I'm here. I might as well do it."

"Suit yourself." She clicks down the concrete walk. Without looking back, she says, "Don't forget to pick up the kids."

High-heels, in Ithaca. Yellow. Can you believe it? "Have a nice day," Armand says after her.

"I'll certainly try."

As if inviting him to imagine. Jesus, the mind boggles. Imagine Leah *certainly trying* to have a nice day. Trying *hard.* It features—what? Early lunch, then spending the afternoon with a—

Armand stops himself. *Don't be stupid.* Leah is the soul of honesty, true-blue, *might still love him,* even if it doesn't show. Married twelve years, two kids, now she works, what does he expect? That she's going to bounce through the door shedding her dress and land in the sack wearing nothing but a smile? *Come on, Armand,* he tells himself, *don't be an idiot.* No honeymoon lasts forever. Besides, she hasn't cut you off completely, even if six times a year feels like never. Desire comes and goes. Only weirdoes like you expect it to be constant.

Armand pops the lid, stirs the paint. Richmond Bisque swirls in the can like soft-serve French vanilla. Doesn't smell like ice cream, however, and of course isn't cold. Armand continues stirring even when he knows the pigment is evenly dispersed and the latex blended. Once he dips the brush, there is no stopping.

It would explain a lot, if she were getting *schtupped* on the side. When he rings her phone in the middle of a nothing afternoon and gets voicemail, where is she, really? *I'm either on another call or away from my desk.* No, really: where is she? Away from her desk, doing what? Long lunches. Unaccounted-for hours: she should be there, but isn't. Leah's desire is not hiding, not in Lost & Found, it hasn't wandered off or died. It is on vacation. Wafted off to parts unknown on the wings of another dick. Or Dick. If it makes sense to speak of a dick-small-d or Dick-D-uppercase with wings. Look, what do you want from him? What do you expect? Armand isn't a Renaissance poet, he's a guy who pored over earnings reports and prospectuses and financial analyses of petroleum-industry companies, then bandied obliquities and half-truths with officers of those companies, then cobbled together the assorted shit with professional boilerplate to produce analyses of his own. A currency of optimistic generalizations shored-up with statistics. To Armand, sure, a dick or Dick can have wings. It can be a bald eagle, all right? Get it? Bald? Or a jumbo jet, all right? get it? a JUMBO jet? Understand? *Capeesh?* Why not? Because isn't that what every guy thinks or fears, that his wife or girlfriend is going to dump him for some dude hung like a horse? Because have you ever seen a twelve-inch human penis sporting testicles like tennis balls? Can you appreciate how such equipment dwarfs an average man? For all Armand knows or cares, a dick or Dick could have bulging biceps, sing opera, speak Latin, own a vineyard, pitch for the Yankees, corner the gold market, live in a 24,000-square-foot villa with picture-window views of Grand Teton National Park. Dick Unlimited. It is not mainly a matter of words, what the Language Police call metaphor. It is a matter of what is, or might be, and how it makes him feel.

He stops stirring; feels shitty, also angry; also sad, as if it means nothing, amounts to nothing, the years and the miles, two kids and a couple houses, the apartment they had for three years after they got married, the condo they had for six, all the way back to when they met, right here in Ithaca, at CU in fact, both of them students and much younger. Most of all, Armand feels helpless. Because if she is, she is. Nothing he can do about it unless he truly is willing to do something crazy, and even then, killing the dick or Dick will not solve the problem. The thing is to win her back. That tends not to work. And Leah especially, once she has made up her mind, is done. And so are you. Meaning, Armand.

Kneeling in the grass, full gallon can of Richmond Bisque open and ready, sun every minute higher in the sky, Armand wonders why he bothers. Why is he here, doing this? Why not forget it and go play golf? As a matter of fact, there is a strip club or two on the outskirts of town. Yet here he is, endlessly Armand. Still loves his wife, still misses her and wants her. Every day. His own dick works fine, thanks, as soon as Leah shows interest. And that circles him back to Why. Why is she not interested? What does she want? What does she need? What should he be doing that he isn't doing, hasn't done? Isn't saying and hasn't said? She does not have to work. Their money is fine. He thinks it is. The ground is solid beneath their feet. They live closer to the vest, or maybe it's the bone he means, or brass tacks, or whatever, but they live damn well all the same. Compared to 98 or maybe just 90 percent of the people in the world, Armand and Leah are rich. They own a house with more rooms in it than people, plus two cars, just that puts them ahead of almost everyone in the Third World, and they have drawers and closets full of clothes, off-season clothes folded and sealed inside high-density clear plastic bins and hanging from wire shelves Armand has hung in the basement. They own a thousand books at least, maybe twelve hundred, accumulated mostly during their marriage, some from before and, truth to tell, mostly not read but present all the same, shelved, waiting, gathering dust and, in the basement, a touch of mold. More CDs than they can listen to, more DVDs than they can watch. Two flatscreen televisions, plus, in Alessandro's room, an old 27-inch Big Tube that Alex uses for videotapes and XBOX. A portable DVD player that currently lives in Julietta's bedroom. Major appliances, color-coordinated. More plates and glasses and flatware than they will ever need: Leah's wedding china, service for twelve Armand thinks it is, complete with serving pieces and an elegant ivory-white teapot they never have occasion for, tall and slim with a swan-neck handle and dainty lift-off lid, all of it hand-painted with red and blue and yellow flowers in a Chinese style. Ditto the lead crystal wine and water—what should he call them? vessels?—also service for twelve, plus varying numbers of assorted cocktail tumblers and champagne flutes and high-ball and juice glasses, plus something called a footed desert dish, twelve of *them,* too, Armand cannot imagine why, meaning he cannot imagine the purpose, the need. Plus, *plus,* a complete set of sterling silver: serving forks and spoons, oyster forks and strawberry forks and ice cream forks and spatulas, although he does not think these things are called spatulas when they are made of .975 silver and longer than ... well, pretty flipping long, ha ha, in addition to formal five-piece silver place-settings, again for twelve, as if Leah and he have ever had a sit-down dinner for more than themselves and one set of parents at a time. Leah's jewelry he cannot contemplate, he can't even begin. Not just the diamond engagement ring and platinum wedding band but also the lesser rings and earrings and necklaces he has given her over the years for birthdays and Chanukah and, needless to say, their anniversary. It's obscene, with children hungry all over the world and dying of malaria and dysentery and clothed in rags, to have spent such coin on baubles.

But Leah likes baubles. And his children aren't hungry. Alex and Julietta crawl into bed with their bellies full and wake up to almost whatever they want for breakfast. Are the world's hungry children, the neglected, impoverished, ill & forgotten children of strangers who are foreigners besides, his, Armand's, responsibility, too?

Nice question. Armand does not answer it, not now, when the job at hand is to paint the lower, east-facing eave, which he has scraped clean and power-sanded and finally primed with a thin, transparent concoction called Peel-Stop that goes on like syrup and smells like glue. Armand dislikes the stuff because it drools down his wrist if he overloads the brush and disappears on contact when he gets it on the wood. He can't tell what he has primed and what he hasn't unless he can get an angle on the slats so that light glints along the grain. Also, he is not sure it works. Armand was dubious, especially at twenty-six bucks a gallon, but when he explained his problem with the eaves—old paint half flaking off to bare wood, half adhering even after power-sanding—this is what they told him to use and sold him at the quoted price, along with a black rubber respirator to strap over his nose and mouth, plus a box of disposable filters. So Armand tried it, jaw clenched, rubber facemask tight against his skin, unbarked curses loud in his throat. Despite the filter, he smelt lead dust or imagined he did and wondered if inhaling it would make him stupid or blind, cause significant impairment, maybe just give him brain cancer and kill him outright. And so what. Right? We have to die of something and this way his family can collect his life insurance, not to mention enjoy the clean, creamy smoothness of freshly-painted eaves.

Armand sets the ladder so that, standing one step below the top, he will have paintable slats and rafter tails on both sides to the limit of his reach. It is important to think of these things. Maximizing coverage saves maybe twenty minutes a day, plus the trouble of re-leveling the ladder each time he sets it. Their lot is sloped seven or eight degrees, so Armand has to toe-nudge shims under the ladder's downslope foot until it stands stable. Also, the ladder is not an ordinary lightweight aluminum step-ladder. It is a Little Giant Ladder System whose design includes a pivoting center joint of machined steel, lockable in three positions, and heavy-duty legs that telescope to four different heights, all of it together weighing maybe twenty times what a typical, perfectly serviceable aluminum step-ladder weighs and costing twelve times the price. As Armand says, they're rich.

He reaches for the Benjamin Moore exterior latex. Richmond Bisque is a proprietary hue that falls, roughly, somewhere between caramel and beige. Leah picked it. She picked all their colors except the midnight blue Alessandro insisted they paint his ceiling and the lavender Julietta wanted for her bedroom walls. Everything else is earth-tones. *To quiet the mind and calm the spirit,* what a joke. Which is how they wound up with Corkscrew Willow, a sort-of mocha with golden undertone, and Light Cocoa, and Autumn Wheat, and Arizona Tan. Travertine: a word Armand had never heard, a color he had never seen. But it looks good in the kitchen and on the stairway wall, which Alex and Julietta *schmutz* with grubby kid-hands. Which reminds Armand, and he reaches behind himself and plucks the brush from his pocket.

Bent over, wire semi-circle of can handle in one fist and best brush in his fingers, Armand looks for no reason at the patched foundation below the lately-painted stucco under the dining room windows—looks for no reason, except maybe he smells it: a moist pile of thick-stooled dogshit glistening in the morning light.

Motherless butt-sucking son-of-a-bitch. Armand has not painted a single slat, hasn't set a foot on the first step of his Ladder System. He hasn't even straightened up from the first of countless times he will have to bend over to pick up his best brush or the 5-in-1 tool he has just dropped, again, and here it is, the day's first add-on chore.

He should have known. A dog of course shits daily, maybe twice. Why would Armand think this day is different? Can he have imagined those mutts would spare him? That Jethro would leash his animals and keep them curbed? Why? For whom? For *Armand?* You have to be kidding. You have to be fucking *shitting* me, soldier. *C'mon Armand,* says the gravelly voice of his former corporate overlord, *whose chain are you jerking? What makes you think you're special? That the world notes your presence, acknowledges your need? Much less caters to you. Much less cares about you. The world isn't here for you, private, it doesn't belong to you, it does not owe you one god-*

damn motherfucking bullshit thing. It does not so much as know your name. It does not care, it couldn't possibly, and about you does not give a single, solitary, infinitesimal fuck. The cosmos does not know you exist and the instant you die and for eons afterward, for eternity, it will go on not only not knowing or caring but as if you've never lived nor loved nor thought nor dreamed, possessed consciousness, drew breath. You are less than a fly, a fucking speck or less, a feckless little fucking dust mite, a midge, clinging to your patch of green-blue orb, tacked-on to no effect, for no purpose and for no one's good, a freeloader using up air and food and water, taking up space and to the sum of existence contributing nothing, nothing, nothing, which is what you are. You quit at forty, you coward, you mouse, you walked away, bagged it, punted, crawled like a worm off a job guys would kill for and the glory of big money. Why? For what? To do what? Live in a past that never fucking was. Paint a poorly-framed horseshit house that should have been torn down fifty fucking years ago. Concern yourself with dogshit. Nice going, bro. Fucking nice move. Swift, as we said back in the day, in the neighborhood, on the block. Joey and Tony, Johnny and the boys. That wasn't too swift, Marconi. *You don't have to tell me, you* gavone, *I got eyes, I can fucking see.*

Armand sees, all right, too well sees a piled load, near-fresh, which means he has narrowly missed the main event, the laugh-out-loud screaming outrage of the pug or lab or that ugly mutt poodle squatting in front of him and letting go—right in Armand's face, in a manner of speaking, as if daring him to fetch it an ass-breaking kick or bean it with a stone slung David-style or drive to Dick's or Dan's, either way the sporting goods megastore at Pyramid Mall, to buy a rifle to shoot it fucking dead.

All right. All right, all right, all right. Let's not get crazy, Armand. Let's not blow things out of proportion. First you mentally accuse Leah of sexual betrayal, and now you want to murder an innocent animal because it defecated outside your dining room window. Come on, Armand. Show some wisdom, a bit of humanity. Exercise a little self-control. Be a man. Grow up, why don't you? It's nothing, less than nothing. A little fecal matter. Here today, gone tomorrow. Or get rid of it, quick-quick, and it's gone right now.

Armand sets the can down and covers it loosely with its lid. He lays his best brush across the top, straightens up and walks around the house to the old garage whose wood studs are decaying into the asphalt. The door is raised because he keeps the paint in here, more strategic efficiency, not that there is really space for five or six cans of exterior latex, what with his Benz and their bikes and a lawn mower, an original door removed during renovation and never re-hung, snow tires for the Benz, bags of grass seed and fertilizer-plus-weed control, as well as a spreader to apply the latter. Also, stacked in the garage's dark back, Armand has eight tombstone-size archival boxes filled to bursting with complete copies of *The New York Times* beginning on 9/11—or rather, 9/12—and running through January 2002 and the end of Tora Bora. Why he is saving old newspapers is anyone's guess, except no one knows. Leah does not know and if she did know would pitch a conniption about clutter and stuff he hasn't looked at in years and will never use again (*Like my penis,* Armand wants to tell her) and make him throw them out, or rather recycle, which is what they do with newspapers. Leah is going to recycle him one day, Armand is sure of it, or just throw him away, set him curbside with a City of Ithaca trash tag gummed to his forehead. Armand himself saves things, some things, the ones that matter, or seem to. On 9/11 and for months thereafter the daily editions of *The New York Times* seemed to matter very much.

Then the manhunt stumbled. Turns out the Marines or Rangers or Delta Force or Black Berets or Navy SEALS or whoever they were had one hell of a rugged time scouring the White Mountains at thirteen thousand snow-bound feet. Meanwhile, Pakistan's so-called army did not exactly run itself ragged trying to seal the border, which it was probably incapable of doing, anyway. And so Taliban loyalists and al Qaida fighters cheated death, eluded capture, escaped to havens unknown. It is humiliating. Armand cannot look at the archival boxes without feeling a hot, red flush of shame burst across his chest, flow up his neck and flood his face. Opening the boxes and lifting out the newspapers and re-reading them are out of the question. He remembers the brave talk, all the firmness and resolve and ardent vows to destroy al Qaida, to starve it of money and manpower, to capture bin Laden, drag him into a court of law and mete out justice, or just plain kill him. Summary execution, as Churchill favored for Hitler. Well, you would have thought so. On 9/11 and for weeks thereafter you had 250,000,000 Americans ready to storm the Afghan brush armed with just their rage. That would have been stupid but the rage was genuine and the impulse sincere. Now the moment has passed. Not quite three years later, that 9/11 rage feels as remote as mountain caves. The national will, if a phenomenon so intangible truly exists, has been diverted to other things. Vengeance does not seem so important anymore. Better to keep the oil flowing, the economy humming, the Internet streaming. Pleasure and profit do not mesh with the machinery of revenge. No wonder Islamists bide their time.

Old Sammie's been hiding. Yes, he has. Except sometimes he shows up on satellite news with another promise to cut off the snake's head.

Rakes and pruning shears, a hammer, a handsaw, two snow shovels and a weed cutter hang from iron nails driven half-way into rotting studs. Armand grabs the spade and walks around front. He thrusts the blade under the reeking pile, this move's being the opposite of a sleight-of-hand-man's snatching the tablecloth without wrecking the china, and carries it at arm's length to the wood lot, where, a second before he flings it in, thinks, *Why should I?* then *Why shouldn't I?*

It is maybe nine-thirty. Leah is at work; he watched her go in that ass-loving skirt. The kids are at camp. No one is strolling the sidewalk as far as he can see in both directions. Birds are singing, sparrows he thinks, is guessing without really having any idea because other than a bald eagle, a crow, a blue jay, an owl, a cardinal, and a hawk, Armand does not know birds on sight or by song. But the air, anyway, is embroidered with it: birdsong; and is warm, and the light is bright. Armand himself stands in the shade created by the maple-leaf canopy. Still, he's visible, clearly visible to at least five houses across the street and anyone who happens to be inside them, looking out. Jethro can see him, too, if he happens to look up from whatever the hell he does all day. So Armand can be seen, easily seen, which means there might be a witness, possibly more than one, of what he is about to do.

And so what. He's nothing, right? We have established that, his no-status in the world's cold eye. And dogshit definitely is nothing, definitively is nothing—is nothing by definition, he means, and besides will rinse off, eventually, because even with leaf cover, rain washes Jethro's house. So it is of no consequence, it really *does not matter,* and even if it did, what of it? Armand is fed-up; no pun intended, he doesn't give a shit. So that's what he does.

Right back at you! And with an overhand motion launches the lately-excreted shit of one of Jethro's dogs at Jethro's house, aiming for the roof. That's what Armand wants: Jethro-dog dogshit on the roof of Jethro's home. Problem is, he hasn't calculated distance, hasn't test-launched several similar loads or even just one to get a fix on escape velocity and lateral momentum, which would have given him a better sense of range. All Armand has done is eyeball it and fire off-the-cuff with no idea how high and far he can plausibly expect dogshit to fly. Guesswork and improvisation: that is all Armand has brought to the task. He does not even have experience to fall back on because he has never flung shit before. And almost wishes he hasn't flung it now because the second he does he can tell the load is falling short. It is too light, or maybe too heavy, or its coefficient of drag is too great or whatever, and he has not started it on a trajectory high enough for its momentum to carry it far enough, and the stools are thudding onto Jethro's lawn. That's not so bad, he figures, it's organic, no real harm or injury there, and probably as much as he should have attempted in the first place. One small chunk, a break-away tip or end, hits the roof's asphalt edge and deflects backward, into the rain gutter. No good. No one can see it, wonder how it got up there, which is the effect Armand was trying for when he set his sights, which have proven myopic, on the roof. And the next decent rain will wash it away. Another half-stool almost makes it, then, hey hey, hits the side of the house just above a window. Armand hears it smack. He guesses anyone behind the window, that is, in the room to which the window belongs, has heard it, too.

Well, fuck 'em. He was willing to be seen, he can't shy off being heard. And what is anyone going to do about it, he'd like to know. Say Jethro sics the dogs on him. Armand can ward them off with the spade. Self-defense, pure and simple: anyone would say so and with luck he'll have witnesses to that, too, maybe the same domestic spies who take vicarious, let's say fiendish, joy in watching eleven cats and three dogs turn Armand's lawn into a manure lot.

That shit on the house will get attention. You can't miss it, a brown glop on the clapboard. Armand guesses he should not have done it. Today or tomorrow he will have to meet Jethro's stare and answer his question and get goaded into an argument and maybe a fight. The guy is his neighbor, after all. They are fellow homeowners and Ithacans, Americans who share pretty much a common lot, no pun intended, although Jethro seems much more concerned about the property line than Armand. As if Armand can pick up the strip of grass and earth, put it in his pocket and walk away, leaving a chasm three feet wide and infinitely deep, clear through Earth's core and out the other side probably in the wilds of China and on into limitless space. Jethro, an eye on his mother's interests, maybe thinks so. The old lady is a shut-in; Armand never sees her. During nights that are otherwise still, a smoker's rattle travels across the disputed side-yard while he lies in bed. That's her, he guesses: Jethro's mother, his old mom. A wicked-bad smoker from the sound of that cough and now paying for it. Armand has her figured for cancer any day now and Jethro he has figured as the sponger son, more ne'er-do-well than prodigal, although he looks as if he has eaten up his inheritance in donuts. Jethro does outdoor chores and keeps Mother company while she keeps him fed—not the worst arrangement if the mortgage is paid and it is a matter of utilities and taxes and daily maintenance.

Thinking it over, Armand almost regrets the dogshit. He should not have flung it at the roof. He should have just shoveled it into the wood lot or dumped it on Jethro's shrubs, which seem to mean so much to him, or flicked it into his queer little garden with the pond.

Now it's too late.

He thinks maybe he can hose the shit off with a good long stream from the high-pressure nozzle. He would have to find it first, the nozzle, and screw it onto the garden hose after first having screwed off the regular one. Still, the shit will leave a stain, call it tan or beige or Richmond Bisque, that maybe no one will notice. But the window: it's open. Whether or not she heard the shit hit the clapboard, the old woman surely is going to hear water drumming against the house. She'll come flustering out and ask him what in hell he thinks he's doing, hosing down her house and spraying water through the screen and all over the floor, or carpet, or whatever. So that's another thing. So maybe he'll just leave it and hope no one sees, that no one has seen, unlikely as that is for reasons that are not just self-evident, not just patent, but cosmic. Because whenever Armand wanders off-base, he gets caught. Even if it's a small thing, something truly little-shit, no pun intended, and not really wrong or just slightly wrong—meaning, even if it is well short of mortal sin and solidly in the gray space of a bent rule—he's nabbed. It is the first lesson of Armand's life: he gets away with nothing. He is the absolute, categorical opposite of these guys he hears about, some of them he worked with, such as salesmen who had legitimate reasons for staying out late, who have an affair or a series of girlfriends over three or four or seven or as many as thirteen years, one of them managed, without their wives finding out or even suspecting—well, it just knocks Armand over, it kills him, despite his not wanting to fool around on a temporary, purely sexual basis with some woman, not seriously wanting, anyway, however he might toy with the notion, because after the fun of physical pleasure he is pretty sure it would make him sad. Not that trying to lob a little shit onto your chubby neighbor's crummy roof is analogous to cheating on your wife. One wrong does not equal another wrong that is wholly different. Even if some of the shit accidentally hit the house and some of this lesser portion even stuck. And that's another thing. Armand has not meant to hang feces on clapboard. That's bad luck. A sort of negative serendipity irrupting from a universe shaped by Natural Selection and driven by chance. Luck cannot be forced, it can't be bought, and bad luck cannot be dodged or squelched and as such cannot be blamed on someone, namely Armand, who was trying to do one thing and ended up *because of bad luck* doing another thing he did not intend. And so he cannot be blamed. Not exactly.

On the other hand: It is hard not to see it as frankly his fault. And a delusion to think he will get away with it.

Armand turns on the spigot and hoses off the spade, letting the run-off seep into the ground. If he had stopped to think, he would have realized he could dissolve the dogshit. But no, he had to complicate, grab the shovel, the spade, as if he were reaching for his gun and it was his wife's honor or his own he was defending. Dead-set on it, and from that point on things got out of hand. Literally. Unless what he means is Actually, this little incident that has just gone down not being a matter of words only. The other thing he sees is that the standard nozzle throws a pretty strong stream that would maybe knock the bit of shit stuck there off. Say he strolls over and blasts away at close range, then darts back. If anyone sees, he'll say he noticed a carpenter bee getting interested in the scraped-down shingles. As Armand knows from bitter experience (so he'll say), carpenter bees do the devil's own job of destruction on dry, unpainted wood, so he thought—no, not thought, just did, he just shooed it off on instinct with a burst from his trusty hose, which is why he did not notice the open window and he sure is sorry about all that water all over the floor, or carpet. Count on him never to do it again.

Just thinking all this wears him out. As a result, Armand does nothing. Suddenly decides *Nope,* and that's that.

He shuts off the water and returns the spade to its place. He goes into the house to use the bathroom. Frees some pee, drops a deuce, and after washing his hands feels ready, he thinks, finally to paint that eave. To start, anyway, and see how far he gets. He is on his way out, actually has his hand on the doorknob, when the telephone rings.

No way.

Somebody saw. Somebody motherfucking saw and is calling him on it, literally, actually calling him. To dress him down. Pin his ears back. Some motherless son of a nosy-bitch-busybody dogfacing *bastard,* Armand can't believe it. He cannot get away with one thing, not one fucking measly little victimless crime, not the least of minor transgressions. A bad neighbor. He is. That is what they say about him, what they already say, and now everyone is about to find out how bad. And then they will punish him. And maybe take it out on his children.

The phone rings twice, three times. Armand does not answer it. Absolutely does not go near the handset. Because it's creepy. Not only did someone see the incident, someone also saw him enter the house and, it seems, correctly guessed not only his purpose but also how long it would take. Which is really creepy. Really. Because it isn't the same two days in a row. Not that Armand isn't regular. A regular guy: he is. So it is a coincidence, or a lucky guess, or whoever is calling means to make him dive for the phone with his pants at his ankles. Which Armand would not have done, if it had started ringing when he was on the can, and as he sure as hell is not going to do now because, one, there is just no flipping chance, he is not answering it; and two, just because the telephone rings does not mean you have to pick it up. Like the doorbell, or even and maybe especially if someone knocks despite a functioning bellbutton obviously just a finger's length away. That seems not just pushy, ha ha, and impatient but plainly aggressive and borderline hostile. *Rata-tat-tat-tat-tat-tat-tat-tat,* staccato-like, rattling the beveled glass of the antique front door annoys Armand to the point of his wanting to pull the door open and punch the arrogant bastard, whoever he is, in the mouth. *What the fuck's your fucking problem?* He knows the type. He used to work with them. Traders and salesmen who were always barking, *C'mon c'mon c'mon,* as if the world could not move fast enough and he, Armand, were stupid. *Whoresons:* that's the word. Another perfectly useful noun banished from standard American English. It describes them to the bone, their hearts, their minds, their greedy cinder souls. The motherfucking whoresons just about drove him mad.

On the fourth ring the answering machine picks up. Leah's hello-leave-a-message cue runs, Armand assumes, although it is audible only to the caller, then the machine beeps and Armand hears the dry rasp of the night before.

"Pervert. I know about you. Hiding with your thing in your hand. You don't fool me. Counting Jew gold. Conniving. Plotting to steal people's homes. A sweet, clean old lady. You should be ashamed. May you drop dead, dirty kike. May your children get cancer. I pray thieves steal your Yid gold. That your wife's tits fall off. Her cunt gets leprosy. That the house you stole burns to the ground. Do you hear me, Jew bastard? The ground."

While the Nazi is catching her breath, the machine clicks and beeps. For a second Armand does not realize it has cut her off. Then he wonders if she will call back to finish. Then he realizes she will never finish because such a message has no end.

It is really something, to hear it. Straight-out-plain, in-your-face hate. Plainly-stated, he means. Outright. Also fascinating, in the way the cobra fascinates the rabbit, and for that reason unnerving. Because the hate is aimed at him.

Malocchio. Can it be this witch is not Jethro's old mom but some greenhorn Italian giving him the evil eye? A peasant type, *una contadina* who never got over it, with a rosary around her neck and Mary Mother of God in a niche above the bed. They give modern Italian-Americans a bad image, these superstitious women who carry on as if they are still in the Old Country. Ancient villages rotten with gossip, stone streets from the Age of Augustus and Feasts of the Saints and forty fucking days of Lent. Christ on the Cross and Satan at large. If they want to live that way, why do they come to America? It embarrasses Armand, as if he himself is nothing more than a made-over ginzo, a Wop with manners who's OK in polite company and knows how to pass.

A red "1" is blinking in the message window. Armand touches PLAYBACK and at the word "Pervert" presses ERASE. A robovoice confirms, "Message one erased," and it occurs to Armand that he has just destroyed evidence. Well, he does not want Leah to hear it. Or the children. He ought to tell Leah. It's their second flame in fewer than twenty-four hours and it's getting worse. The witch has singled him out, wished horror on his beloveds.

Curses on his head.

The evil eye.

Leah will want to report it. Call the IPD, have them send over a squad car so the cops can write it up. She will be annoyed that Armand has erased the tape.

A hate crime. In the so-called privacy of their home. He will have to remember to draw the curtains. Funny, the Nazi did not mention dogshit.

Fat Jethro and the Wicked Shut-in of East Hill.

Cats scamper from interior shadow to golden pollinated light, a cream-and-amber American wirehair named Roosevelt leading the rush. Luke brings up the rear, mug of apple juice icy-cold in his hand, blue-and-white checked bandana knotted four-square on his head. Roosevelt sets the pace, which the other cats feign not to notice. Boris and Natasha, a pair of Russian blues, lie in the grass and begin to tangle, claws retracted. In less than a minute they stop—because of the heat, Luke figures, which has really set in. Ten o'clock in the morning and the big man is sweating.

Tennessee, a blue-banded, golden-eyed Somali, stretches out under the trunk of Luke's smoke-gray LeSabre, a 1989 model rusting at its wheel wells. His father died six months after buying it, the only new car Walter Robideau ever owned. Its leather seats have cracked, its clear-coat is long gone and the paint has faded. Luke parks the LeSabre on a packed-dirt space a half-dozen steps from their front door. The driveway, all ten feet of it, is gravel. The parking space used to be grass. Over years too many to count, tires of forgotten cars have ground the dirt as fine as talc and the sun washed it almost white. Tennessee seems to find it comfortable, there in the shade under the LeSabre's back end. Kookla, Fran, and Ollie, a trio of white-and-black American short hairs, pad after a mature white-and-black named Lola, their mother. A silver-gray female Korat with green eyes called—what else?—Korey stalks around the house and heads for the trees—to be alone, Luke cannot help thinking. Despite Mother's favoring her, or perhaps because of it, Korey is a *prima donna* and acts the part. As if to balance their collective karma, Pavel, a magnificent Havana brown, is friendly in a way that is heartbreaking and strange. Generally it is a dog that loves you. A cat tolerates you. Sometimes. Pavel, it seems, is a dog in cat form. Having appeared one day, he has never left, has learned to avoid Vladimir, and caterwauls after every she-cat in the neighborhood. And Vladimir, a mature orange and white male, fears nothing, hunts everything, gives no quarter and with his green stare terrorizes every animal within a two-hundred-foot radius of the Robideau Cape.

Luke never planned on so many cats. The house cannot hold them, not with three dogs skirmishing for turf. As a matter of fact, Luke does not especially like cats. He does not much like any animal, although if forced to take something he would take a dog. One dog, preferably a Rotweiller, which he can neither afford nor accommodate. Rex and Speckles and Barney are pound strays; to Luke they have always felt temporary. Stop-gap companionship. The things he has settled for rather than the thing he wants. The cats Luke has grown used to, mostly because Mother enjoys them. To trim costs, he has not had them de-clawed or spayed, with the result that they hunt and kill and propagate in a virtual state of nature. Luke gives away litters once the kittens are weaned, those for whom he finds takers, and keeps the rest. He does not drown kittens or abandon cats along rural roads. Cars skirting Cooper Circle Park—for no reason, Cooper Circle itself leads nowhere—

have killed several that have dashed into the street, not wholly to Luke's regret. Cats, supposedly, are intelligent, but he does not see it.

He sips the apple juice, deliciously sweet. The grass, he sees, is overdue for cutting, and he is going to have to clear the garden of weeds. Quackgrass and hogweed will run wild if he neglects it much longer. Also, he has to prune—just an inch or two to smooth ragged tips of forsythia, pare back mountain laurel and red oleander. The lilac he'll leave. It looks better un-fussed-over and borderline unruly. Now is not a time for aggressive pruning, what with everything growing and blooming except the tulips, which poked through early in April and have already spent themselves in the wan spring sun, and the Montauk daisies, which show their bright faces only when summer, true summer, is gone.

Circling the house, following more or less in Korey's pawprints, Luke takes stock. His azaleas are thriving, evidently happier in the new beds he built with better drainage than their native clay-dense soil otherwise allows. Acidic food helps; the pink and purple flowers are big and vivid and look luscious enough to eat, except they're poisonous. The bed is in a good shaded spot, sheltered from the street and also from his neighbor's front walk and its ungoverned foot traffic. So no excuse if those pesky kids trample it, although to get satisfaction Luke would have to step across the side-yard and knock on the door and register a complaint face-to-face. As if it would do any good. His neighbor would likely claim his kids went nowhere near the bed. On the other hand, it would give Luke an excuse to mention the devastated redbud in his neighbor's backyard. The tree is in shock and getting ready to die. It is twenty-seven years old, which Luke happens to know because he planted it. 1977. He was eleven and a Cub Scout, and his troop was doing a Green Thumb project. The redbud earned him a merit badge, although he forgets which one. Was there a badge just for horticulture, or did it also involve neighborliness or community service? It does not matter anymore and probably never did; being a good kid, Luke has learned, does not get you anything in the long run, and short-term it's just those worthless badges. He had a navy blue sash covered with them by the time he quit, weary of doing-good and paper drives and all the yes-ma'aming and red-wagon-collecting of canned foods and assorted non-perishables for poor families living amid the green hills and purple valleys that surround the town of Ithaca. Not that Luke was reluctant to help. He could see the purpose of it, and the necessity. It was a straight-backed, square-shouldered feeling, to walk into an unpainted, five-room house carrying a box of canned pork and beans, tomato soup, tuna fish, chili, and see four kids smile when he set it on the table. "Compliments of Troop 130," he would say. As if he were eight feet tall and wearing Santa's suit, the kids would say, "Thank-you," all together on mom's cue. And their mother, who was sometimes not bad-looking and once or twice damned pretty, might kiss him a quick one on the cheek.

Those days are gone. Now it is Luke who could use a free box of canned foods, even if he and Mother are sitting on a tidy pile of gold, supposedly, with this house in the current market. They call it a bubble and maybe it is, in the sense of things being overvalued for reasons that have nothing to do with the things themselves. But the house is real; it exists; it is worth something. A tangible asset. They are nowhere near as poor as those country people, who really had nothing or the next thing to it, only their land and what they could grow, corn or strawberries, in this climate mushrooms thrive, and as far as livestock maybe pigs, or chickens. By comparison Luke is rich. In practice, of course, he is so not-rich that just thinking *I'm rich* feels ridiculous. Except he grows things purely for pleasure. Foxglove and belladonna, hyacinth and chinaberry. Ornamentals. They are generally poisonous and serve no purpose other than to please him. The eye: these flowers feed the eye, especially when arranged just-so. That redbud tree needlessly dying in his neighbor's yard was the first planting Luke did on his own. Not only did it take, it thrived, grew and spread and until this year gave forth large, heart-shaped leaves. A hardy tree that should have lived longer than any of them, and would have if his asshole neighbor had not attacked it with a saw. Luke shouted when the first limb fell, sap oozing from the wound. He was up in the sniper's nest, keeping watch. He thought the guy would see the sap and understand what he was doing and stop; but no, he went ahead and severed three more limbs and two branches, all in all about half the tree. When he finally quit it was too late. Sap was running like blood. Luke could hear the redbud scream.

Now at the end of June the tree is nearly bare. Branches gone black. Small, attenuated leaves. Luke expects it to drop those leaves by August. He wonders if his neighbor can distinguish a living tree from a dead one.

Bending his steps around the Cape and turning into the sideyard, Luke notices something in the Zen garden. The hedges are intact and the meditation bench looks untouched but the smooth stones, three or four of them, are less white than they were. As he comes closer, Luke sees some mud has been kicked up. One of the dogs marking turf, although he has trained them to keep out. A stray? Some negligent person's mutt? He has almost made up his mind to visit Agway for animal repellant when, now inside the garden, standing close to those stones, Luke sees it is not mud. It is shit.

Shit in his Zen garden. On the smooth white stones that ring the pool. Some mangy tramp has slunk in here, where Luke allows no dog to be, and defecated. In this sheltered, peaceful spot, beside this still water, a stray brute has relieved itself. The turds are medium-sized and dark green, fecund and ripe, and seem not so much deposited, Luke thinks, as tumbled. Almost as if they have been brought there.

His eyes move from stones to pool. He looks down through its crystal water and sees four turds at the bottom.

Luke sets his apple juice on the bench, mug carefully centered on a slat, and circles the pool with his hands on his hips. He inspects the stones, the grass fringe—fescue, it is, a nice medium green, medium-fine blade that can live in shade—and the privet hedge that stands eight feet high on three sides. Nothing else looks messed with, nothing crushed or broken, no snapped branches or matted grass, no paw prints in the loamy soil under the hedge. It is possible a dog walked through the entrance and out again (for it is dogshit, Luke notes, distinctly canine fecal matter) but it makes no sense for a dog to shit on stones. That is something a cat would do, to let you know she is not impressed by your precious arrangement and not too bowled over by you, either. But it is definitely dogshit. And dogs prefer grass.

Luke goes to the garage for a shovel and a plastic bag. It really is an eyesore, the garage, with its peeling clapboards and disintegrating roof and sagging walls, but where is renovation money coming from? We are not talking about patchwork repair. The whole roof needs to be replaced, the green clapboards need to be scraped to the wood and repainted, the windows need new panes and, for all Luke knows (he hasn't checked in awhile, afraid of what he might find), the posts are rotted—which means the frame will have to be jacked up and a foundation built and the old, rotted posts replaced with new, pressure-treated 4x4s. A domestic disaster, a cash leech. So ignore it. Pretend it isn't there, that nothing must be done, that it has nothing to do with him. Maybe he should burn it down. One night, when no one is around to see, or in broad daylight so the whole world can watch if it wants to. Where would they put all the stuff, the odd this-and-that and Robideau clutter that serves no purpose except to make it impossible to garage the car? Which is past garaging, anyway. And a fire might get away from him, spread—what then?

The shovel Luke finds hanging from its nail. For a trash bag, he has to hunt. After ten minutes he decides the hell with it, shit is organic, and carries the shovel and a bucket of hose water and two chlorine pellets out to the garden. He shovels shit off the stones and shunts it under the hedge, then with the shovel lifts each fouled stone in turn and slides it into the bucket for a wash. Again with the shovel, he removes the abomination from the pool, one-two-three-four, and is about to shunt it under the hedge; then thinks, *Wait a while* and carries all four soggy nasties away. Moving at a normal pace, Luke looks around as if he is trying to decide where to plant, say, a redbud sapling, when really he is looking for a clear shot.

Cool Luke, loaded shovel hot in his hands.

It is maybe half-past ten. The asshole carted off his noisy kids early this morning. The sexy wife walked past his window two hours ago. The asshole himself is nowhere in sight. Not sanding eaves, not power-washing stucco. Not painting at all, unless he is working inside. A door, a radiator. Or just sitting in an easychair with his feet up, reading a book. Whatever he's up to, what are the odds he is at a window, looking out?

Four wet stools are melting on the shovel blade. So Luke, *and why not?* he would like to know, lifts his arms and snaps his wrists and steps into the fling, basic lacrosse technique, and shit-gone-gooey shoots off the blade and becomes a brown smear in flight. It lands near the middle of his neighbor's yard, which is half-mud, anyway. So who will notice? Who will care? And anyway and anyway and anyway, they are broken-up and nearly dissolved, and ANYWAY dogshit is organic, and all other shit, too. So how can it hurt grass that is already half-dead? Luke almost smiles, so close is this feeling to something good. Savoring it, he considers possible spots for that redbud.

*

Over the next week he keeps an eye out for a freeloading dog. One doesn't show but that settles nothing. Luke is at work through the evening and when he is home he is not nailed to the window or posted sentry-style in his garden. *Absence of evidence is not evidence of absence.* Anyway, he has evidence. Shit on the stones and in the water. He'll be damned if he is going to take it. His meditation pool is not a latrine. Those stones are not cakes of lime. It might be a stray that college kids kept for fun, then abandoned. Each year after graduation you see a few wandering around. The SPCA has to pick them up, screen them for sickness, cage them in the shelter way the hell out on Hanshaw Road. Sometimes they miss one and it becomes Luke's problem.

He could put up a fence with a gate but fences run against Buddhist notions. It is about Oneness. Unity. This sky and that grass and all water inter-are. So, too, are the stones and trees, the talcum-fine dust and lethal flowers, all animals and Luke himself. Ditto dogshit, which is harder to accept. Only a Buddhist sage could go misty-eyed contemplating the inter-relational wonder of fresh shit. But the clear pool, the white stones. Stones in a circle help us focus on the center. A fence ruins it. A fence separates, is exclusionary, draws a line that divides one thing from another, this from that, a man from his neighbor—maybe not such a bad idea, Luke thinks, even if it isn't Buddhist. As if anyone outside a monastery could survive as a Buddhist in these United States. Luke does not really try to be Buddhist. He would not call the feeling he lives with faith or describe his practice, such as it is, as devotion. It is more along the lines of a better self to which he aspires. The selfless self, the soul centered and contemplative, at peace. *Teach us to care and not to care. Teach us to be still.* He will never attain it—not with the tests and tasks, the insults and indignities every day throws at him. A dirty job, taxes, always cash-poor. Not to mention that guy next door, a walking, talking invitation to envy if ever Luke met one.

At dinner he asks Mother about it. A trespassing stray. Has she seen, noticed anything? Has anyone mentioned it?

Mother cuts her chicken into twelve pieces before she begins forking it into her mouth. "Who do I talk to?" she says, chewing. "No one but you. Cindy on the phone. Matty and John once in a blue moon."

"No one's called, asked about a stray?"

"What dog? Ours are the only dogs running loose around here."

"Yes, Mother. Only some stray crapped up the pool."

She stops chewing. "You cleaned it, I hope."

"Of course, Mother."

"Don't mind me. I wouldn't mention it, except the grass and plantings do seem to have gotten away from you."

Luke stares at her, then drops his eyes to the chicken, breaded and pan-fried, on his plate. He picks up his knife and fork and cuts through the first breast to make sure the liquid runs clear. He sees no liquid at all. Mother has overdone it, again. What was boneless breast of chicken and not cheap even coming from a factory farm has turned more or less into wood. "What's that supposed to mean?" he says, and forks a piece into his mouth.

"Nothing, nothing." She sips her water, waves him away. "Only our neighbor has been mowing our side of the line."

"Slaughtered some wildflowers, did he?"

Mother nods.

"We'll want to put a stop to that. What's ours is ours."

"Well. I think so."

Luke, nodding, cuts a second chicken breast into quarters. He has noticed his neighbor's mower-line, its encroachment, and when it did not retreat on its own, gouged six three-inch deep, six-inch long divots in the turf to mark the boundary of their respective worlds. Which the asshole has ignored.

Luke chews. Mother cooks chicken to death, what with her own mother's horror stories about food poisoning from before the Flood and now a kid in Texas and his grandmother supposedly dying from salmonella. Wooden chicken clumps in his mouth. He does not say a word about it, never has. She has been cooking for him for thirty-eight years. When he fixes his salad, he splashes some Caesar on the chicken.

"You might mention it," Mother says.

Luke forces the tines through a sawed-off piece and backs it up with a clutch of lettuce. "I guess I'll have to," he says. He puts the combo in his mouth, slowly chews, swallows hard. "I'd rather not start an argument."

"Bring it up nicely. Say if you happen to be outside when he is."

Luke nods. Advice is easy for her, who talks to no one. Not that he blames her; talking to people wears him out. Listening takes energy, especially when you have to watch a stranger's face while you follow his words.

"Besides," she says, "the lots are posted."

"It isn't property lines I'm thinking of." Her eyes, now scanning the gray-paged *Pennysaver* that arrives each Thursday folded into their *Ithaca Journal,* let him know that Mother has moved on. What makes Luke pause is the anger he sees each time his neighbor scrapes shit off his walk. The man's tense neck and tight shoulders, his clenched fists and lips are a silent shout. As if animal crap were a personal insult he might answer in kind. He is careful to shovel-up every stool and toss it back, usually into the woodlot.

Luke, chewing, looks at the kitchen clock. Its black hands are metal although the clock is made of wood. He tells the time to himself; it is important to know the time. He understands. He knows what it means. Animal feces in his garden. Turds in his pool, on his stones. Now that he reflects on it, Luke decides it is the sort of thing an asshole would naturally do.

E arly summer twilight is Mary Robideau's favorite time and here its peace is ruined. A roaring engine spins the blades that cut the grass of their neighbor's splotchy lawn and, Mary notices, the border of her own. How many times will she see this and say a word to Luke, who does nothing? Why can't this unpleasant person mow his own grass only? Mary eyes him through the space she pinches between the curtains. He is wearing those shorts again, blue they are and look like cotton, with pockets to the knees, and a sleeveless shirt gray like granite with words she cannot read and a sort-of picture or design she can't make out printed on the front. In her day a man would not have been caught dead in such a get-up.

In Mary's day men dressed like men, not boys or, what's worse, tarts. A sleeveless shirt is a blouse. Tart garb. This neighbor is Luke's age at least, and here in broad daylight he parades about like a five-year-old or a chippie on the make. Disgraceful. He should be embarrassed—might still be if he would leave off lawn-mowering and think. As Mary thinks, trying so hard, for all the good it does her. She knows what she sees but is not sure what it means. Her neighbor is married and a father, not the gay blade such clothes might lead you to expect. His children are beautiful, she must admit. A little boy and a younger girl. Not beautiful in the way of her own grandchildren, whom she sees less often than she wishes, but as all children are beautiful. Silky hair. Custard-smooth skin. Eyes so clear they seem inner-lit. Not that Mary has been close enough to see their eyes. She just knows.

When she drops the curtain dust swirls in the air. Mary drifts around the room, tidying cushions, wiping sofa arms and side tables with tissues she pulls from her apron pocket. The thing she must do is get rid of these collectibles. Ceramic cats and quilted cats, cats made of brass and glass and iron, an ivory cat balancing atop a porcelain ball, cats carved of soapstone and hardwood, coats of the latter simulated in the wood's grain. Life, they say, is a casting-off and Mary does not disagree. Still, she finds it difficult. How many hours has she spent pondering at farmers' markets, garage sales, rummage sales, antique stores, souvenir shops crammed with knick-knacks, only to buy both or all three? Always the least expensive items, which seldom were the ones she wanted. She lives with the result. How many cat-items clutter her home? Her thinking is tending toward a clean-sweep, what they call a purge. Out with what's old, the useless or broken. If she does not need it to live, she does not need it at all.

In her day, a man wore pants. Even on vacation Walter had chinos, lightweight with a crease, in blue and green and khaki. For yard work there were dungarees, now they call them jeans and wear them everywhere, including to a movie theater, which used to be a place people dressed-up to go. No more. To Mary it seems the younger people, by whom she means everyone younger than she is by twenty years or more, do not want to face the fact that they are no longer children. They dress and speak as if still teenagers, or think they are, or want to be. Not that she goes to movies anymore or sees much of anyone apart from her youngest child, long since a man. But she has heard-tell. If you judge by television the whole country is stuck in childhood. Oh, it's fun, she supposes, this pretending you are not an adult, but to her it's silly. Shirking. Might even be immoral, although Mary does not go so far. She is not ready to say that. Oh, to whom? Luke only is here and he would disagree.

If she were their age, she thinks, thirty-five or forty or even fifty, maybe she would do the same. But now here is something: plastic breasts. Mary cannot get over it. She does not understand or maybe just cannot imagine. That young and also, sometimes, middle-aged women pay surgeons to cut open their chests and install plastic whatever-it-is, bags of oily-plastic something. Gel. To make the breasts larger, also firmer. Well, yes, they're firmer because they're plastic. And how, Mary wonders, is that appealing? To the touch, she means. To a man's hand or his cheek. Because isn't that what this craziness is about? But now, plastic, what they call silicone—in what sense is it a substitute for human flesh? *What God has created,* her mind recites, almost there, *let no man rend,* confusing herself a little and knowing she is confused without knowing just how. But finding some comfort nonetheless. The verse tells her it cannot be right, this business of plastic, of installing plastic in a woman's body. Ten years down the road they expect—what? Take for example that woman, the blonde on TV, always wearing heavy mascara and a torn tee-shirt or scanty blouse. Mary knows her name, how could she not, the woman is all over the tabloids, but she will not say the name, will not think it. Not that she begrudges the blonde her success, which is tremendous. A mansion in Beverly Hills, Mary guesses, and what must seem like all the money in the world. On the strength of what? Call it jealousy or plain cattiness but Mary does not see talent there. Oh, she's pleasant, the blonde, she laughs and smiles and has a girlish way of speaking, which is maybe just part of her act, the whole perky-chirpy thing. But the woman fancies herself up like a whore. Mary does not say that word aloud. She is perfectly capable of saying *whore,* she is capable of saying anything, but she chooses not to. Luke likes to look at the blonde and how can she blame him, when the woman parades in front of cameras with most of herself on display? Curvy figure, jiggly flesh. A man always is just a man even if he was once your baby boy. Luke stares at the blonde's breasts, obvious fakes if ever there were one, or rather two, which are so large Mary is surprised the woman doesn't tip. She has a hard time believing they allow this person on television, where the whole country, her grandkids included, can see those giant phony mams. She tells herself that John and Debbie, that Cindy and Frank, do not allow the children to watch.

Sometimes she thinks she has turned prude. That age has made her one. She was young once. In her day it was Marilyn Monroe. Mary never thought of Marilyn as a whore, despite her marriages and carryings-on. A sex symbol, true, they called her that, but Marilyn never had her chest inflated with plastic gel and, apart from a few not-very-revealing photographs and some sort-of artsy nudies, kept her clothes mostly on in front of cameras. She never had children, which in the long run was maybe the right thing. Marilyn watched her weight just like a regular woman and hid her laugh-lines with make-up. Yes, she did have her nose fixed. No one is perfect. Maybe the real difference, the one that matters to Mary, is that Marilyn, whatever wasn't going right for her and despite the mistakes she made, had talent. Not the greatest tragic actress, all right, in the history of cinema, you would not cast her as Lady Macbeth or Mary Tyrone or Martha What's-Her-Name, that sad, unpleasant woman who's afraid of Virginia Woolf. But for what they called comic turns Marilyn was terrific. A bombshell, no doubt about that, and happy to show off what God gave her. Just a tease, a hint, a touch naughty and good, clean fun.

It was. Years and years ago, when Mary was Marilyn's age. Even if she did not look like her, and who did, Mary often thought she felt as Marilyn felt, or at least knew what Marilyn might be thinking, or wanting, or hoping because she had thought and wanted and hoped the same.

Lawn mowers annoy her. Never mind that the season calls for it. Mary wishes for a time that was, when all you heard of a summer evening was the crisp, well-oiled clipping of push-mowers, like a dozen neat scissors snipping all together. That was a pleasant sound, if your husband was home and your children were fed, dishes washed and dried and stacked in cabinets, and you yourself were twenty-five years old or twenty-six, and were sitting in an Adirondack chair your father had carpentered when you were a child and your first family, your mother and father and brother and sister, spent summers at a cabin near a lake; and you sat in that chair twenty years later, on your clean-swept porch in Ithaca with your tall glass of iced tea with sugar and lemon, and listened to your husband clipping the grass with the delicate mower, listened and watched him, who was young when you were young and your children were barely more than babies or not yet born .

The prime of your life. They call it that. The years when you are young enough to have children and love each other, and grown-up enough to solve problems and provide. Nurture your family. Protect it, by any means necessary. *Protect it.* And it passes so quickly. Blink and your babies are grown. Blink again and your children leave home, they marry, they start families and seldom visit. Turn your head and see: your husband is frail; his hair is white. A year from now, three at most, he will not remember your name, or that your own hair was once jet-black, your spine straight, your clear eyes alight with emerald and gold. Then your husband dies and you are old and gray and full of sleep, drowsing on a couch in front of the television and afraid to go to bed. The fact that you knew him almost your whole life, his presence feeling like breath to you, means nothing. Death takes him as if he were nobody. You live in its company thereafter. And your closest companion is absence. And your memory of the man who was your husband fades. And your own death seems imminent and, sometimes, you pray for it.

Go quickly, time. Let it be soon.

Mary, out of tissues, crosses the room and sits in Luke's chair. Dust and tears, she is never done with dust and tears. It smells of him, the chair, exudes his heavy, round-shouldered scent of sweat and topsoil. It is not a bad scent but Mary dislikes it for coming off her son who was once a baby smelling of milk and talc, then a little boy who smelled of grass and peanut butter. Now Luke is a large man who often seems like a stranger yet lives in her house and eats the food she cooks and calls her "Mother." He looks nothing like Walter and has never resembled her. Sometimes she wonders where he has come from, if he was left by gypsies or laid in the wrong cradle by a maternity nurse blinded by double-shift fatigue, or if she herself was taken unawares, in her sleep after too much wine. Oh, by whom? This one Mary can think on with no trouble because, truth to tell, there is nothing there. She and Walter kept company for two years before they married and that's that, that's all, not even once with the milkman, when they still delivered. The glass bottles then had an egg-shaped bulb at the top to collect the risen cream. Straight from the diary, not homogenized. Not like now, with everything wrapped in chemical sheets or sealed in plastic from God knows where.

Mary realizes, if that is the word for remembering what you do not know, that how to use the television's remote control is a mystery to her. ON/OFF is easy but once the picture appears she is in doubt. How does she change the channel? They pick up signals, Luke has explained, through a satellite dish. Then the black box that sits beside the television decodes the signal and a cable carries it to the TV. The flatscreen's remote control has a pair of arrow buttons marked CHANNEL but whichever arrow Mary presses makes the flatscreen go black or fill with snow. So that isn't it, despite seeming that it should be. More confusion. When she thinks of her dwindled, slipped-away life, this difficulty with the remote control seems to sum things up by way of for-instance. Also: it frightens her. Because what might it mean, her inability to remember what Luke tells her about how to change channels? Alzheimer's means she cannot be left on her own or care for herself or take responsibility for anything. And that means Luke will put her away, shut her up in assisted living, and Matt and Cindy and John will agree. Which means that Mary, after fifty years with her own things and family around her, will wash up in a one-room limbo of flame retardant carpet and sponge baths. Boiled chicken and creamed corn at five o'clock. Scent of twice-worn cotton. Large square elevator buttons: more plastic, she cannot escape it. Brushed-steel handrails bolted to every wall. A red plastic knob on a slim metal chain hanging beside her pillow, in case, in the night.

She tries to remember, for five minutes tries. Once or twice it seems she nearly has it, her mind almost there ... then her attention wavers or quavers, her thoughts break and fall into darkness, scatter through cracks, and Mary is lost. She touches buttons at random, the screen jumps from picture to black to snow, and she has trouble believing it will not just happen—that she will change channels by accident, then keep changing until she finds the thing she wants to see. Just a click away, it must be—but which way? She cannot get there. Her attention is brittle and will not hold.

Finally she presses POWER, of that she is sure, and smiles at the decisive *POOF!* that accompanies the picture's flash-disintegration. TV, anyway, is hardly worth watching, what with commercials making a person forget what the show is about. Sometimes Mary thinks television is not about shows. It is about commercials.

She does not want Alzheimer's. She does not want to forget the faces and the names, why things matter, everything that has happened. Her life. To live a long time only to forget her life seems to Mary very wrong. She wants to die, when the time comes, with her eyes open, aware of what is and what was. Most of all, she hopes to live a while longer, in something like clarity. How did she get so old? When did it happen? She was a girl, then a wife and a mother, then a grandmother, now a widow with more years on her than she feels, many more years than she feels inside. Inside, Mary is eighteen. Oh, she knows more and wants less, desire has a way of backing off, but still she enjoys her coffee and misses her cigs, loves fresh flowers and new shoes and perfumes she will never buy. Young men draw her eye and a thought, although not as before. That's over: it ended long ago. Still, youth is seductive, its fine lines and balance, its rose-blush glow.

She does not want to die, not yet, not for years. She expects it to be a relief when it comes and maybe not so bad. Nothing more to cook or clean, no neighbor to vex her, no gadgets to puzzle her, no Luke to worry over—or rather, no Mary to worry. In death she will lose everything, herself included. But it is not her time. That her time is coming Mary does not doubt. She cannot deny what her age means. Her mother passed at seventy-one; her father, at sixty-four.

She drops the control on the sofa and heads for the stairs. She ascends slowly, hand tight on the banister, legs working, back and shoulders holding her upright, arm pulling body against gravity's drag. Slow thighs make for heavy lifting. A curved spine is a trial on steeply-pitched stairs, treads too shallow for Mary to climb in comfort or safely descend. The charm of old houses, she thinks, is felt mainly by people who do not have to live in them. Give her an elevator any day, even if she cannot remember hearing of one in a single-family house, and central air-conditioning as John and Cindy each have in their homes. One in Florida, one in California. Two children in sunshine states ought to make it possible for her to miss winter, Mary thinks, but invitations are scarce. If one of them asked her, she would sell the Cape and live with him, or her, whoever offered, and from her profit make cash gifts, if that is the issue, if cash is what it would take. She does not call such gifts bribes because it is family money and these are her children. Mary calls it a consideration. A sharing. Except what would become of Luke?

In her bedroom she clicks on the small television, switches to her channel, turns up the volume. So simple, although the picture is nothing as good. But she can see just fine the beautiful faces. There is, it seems, no shortage of men and women who are miracles to look at, all of them younger than her children now, as young as her eldest grandchild, although none of her grandchildren, not one, has a face so magically gorgeous as the faces on TV. She has to admit it, no matter how much she loves Cheryl and Josie and Imogen, David and small George. Given a clear shot, she would dote on them. That is what she wants: to spend the rest of her life doting on her grandchildren. But to be doted-on, grandchildren have to live local. Cindy and her family, and John and his, will never move to Ithaca. And Matty, like Luke, is unmarried, although Matty, thank God, has lived on his own for almost twenty years. Whereas Luke—well, since his father died Luke has seemed like a lost boy.

Fifteen years is a long time to miss a person. To be lost.

Her baby. It is ludicrous to think of him that way. But Luke is, even if a kitchen chair just holds him. What is it he eats when she isn't watching? Donuts and muffins, cake and pie? Also soda, Mary suspects, despite her pains, all the years growing up, to give them as little sugar as possible. Baked her own bread, which she made rise with her own starter. Brewed soups. Chili in winter. Why does everything that comes in a can or package, from salad dressing to tomato sauce, have high fructose corn syrup? Worthless calories, which have made her baby huge.

Mary is not watching the television. Or is watching but is not seeing. When she hears the lawn mower stop she understands she has been hearing its engine through her window. She gets off the bed, pinches back the curtain, peeks. Below, her neighbor is emptying grass clippings into a green plastic bag. The mouth of the catch-bag is clogged and he is shaking it hard from its wide bottom while the other hand holds open the plastic bag. Mary clicks her tongue against her teeth. *Such a stupid man.* Easier it would be if he flattened the plastic bag, like pants puddled at your ankles, and scooped out the clippings. It surprises her that he has not thought of it. That he seems not to understand.

After struggling a minute more, he clears the clog. Cut grass pours into green plastic. Catch-bag reattached, he pushes the mower onto the walk and leaves it. Mary watches as he takes a spade from where it leans against his house. He soft-pedals over his scruffy lawn as if it were a minefield. She sees him stop, scoop something, lift it clear. At this distance she is not sure what she sees lying on the spade's concave face. But it looks like crap.

She has told Luke a million times not to let the dogs run loose. She has said, Mary is sure she has, that he should leash them and curb them, and afterward bag the mess. But Luke will not do it. Can't be bothered and anyway is at work when a dog needs a walk. So it is Mary who lets them out, because who is she, at threescore and ten and then some, with curvature of the spine and arthritic hips, to be walking a rambunctious poodle or that lab? It is cruel to make them wait, whimpering, until Luke returns, perspired and weary. What is Mary to do? Does her neighbor really expect her to dress special and step into public just to walk a dog? He ought to consider it humane, to let Rex and Speckles and Barney do their business in his yard. A community service rendered to a senior citizen. A good deed.

Where is he going with it? Why doesn't he let it melt into the ground? *Stupid man.* House painting and lawn chores and children, judging by what Mary has noticed on the sly, have him bamboozled. Now he is creating work. It's needless, but not as needless as what Mary sees next.

As her neighbor comes closer, Mary sees shit-stools on the spade's curved face. Soft-looking they are, dark, fairly fresh. She watches him walk to the privet hedge and, without breaking stride, pitch the crap over the hedge into Luke's garden. Then he turns and walks off. Cool as you please.

Her hand goes limp, her arm drops. The curtain falls across the window as if erasing creation. Mary drifts to the bed, sits on its edge. She feels weak, heart-weak, her arms and legs hollowed. What has she seen? It is important to be sure. So she can tell Luke—if she tells him. How can she not? She knows a vandal when she sees one. An enemy. Someone who has it in for her, means to do her dirty. Already has. She cannot let him get away with it.

Dogshit in Luke's pool. When he sees it again and asks her about strays, she cannot pretend not to know.

Mary worries a thread loose in the patchwork. It might have been a mistake. Her neighbor might have meant to do something else—just what, Mary cannot imagine—and mistakenly did that. What she saw. Possibly he does not realize Luke has created a garden behind the hedge. Except the hedge is not so dense it is impossible to look through. And anyway, he should not be throwing dogshit over it. And that's another thing, mister. Throwing dogshit. What kind of man does that? And how does he know one of their dogs is responsible? Strays do wander by. It is not as if Rex's crap has Rex's name on it.

She is pressing CHANNEL UP repeatedly. Nothing she wants to watch. Game shows. Soap operas. Home shopping. Worldwide satellite news, all of it bad. She is about to snap off the TV when something catches her eye. She is far into the three-digit numbers, rare air for a woman who sticks mostly to stations she used to hand-tune with a plastic knob. Mary presses CHANNEL DOWN and it turns out that, yes, there it is: people on her television having sex. On her television, in her bedroom. Mary is aware such shenanigans are permitted but she has never expected to see them. Intimate behavior is kept hidden—what used to be called *under wraps*. Interested parties, call them customers, are put to some expense to view it. Yet here it is. In the privacy of her home. As easy as pie.

A young woman is sitting on a red carpet, *broadloom* is the word Mary remembers from 1960 or thereabouts, with her back against a black couch that seems to be leather. She is naked, this tart, but that isn't the thing, despite the fact that her breasts are weirdly large for someone so young and slim. *Plastic.* The thing, which Mary has to study for a minute before she understands, is the penis some man is feeding her—not that fellatio is unusual or to Mary unknown, except here this fellow, whoever he is, is standing. Which does seem unusual. Because in Mary's experience, which admittedly is not great and dates to decades past, a man likes to relax. Not this brute, who is 95 percent invisible, that is, out-of-frame, some smart-aleck having set the camera close to the floor or maybe on it—as a matter of fact right under the man's out-of-frame ass. So what we see, what Mary sees, looking up through the lens, are a woman's perspiring torso and gleaming breasts and stretched lips wetly encircling a glistening penis, which blocks Mary's view of the woman's nose and most of her face below her jaw, the cad's testicles bouncing against her chin.

On her television. In her home. She is surrounded. What does she do all day but mind her own business? Maybe, okay, a peep here and a peep there to keep tabs, make sure nothing wicked is afoot. Yet here she is, under siege.

On the numeric pad she presses digits at random. The channel changes and a commercial appears for a law firm whose specialty is personal injury compensation. It is workplace accidents and car wrecks they mainly are talking about but Mary wonders if she ought to call. Spengler & Spangler, Attorneys-at-Law. Pick up the telephone, dial, and inquire. Just to run it by him. Mr. Spengler or Mr. Spangler. Or both of them, Spengler & Spangler, or Spangler & Spengler, and inquire as to redress. Explore possibilities, to such extent as these exist. In terms of, What level of award might she be in line for? As a victim, her thinking runs, specifically of vandalism, which no one could deny. Dogshit over her hedge. Who ever heard of such a thing? Showered with shit—or, no: besotted. Beshitted. Yes, that's right. Pelted. Walter, she is sure, never would have imagined it. Although Walter, she is sorry to say, to remember, never imagined much. Because books, you see, what he called literature, told him what to think. And this, Mary is dead certain, is a thing outside the margins. Defaced by feces. A lawyer will know how best to say it, how to imply that some of the dogshit her neighbor tossed, *negligently* tossed on Mary's property, actually almost hit or practically landed on her, touched her skin, without stating so in bald terms because, of course, it is not true. That's why you hire a lawyer. To make your enemy out worse than he is, render him in the darkest colors, show that he is without conscience, lacks lovingkindness, is possibly a sociopath. And so put the screws to him.

Negligently pelted an elderly woman with canine fecal matter. Along those lines. *Imagine,* Mr. Spangler & Spengler will say, *just imagine, ladies and gentleman of the jury, a grown man in the healthy, well-off prime of his life, flinging dogshit at your mother.* Or grandmother, Mary thinks, for that's about the size of it.

She has to get it straight in her mind. What is her boiled-down story? She has to be sure of details but only those she could have plausibly seen. For example, his face. Did she see his face? From that distance? With her glasses or without? How does she know it was, in fact, him? Her neighbor. Why, by that shirt, Mary argues, that sleeveless thing like a woman's blouse. And those ridiculous shorts. Pockets to his knees. Very good. Now this shit, what she is calling shit, has convinced herself was in fact the genuine article— she knows this, how? Got a good look at it, did she, peeping from behind the curtain of her upstairs window, old face peeking out? And so knows? Is sure? Would swear to it?

On stacked bibles. You just try me, mister.

And, oh: He has done it before. Of course; now she understands. Her neighbor, this vandal, has pitched dogshit into Luke's garden once before. That is, Luke found dogshit in his pool and asked her about it. At that time she did not know. How could she?

Luke himself thought it was a calling-card from a filthy stray. But now it makes sense. You have one thing and then you have another thing just like it. So you put two and two together, circumstantial-this and coincidental-that, which Mary has just happened to see, and there you have it. A rapscallion. Living next-door in a house he virtually stole from an old woman who did not know she was sitting on gold. But he is not content, this Visigoth, with his steal of the century and Marilyn-type wife and beautiful children. No, not yet satisfied, he wants more, is hunting it, is hell-bent on having her home as well; and so is using terrorism of a domestic sort to drive her out. *Sell,* she imagines him calling across the yard at night while Luke is at work and Mary, soul-lonely and alone, locks the doors and opens the windows to lake-cooled air flowing along the valley and creeping up the hills. *Sell.*

At her age, a person wants peace. Wants to live in her own home and feel near her family and have nothing pressing her. What would he do with two houses? Rent the Cape to students? How much trouble might it be worth, to have rent-paying college kids living next-door? Mary suspects her neighbor of coveting her house not for the house itself, which let's face it is hobnailed and downtrodden, but for its property, a corner lot that faces a park. She would not put it past him to buy the house to tear it down, raze it, bury the cellar with clean fill and plant grass, maybe trees, small ones so as not to block his view. Coeds sunbathe in the park. Mary has seen them from her windows. Tiny shorts. Bikinis. Unless this rapscallion wants to add-on. His lot is too narrow. Without her property, he is stymied.

Mary presses POWER and her television goes dark. She must try to forget that woman, letting a bad man gag her with a penis that looked ... well, like nothing Mary has ever seen. Yes, her life has been limited and she has been sheltered. Hemmed in. If you are, as she is, a woman who has known only one man, you just cannot have an accurate idea. Which is worse, she wonders? A spectacle of freaks and sodomites performing abominations on her television? Or the fact of her neighbor heaping shit on her head?

Spangler & Spengler. Mary descends, fingers tight on the banister, feet careful on the stairs. Safe in her kitchen, she picks up the telephone, dials the lawyers' number. After the third ring a machine voice informs her that their office is closed for the day. Mary checks the kitchen clock and sees the time is after eight. She hangs up, not wholly disappointed because it is the sort of thing, hiring a lawyer, that Luke has asked her not to do without telling him. There is the money, first and foremost there is always the question of ready cash and how much a thing costs. Then there is the possibility of papers to sign, agreements likely binding, a contract. But more than anything practical it is, she suspects, Luke's fear that she will do or say something foolish that will make him, in his effort to set things right, look foolish in turn.

Cautious boy. Luke has been too careful, too reserved, and where has it left him? Cleaning floors after-hours. Building flowerbeds. Sitting on a slat bench beside a still pool, humming a single note with his eyes shut and waiting for Krishna to descend, to help him riddle-out the mystery of a missed life.

What they need, Mary decides, is action. A little something to shake things up.

She hunts up the Ithaca directory and flips to the Ts, trying to remember the hard compound of *a* and *r* the old lady mentioned as the name of the family that was buying her out. Began with a T, ended in a vowel. Typical guinea, with his muscle shirts and hairy arms, a propensity for acts of petty violence. Imagine a man, a husband and father, flipping shit at her. But the wife is Jewish. Mary is sure the old lady said so. But how? Don't they marry their own kind? Yet, it must be, she has not seen a Christmas tree going in the front door or out the back. So the husband also must be not an Eye-Tie but some sort of Jew. Because they do, Mary thinks, marry each other. Are supposed to, she is sure of this. To have Jewish children, when she isn't playing Jezebel bare-assed on the broadloom.

She finds the number as much by address as by name, which she cannot retrieve from the silent, mostly empty spaces of recent memory. Even after she reads it, their name seems strange enough for her not to have known it before, that is, never to have known it. But it also seems familiar, as if she has known it and forgotten. And it does, indeed, begin with a T, end in vowel. Pure Eye-Tie. And the wife a Jew. Cast-offs. Or cast-outs, is what she means, or rather outcasts. Yes. For marrying outside their kind. Disowned, banished. Traitors to their people. Respectively, to their peoples. Their respective peoples, outcasts all. This is what she has living next-door. A kike and a wop, friendless, without family. Whom no one wants to know. Whom respectable Mary, a decent woman, shameless debauchery on her television not her fault, has to put up with.

She notes the number on a scrap and slips it into a pocket. For later. After the children are in bed and the wop has finished sodomizing his kike and he, the wop, can pay attention. Slumbery summer midnight, not a whisper, not a breath. Just words on the telephone, simple words across a wire that he must understand yet of which he cannot be sure: of her voice, its sound, where it comes from. Just as she still has a doubt about what she has seen.

Tricks of uncertainty. How confusion cheats us of what we need to know.

High above the Milawa Valley, Army Rangers hunt Old Sammie in caves hidden in the sky. At 13,000 feet, the White Mountains rise as if to heaven's threshold and snake for several hundred miles along Afghanistan's eastern verge. Here is where al Qaida lurks, in bunkers built inside living rock. Keen to kill Infidels, jihadists hunger for martyrs' deaths. Forever young in Paradise: heavenly splendor and seventy-two virgins to soothe eternity. It is the Rangers' job to speed these eager, other-worldly lovers to the consummation they so devoutly seek.

Alessandro Terranova toggles to **Deployment**. He scrolls down the *SPECIAL FORCES* menu to Operational Detachment Alpha and on the black handset thumbs A. On a pop-up submenu, Alex toggles to *AIRBORNE INFILTRATION* and thumbs A again. The submenu self-enfolds and the main game screen appears. In a virtual environment of snow-capped peaks and hardscrabble slopes, twelve parachutists in camouflage khaki waft groundward from a silvergray sky. Below, forward-deployed two-man teams laser-target smart-bombs at AQ strongholds. Alessandro toggles the crosshairs over a cave mouth and thumbs A.

"Ordinance clear," says a voice, transmission-fuzzed, as a red tracer bends toward the target. An orange-white flash covers the cave mouth, then a boom, heard from a distance, seems to rattle Alex's screen. Smoke roils from the cave. "Attention Warrior One," and Alex is toggling even as this voice—firm, impersonal, its urgency fogged by battle-static—says, "Acquire fresh target." From the cave just hit, crumbly debris rains. Another voice—hurried, elated, high-tenor, nasal: "Six AQ confirmed killed, repeat, six terrorists EKIA." Alex thumbs B to pause, thumbs B again to bring up his real-time statistics, laid with semi-transparent ghostliness over the riven mountain. The table that tallies casualties also registers that Alex's arsenal is light by 71 AGM-86D "bunker buster" missiles. UNNEUTRALIZED CAVES are 34; NEUTRALIZED CAVES, 11, although Alex has hit more than twenty in addition to uncovered al Qaida and Taliban positions. The line item, Enemy combatants, is broken down into a roster of uncertainty:

al Qaida commandoes	?
Taliban fighters	?
Foreign Jihadists	?
Others	?

The question mark opposite each combatant class is flashing red. When Alex toggles to **Battle Status** and presses A, he learns that his performance to this point is **Fair**. He toggles to **Fair**, palely glowing in cool blue, and touches A.

Words unscroll on-screen as if someone is speed-typing. A new voice—female, calm, moderate, stern—reads the assessment:

Warrior One, you have scratched the armor of al Qaida's defensive stronghold. Ground forces in effective numbers must be introduced to this theater for SOCOM to meet U.S. Army objectives. These forces must be fully supplied and redundantly armed. In tactics of unconventional warfare they must be expert. Understand that fighting the battle of Tora Bora via proxies is a Weak Strategy whose chance of achieving operational success is assessed at ten percent: Probable Failure. At the same time, American Special Forces must work hand-in-glove with anti-Taliban Afghans and mujahideen to conduct ground operations in unfamiliar, physically taxing terrain under extreme climatic conditions and sensory deprivation. High casualties will undermine morale. Enemy Combatants will use ancient smuggling routes to slip across the Pakistani border. Shepherds loyal to tribal warlords will guide them. Foreign jihadists will infiltrate the country by these means and conceal themselves by blending in with local populations. Your task is complicated and difficult. Its triumphal completion will demand the respect of a grateful nation. We at SOCOM commend your can-do attitude and applaud your unflinching courage. Those of you who are about to die, we salute you. To those who will survive, we offer congratulations in advance. Rest assured that the American People is proud of its Patriot Warriors. Good luck!

Alessandro's sky is deepest blue spangled with glow-in-the-dark plastic stars. His bookshelf overflows with comic books, videotapes, DVDs in plastic cases. His playdesk, a 3-by-7-foot hollow door, is covered with Legos that, when assembled, depict set-scenes from Harry Potter movies and the Star Wars saga. These lie in pieces, randomly configured in mysterious shapes, scattered as if bombs have detonated. The playdesk is his father's gambit to keep Alex's Legos off the floor. As much as Alex loves Legos, it is video games he enjoys most. The realism, the options, the free-falling sense of creating events, of creating reality, all together ignite firestorms in his mind.

Alex thumbs B, B, B and returns to battle. He toggles to Alpha 77 as it is parachuting onto a flinty slope and watches each member of the 12-man team touch down. A-Team commander Captain Michael Stokes is first on his feet, already detaching the now-useless parachute. Captain's bars are pinned to the collar of a camouflage jacket that does not otherwise distinguish him from his men: Bryce, a warrant officer and second-in-command, and ten ser-

Hunting Old Sammie   131

geants, hierarchically paired, with responsibility for Operations & Intelligence, Weapons, Demolitions, Communications, and Medical, respectively.

Alex selects Captain Stokes and thumbs A. Blocks of data crowd the screen: date and place of birth, mother's name, father's name, wife's name, name(s) of children; years of education and schools attended, grade-point averages, earned degrees; details of his military service, performance assessments, weapons competency, major campaigns, decorations and awards. Captain Stokes, Alex learns, is a graduate of the University of Pennsylvania, is thirty-one years old, is married to Susan. Under Personal is a note that Stokes worries Susan cheats while he is in-country. Hobbies are movie-making, computers, and deer hunting. Likes to read science fiction, especially of alternative realities and time-travel, but prefers movies to books. Would enjoy visiting the early Christian era to assume command of a Roman Legion and prevent the Empire from being overrun by barbarian hordes. Equipment includes Kevlar vest, Cyclops Night-Vision, a Colt M4A1 carbine with 4x combat optical scope (accurate to 360m) and M203A1 grenade launcher. Captain Michael D. Stokes, United States Army Special Forces, Operational Detachment Alpha 77. Father of two, Joseph and John.

Alex wonders what it means, "cheats." What game can Susan and Michael play while they are so far apart? Nothing so cool as *Hunting Old Sammie,* and anyway Captain Stokes is a character in the game. He cannot also play the game. Not in the sense Alex plays it, hours each day. *Hunting Old Sammie* became his favorite the second his dad bought it for him. *A hundred bucks,* his father kept saying. But that's what stuff costs, Alex figures, especially a great game you can't get just anywhere and not everyone can have. There is nothing like it: the levels of increasing difficulty, each scenario more complex than the last, how it goes on and on. Risky missions: search-and-destroy; recover-and-rescue; infiltrate-and-kill. High-tech weaponry and lightning assaults, different ODA units competing for kills, shadowy Delta Force, accessible only through Cheat Codes, whose activities the manual describes as "spontaneously created and independently pursued on the basis of instigated opportunities." The faceless authority of SOCOM, remarking, judging, tasking, meddling. Scenarios he, Alex, can modify; personnel substitutions, strategic reassessments, indigenous assistance or resistance, foreign interventions, theater nuclear options. A dozen virtual environments. A cast of thousands.

The world of the game. Alex does not want to live anywhere else.

Toggling through Alpha 77, Alex finds that Weapons Sergeant Sloan and Assistant Weapons Sergeant Richards each have sniper ability with Proficiency Quotients approaching 100 percent. On Sloan's screen Alex selects Small Arms and hits A. Using the sub-submenu, he swaps Sloan's M4A1 for an M25, the new Special Forces sniper rifle. It is the coolest thing Alex has ever seen, judging from the graphic: a sort-of carbine with classic green camouflage mottle on the stock and a big-eyed, top-mounted 10x scope. Under Specs, Alex gets the giddy skinny: Sergeant Sloan's M25 is a rotating-bolt, gas-operated, air-cooled, semi-automatic Light Sniper Rifle firing 7.62 x 51mm NATO rounds (equivalent to .308 Winchester) fed via a 20-round box magazine (detachable). Effective range is 900m: pretty damn far, Alessandro thinks, although he can't exactly picture 900 meters despite having learned in school that one meter equals one yard plus a near tenth. Say a thousand yards, roughly: ten football fields without end zones. Just as he's figured: pretty flipping far. The wild-ass kills he has pulled off in previous scenarios, mostly in remote regions of Iraq, prove it.

Hunting Old Sammie

Even so, Alex is a little disappointed. As wonderful a weapon as the M25 is, it does not have the reach of the truly big guns, which Alpha detachments do not carry except on top-secret missions of rare and singular focus. Such as the M88. Portable at 30 pounds, the M88 is a bolt-action, single-shot, .50-caliber Special Application Sniper Rifle with a 33-inch barrel and an effective range of 1.2 miles. Which Alex, school-wise, calculates as 6000-some feet. Two thousand-plus yards. An outrageous muzzle flash, like sending up a flare. Alessandro wielded an M88 in *Gulf War Pride,* an old game in which he has mostly lost interest. In *Gulf War Pride* he was USMC sniper Greg Forest, who was all about clean, quick, single-shot kills. Sergeant Forest's M88 set up on a bipod and fired, among other ammo, armor-piercing depleted-uranium rounds that could ruin a personnel carrier and smash through body armor from the aforementioned frightening remove. Through the 40x Leupold scope Alex would acquire his target, an Iraqi sentry, say, guarding whatever, and onscreen the man was invisible, not even a dot. Once he had compensated for wind, distance, and differences of elevation, Alessandro as Sergeant Forest would hold his breath as he gently thumbed A. The gun would roar, the onscreen picture jolt to simulate recoil, and not instantly but a few seconds after, the Iraqi sentry or enemy combatant, a red-eyed jihadist wearing crossed bandoliers, or just some fool in a turban and robes, would take the screaming bullet in the head, if Alex's calculations were accurate, or in the chest if these were slightly off or the wind had shifted or the fool had moved, and his, the target's, head or chest would soundlessly explode within the intimate circle of the scope. After watching the kill, Sergeant Forest got out pronto because the hellacious muzzle flash would have given away his position, which would presently draw all manner of retaliatory fire.

That was then. A different mission in another war. In *Hunting Old Sammie,* Alex runs covert assaults on al Qaida mountain hideouts. Honeycombed with caves, riven by protected passes and claustrophobic défilés, it is a landscape ripe for ambush. When Alex calls in an airstrike, B-52s roar into the frame. Once the target is cross-haired, the bomb-bay doors open and BLU-82 "daisy-cutters" drop as if from the clouds. On the Ordinance submenu, Alex learns that the BLU-82 is twelve feet long and six feet high, weighs 15,000 pounds and needs a parachute to control its fall. A four-foot trigger that protrudes from its nose insures that the BLU-82 explodes just above the ground, erasing everything within several hundred yards. Rocks become sand. Alex can also guide Predator drones, each armed with two Hellfire missiles reserved for targets of choice. He cannot access close air support from Apache attack helicopters or A-10 Warthogs because *Hunting Old Sammie,* for the most part striving toward historical accuracy, does not let Alex bring resources to bear in the battle of Tora Bora that the actual U.S. Army did not have in-country until Operation ANACONDA. So when it comes to whites-of-their-eyes engagement, Alpha 77 is on its own.

Not optimal; not the way SOCOM would draw it up. But, as everyone now knows, you go to war not necessarily with the army you want, but with the army you have. And what we have, what Alessandro has in the hunt for Old Sammie, are thoroughly prepared Special Forces. Operational Detachment Alpha specializes in infiltrating hostile territory, which Tora Bora is in spades. Captain Stokes and his men are capable of carrying on independent operations without external support or command; of recruiting, organizing, equipping, and training indigenous volunteers, should any materialize, to seal the border and search the caves; of taking the initiative always; of improvising when improvisation is called for;

of implementing tactics that are not, strictly speaking, by the book. Alpha 77 is cross-trained in free-fall parachuting, demolition & explosives, battlefield surgical procedures and dentistry. Also underwater and waterborne infiltration, which, Alex can plainly see, do not apply here. But just flipping imagine the damage these guys can do. Engineer Sergeants Drew and Pascoe are demolitions experts capable of destroying almost any structure—and capable of building them, too, although at the moment Alex is not interested in building. His father seems never to be done with it even now, more than two years after the big renovation ended and they moved into the house. Although painting, well, that's not exactly building, despite the time it takes. So much time that his dad can hardly drive Alex to Pyramid Mall on days he paints, which are most days. And a mountain cave, Alex understands, is not exactly a structure, even if improved with floors and walls. And mountain rock might dull the blast power of Drew's dynamite and Pascoe's plastique.

Except it wouldn't flipping matter, Alex thinks, if these Arab bastards would crawl out of their holes and fight like men. Sloan with that M25 accurate to 1000 yards. That's the thing, Alex decides, manipulating Alpha 77 along a mountain pass, the magic thing: to be a sniper. Cool, calm, deliberate, choosing unique targets with judgment and care, calculating aim, all steady, everything controlled. A way of dispelling the fog of war, its sudden chaos and fear, its confusion and panic and mayhem. In battle, you do not always know where you are or what is happening, only that you had better shoot and hide and run and shoot and shoot and hide and shoot and run. Grenades if you have them, close air support if available. The 25mm, six-barrel Gatling gun mounted on an AC-130 Spectre gunship lays down a withering fire of 30 ten-inch high-explosive rounds per second. Thirty, *per second.* That's 1800 rounds a minute, Alex figures, and that's no joke. Plus a Bofors 40mm gun and a 105mm howitzer. A cannon in the sky. A Strike Eagle tactical fighter strafes enemy combatants with an M61A1 20mm Gatling gun. Six barrels each firing 940 rounds a minute. Each member of Alpha 77 has a 40mm grenade launcher underbarrel-mounted on his gas-operated, air-cooled, rotating-bolt M4A1 carbine. Sloan and Richards can operate to lethal effect nearly every small arms weapon in the world.

Sergeant Johnson, "Daddy" of Alpha 77, shouts "Ambush!" and the next thing they know rifle fire is coming down hot and heavy from all sides except, thank God, from above. They form up, Stokes and Richards firing forward, Sloan and Bryce covering the rear, the remaining eight back-to-back and shoulder-to-shoulder defending the flanks. In a firefight Sloan's sniper rifle is unwieldy and once the shooting starts it is too late for Alessandro to revert to the carbine, so he, Sloan, resorts to his side-arm, the M9 Beretta semi-automatic they all carry, capable of blasting off a jihadist's head at twenty paces. Except enemy fire is not incoming from twenty paces, it is kicking up flint from 200 yards away. Alex cannot toggle accurately enough to acquire targets quickly enough to thumb A rapidly enough to cut down these black-robed, turbaned sons of bitches who are jumping out from behind boulders and firing a burst and jumping back. He stays with Stokes and does his best, reloading the carbine twice, while the COM plays Bryce and Sloan and Richards and the others. When Johnson and Savage are hit and go down, Alex thinks, *Mistake.* He should have played Johnson, whose Profile distinguishes him on relevant points of combat experience: a savvy veteran who went into Operation Desert Storm a pup and came out the toughest dog on the porch. Alex remembers Johnson from *Gulf War Pride,* sure, he should have known. Now Johnson is hit and it's too late.

Hunting Old Sammie

In two minutes it is over. Johnson and Savage are down with a leg wound each. The others are shaken, adrenaline-juiced, set for whatever comes next. Alessandro selects Grant, Medical Sergeant First Class, to attend Johnson; Clemens, a Medical Staff Sergeant, patches up Savage. The medics work quickly, cleaning wounds, injecting anesthesia, plying sterile oversized tweezers, antibiotic salve, suture kits and bandages. Shot-up Taliban no one attends until Johnson and Savage are stabilized. Then Stokes and Bryce, Sloan and Richards, Communications Sergeants Davenport and West, Engineer Sergeants Pascoe and Drew, reconnoiter enemy casualties and find seven killed, five wounded. They leave the seven. The five they end, one-by-one. Two bullets each through the turban. Each man participates in no special order and without malice. Alessandro selects each in turn, levels his weapon, presses A. The Taliban die soundlessly, although the pistol reports open seams in the mountain air.

The wounded cannot walk. It is a problem, to have both Operations sergeants incapacitated, but nothing the unit can't handle. Alex is busy improvising crutches when his sister comes pounding up the stairs. Julietta is six-going-on-seven and in no way overweight but when she is coming it sounds like beef on the hoof. The thundering herd. Their father calls her Twinkletoes but Alex doesn't get it. As far as he knows, it's eyes that twinkle. Also stars. This is just Julietta. And now she runs into his room.

The little girl stares at the screen, sees hurt soldiers and turbaned corpses in the background. Explosions echo in the distance as Warrant Officer Bryce contacts SOCOM on Davenport's satellite radio and Captain Stokes studies a map along the top border of which TOP SECRET is stamped in red. No one barks orders. Everyone knows what to do.

"What are you doing?" says Julietta.

"Playing a game," Alex says with a sigh.

"Can I watch?"

"No."

"Please?"

"I want to play in peace."

"I'm only watching. I'm not going to bother you."

"You're bothering me now," says Alessandro. "Why can't you stay in your room and leave me alone?"

"All right, fine!" Julietta stalks out. She turns hard right, into her bedroom, which she has not failed to notice is one-third the size of her brother's. She does not understand why. Something to do with the renovation, their father has explained; how they moved the wall as far as they could, given the placement of windows, to make her bedroom as large as it could be; and installed radiator heat and a closet, neither of which the room had before; and raised the dormer so her ceiling would not slant; and added new thermal-pane windows to match those the house already had. A new bathroom also was carved from Alex's oversized bedroom, which despite these alterations is still one of the largest rooms in the house.

So, fine. Julietta doesn't care, she has a room of her own. Except she does care. Just because she is smaller, younger, a girl, does that mean she needs less? deserves less? should be happy with less? What makes Alessandro so special, that he gets everything?

"I don't like you anymore!" she shouts through that new wall.

"You always say that." Alex's eyes are pinned to the screen, his thumb busy on the buttons.

"I mean it! I always don't like you! You're just a big ... a big ... meanie!"

Alessandro sighs. Why does he have to have a little sister, he'd like to know, and why does she have to be such a pill? It isn't as if he is ever lonely, what with his games and videos and TV shows and comic books and, when these start to bore him, his imagination.

"Do you hear me? I really, really mean it."

"Okay." Alex is not interested. How can he be, with two men wounded and an impossible mission? She is distracting him and he cannot afford to be distracted because distraction causes error and error leads to death. *Hunting Old Sammie* is tough enough without his little sister yelling at him.

"Hummpf!" he hears her say, or maybe hum, it isn't a word but a sound that tells him she's peeved.

Alex pauses Alpha 77 and brings up the panel that lets him enter Cheat Codes. These long strings of alphanumeric gibberish are supposed to reveal exact positions of al Qaida leaders, including al Zawahiri and Old Sammie himself, as well as to access scenarios of prisoner interrogation that are not officially present among the levels of the game. The trouble is, Alex does not have any Cheat Codes. The regular game guide does not list any. As far as Alex knows, Cheat Codes are available only in a special *Hunting Old Sammie* Cheat Codes manual that costs $19.95. Alex's asking for it the first time they tried to buy the game ruined everything. His father had a mini-fit, as if another not-even twenty dollars were some kind of big deal. Alex kept saying, *But dad ... But dad ... But dad* until Dad threatened to put *Hunting Old Sammie* back on the rack and buy it exactly never. At which point Alex stopped asking for the manual and called his father, "Blackmailer."

Alex tries not to think about what happened next. He knows that thinking about it is exactly what his father wants him to do: how his father did, indeed, put the game back, and took Alex by the arm and marched him out of the store, across the food court and through Pyramid Mall to the exit outside which their car was parked; and put Alex into the back seat and shut the door and got into the car himself and fired it up and drove them home, all without a word.

That mistake, or those mistakes, cost Alex two weeks. He could have been playing the game, learning its tricks and glitches, best strategies and work-arounds, getting better, capturing more caves, losing fewer men. But no. He was careful about what he said, *watched his mouth,* his father calls it, and asked for nothing, almost nothing, tried to and almost made it. A comic book for three dollars. A water cannon for $12.95 to use at Cascadilla Park pool to soak any kid dumb enough to play, or to blast Julietta when they played in the lawn sprinkler on hot afternoons. Twice she slipped on dog poop. The second time it happened, after his father cleaned her foot in hot water and soap, he had them change out of their wet bathing suits back into clothes and put them in the Benz and drove to Pyramid Mall, where he finally bought *Hunting Old Sammie* for Alex and stretchy, rubber-soled pink nylon pool shoes for Julietta and, at the big sporting goods store, a cool and scary shotgun for himself. He let Alex hold it. A real gun, it turns out, is much heavier than he has imagined.

Using the onscreen keyboard and handset toggle, he types letters and numbers at random. Cheat Codes vary from a virtually unguessable fifteen characters to a tantalizing six, indicated onscreen by yellow hash-marks that appear above a virtual keyboard. Just *six,* you would think he'd nail at least one. Even when Alex seems to feel it coming, on the way, in the wings, picking letters on ESP, numbers, picking blind, guessing without thought, without rhyme or reason, wild-ass guessing by the seat of his pants that's primed to trip the tumblers just once, he gets the razzing tone and **Invalid Code** smackdown. And so he is stuck with Alpha on crazy terrain, going cave to cave.

They are where he has paused them, Stokes and Bryce, Grant and the others, on a mountain pass hemmed in by pine trees, with two non-ambulatory sergeants and a dozen dead Taliban. WO Bryce has advised SOCOM of their situation and Captain Stokes has determined that half of Alpha 77 can mount an effective assault on a certain cave, designated PCP250 on the **TOP SECRET** map and lying a mile beyond the next ridge. The idea being that four stay back with Johnson and Savage until MedEvac arrives. Alex OKs the plan and divides the squad. Stokes will lead the mission, which means Bryce stays back, he and Stokes being officers. Of the two Medical sergeants, Grant seems like the better choice to treat gunshot wounds under fire. From that point the selections are clear, except that with both Operations sergeants down it's a cinch both Weapons sergeants will take part in the assault. So Sloan and Richards are going. Alex can see it coming, the ineffectiveness of the sniper rifle in a close-quarters fight, and switches Sloan to the carbine. It's a little like cheating to make sophisticated small-arms materialize and vanish into thin mountain air, but it is part of the game. What the rules let you do. Anyway, it is not as if Sloan could not take Clemens's M4, for instance, if this were real life, and leave the M25 behind.

"I don't like you anymore!" Julietta reminds him.

"I know! Would you please shut up? I'm trying to concentrate."

Stokes tells his contingent, "Remember what these dogfacing ragheads did on 9/11. Take no prisoners. Good luck." He nods at Bryce, says, "Sit tight. We will return for you," and Bryce nods back. The detachment falls into line and off they go, one-half of Alpha 77: Stokes, Grant, Sloan and Richards, Drew, and Davenport, eyes sharp, ears keen, guns ready. They cover the distance without incident or visible strain, circle up 500 yards from the cave mouth and run through the plan. They will fan out, Stokes tells them, get close enough, and when everyone is in position, Sloan and Richards will let fly three grenades each right down the throat of the cave. Alex thinks, *Straight up jihadist ass,* its being something he has overheard his father say while he watches TV news. He tries it himself. "Up jihadist ass." A whisper, barely more than a breath, and none too confident of that strange word, *jihadist.*

"I can hear you!" Julietta cries.

Another confusion. Like their unpronounceable names: Ahmad Kahlil Ibrahim Samir al Ani. Tawfiq bin Attash. Anwar Aulaqi. Ramzi Binalshibh. Abu Hafs al Mauritani. Riduan Isamuddin. Abderraouf Jdey. Abdelghani Mzoudi. Ayman al Zawahiri.

Old Sammie Been Hidin'.

After the grenades go off, Alpha's thinking is, AQ commandoes or Taliban fighters or whoever is holed up in there and hasn't been killed will panic-counterattack and bull-rush the exit, at which point this six-man A-Team will cut them down. Afterwards they will search the cave for survivors, back-hangers, cowards, and neutralize them. Sloan and Richards will drill into the interior ceiling and that part of the mountain that defines the entrance, and set hellacious big charges that from a prudent distance they will ignite, the better to dislodge the rock that will seal the cave.

So that is what they do, Alessandro toggling and pressing A, *blip, blip, blip,* and sure enough the ragheads swarm out, Kalashnikovs blazing. Kneeling behind boulders that a thoughtful someone has dispersed in a useful pattern at a convenient distance, Stokes and Sloan and Richards, Davenport, Grant and Drew open up with their M4s, and *goddamn,* Alex thinks, *Jesus H. Christ God All-fucking-Mighty,* something else he is not supposed to overhear, much less remember, much less say. But the jihadists do not have a chance. Not a shadow of a dream, echo of a prayer, hope in hell. 5.56 NATO rounds cut through flesh like ripe melon, shatter skulls like eggshells. With Dari-inflected screams as soundtrack, blood and brain spatter antediluvian rock, congeal in dust otherwise unaltered since Earth's first age. Onscreen the kill zone is halo'd in pink-gray mist that does not clear for a minute after Alpha 77, Alessandro, ceases fire.

"It's awfully loud in there!" says Julietta.

Something she has heard their mother say. Or their father. Alex ignores her.

"I said, it's awfully loud!"

"Mind your own business," says Alessandro.

"Alessandro, you are so rude."

Why, if he had to have a younger-something, couldn't it have been a brother? A pint-sized snot-nose who would think everything he did, said, liked was just great. Julietta is like having a second mother, the way she listens, watches, pretends to correct him when she thinks she has noticed he is doing something not-quite-just-sissy-so. *Ignore her.* It's all he can do. Argue with a girl, even a little one, even your sister, and you lose. It's automatic. Even if you happen to get the best of her by some crazy chance or cockeyed luck, you lose. When there is no way to win the only smart choice is not to play. His hope being that, in the long run, Julietta will get bored and leave him alone.

Twenty dead in the kill zone. Alpha meanwhile has taken no casualties. Cautiously, they approach the cave. It is impossible to know if anyone is alive in there, cowering behind a rock with an AK-47, waiting for the Great Satan to show his horns. Richards pops in two more grenades. Detonations echo in a darkness that feels empty, dusty debris billowing from the cave mouth and rising in the wan, high-altitude light. Stokes ignites two chemical flares and throws them in. When nothing happens he ignites two more, throws them in. Nothing. Each man ignites a flare and, holding it at arm's length, enters the cave in staggered formation, a shuffled asymmetry with guns at hips, fingers tickling triggers. Stokes sees immediately that the cave is empty. It is small and unimproved except for a pine-plank floor on which meager sleeping mats are laid. There is no electrical generator or propane stove, scant provisions of water, figs, pistachio nuts, hard cheese, coarse bread.

"This is it?" says Davenport.

"Seems like all these ragheads can do," says Stokes.

The image angle shifts. Drew says, "It's embarrassing to fight such weak-ass losers," a sentence he has opportunity to retract only in his mind when seconds later AQ foot-soldiers open up and bullets are zinging past and ricocheting off the walls, catching Alpha 77 dead-to-rights.

It happens so fast Alessandro does not know what he is supposed to do. He thumbs A as quickly as he can, emptying the M4's 30-round magazine. Stokes, trying to reload, is hit in one shoulder, then the other, and knocked backwards off his feet. The Kevlar, he figures, has saved him from mayhem but still it hurts, taking rifle-fire at close range. Maybe one shoulder is dislocated; maybe both are. Maybe bones are broken. Stokes thinks this is how broken bones feel. The others are blazing away when a grenade bounces in. Everyone shouts, "Grenade! Grenade!" and dives for cover that does not exist. The grenade goes off with a flash so bright and a sound so loud Alex thinks for a second the television has exploded, has in fact exploded rather than just depicted an explosion in virtual fact. The onscreen air is full of smoke and dust. Stokes and Sloan and Richards and Grant are coughing and trying to wipe crud out of their eyes. Davenport and Drew lie still on the pine planks. AQ guns open up and in thirty seconds Alessandro learns that one move you never make is to let your A-Team enter the same cave all at once.

WARNING: Mission Failed.

"Oh!"

Alex looks up. Julietta is standing in his doorway, wide eyes fixed on the screen. "That's horrible!" she says.

"No kidding." Alex presses B. From **Game Options** he toggles to ***New Mission***. And hits A.

He came so far, accomplished so much. Now he is back at square one.

It is a lot tougher than he expected.

Leah Goldman crossing Collegetown under a brilliant sun remembers who she is. There are her children and her home, her job and the education she has earned, the years with Armand: a critical mass of experience and memory no admiration from Max Obermann can match. Her life makes sense to her. If it is not completely happy, whose is? Max's? Leah doubts it. If she lets something happen, something more than the emotional cheating she has already done, it will not be about happiness. Excitement will be a side issue. Even lust will have little to do with it. Leah likes Max but does not feel powerfully drawn. No, anything that still could happen if she let it—despite having deflected his intentions along these lines some weeks ago—would be less about pleasure and more about change. Because whatever else it was or did, even if they knew the instant it happened that each secret kiss, every hidden touch meant nothing, a real affair would change everything.

When she reaches her office and finds her message light blinking, *already* blinking although it is just nine o'clock, Leah feels the tedium of another workday fall across her shoulders and settle around her neck. Maybe she will not be interested in alumni affairs much longer. Maybe she should start looking for the next thing. Maybe they will leave Ithaca, after all, say good-bye to its long winters and grayed-over sky, the Commons and Collegetown, East Hill and Cayuga Lake, the Farmers' Market and Pyramid Mall, all the people they have never come to know, and go to a true city of sparkling glass and chromium steel, big museums and professional sports, taxi cabs, a subway system, and—most importantly—a diversified job market. Or maybe she will take Armand at his word and not work at all. What would fill her days? Shopping sprees? No store at Pyramid Mall sells clothes she wants to wear, much less buy. Leah stages her retail raids online. Spending hours on the Web, passing the afternoon with television. Lunch at home with Armand, every day.

The message insistently winking at her turns out to be one of his rants, along the lines of why has she highlighted honey on the grocery list when they have a new bottle in the pantry. The same goes for lemons, he claims, and packages of organic baby spinach, both of which, or rather all of which—it seems they have two packages of spinach and four lemons—already occupy major space in the Crisp & Cool bin. Which she would have discovered, Armand snarks, if she had bothered to open the refrigerator before rushing to highlight.

Implying that she is lazy. She, who works all day. Or careless, or neglectful. Or something. All of the above.

So helpful. Armand's messages, his little notes and reminders, email sparks and blow-backs that pepper her Inbox like sniper-fire. Leah is about to punch the speed-dial to tell him, *really* tell him, then decides she does not want to hear his voice or listen to his words or speak to him at all. Twelve years. Their conversations circle a dozen topics, each known point and fated counterpoint like pins in her eyes. What she imagines pins would feel like. Most of what Armand says slides toward mumble, unfinished. Ellipses of the not-worth-saying. Leah tunes out, having heard enough to get the gist. Armand uses too many words and Leah already knows what most of them will be. They have known each other a long time and maybe cannot surprise themselves anymore.

Leah wakes her computer to type him a quick, hot burst she hopes is terse enough to convey her annoyance while letting him know that grocery shopping is in his bailiwick now and she does not always have time or energy or, frankly, any interest in combing through their accumulated stores of lemons and honey and what-all-else she does not know and does not care, could not possibly give a plausible damn *(not a flying fuck,* although she does not type that), and anyway is at work all day, works all week in case he has forgotten or hasn't noticed, does he expect her to get groceries, too? *Just take care of it any way you want, dear,* she finishes, *and spare me the grousing.*

She clicks Send. As she returns to her Inbox the computer pings and a new subject line appears:
lunch?

Leah clicks Reply, types, *You bet. Asia House? -L.* No smiley-face this time. And clicks Send.

Is she about to …? Does she intend …? Just because she is hacked off at her husband and looking forward to moo goo gai pan and an eggroll does not mean Leah is bent on adultery, which sounds so final, being a transgression of a Commandment people still take seriously. In fact, she is planning nothing, just lunch. Yes, she cheated—although she really does not believe anyone can call it that—before she and Armand were married, during a long-distance separation. She is pretty sure he did, too. They have never spoken of it and she has not thought of it twice in fifteen years. How can it matter now? Anyway, Armand never seemed to suspect. How could he, with a continent between them and Leah a pro at playing innocent? She knows how convincing she is, has listened to her voice suggest promises she has no intention of keeping. Unless she changes her mind. It is all about tone: pitch and cadence and the mood these create. Affection loaded into a long, rounded "o," a softly sibilant "s." No man doubts her and few can resist, although her husband has heard her act many times and, she believes, caught on.

Still. Leah can finesse her way around Armand any time. If all else fails, she can hold her nose and close her eyes and play beauty and the beast until his eyes cross. Trying not to gag. She hopes it won't come to that and anyway it is all beside the point. She does not intend to have an affair with Max Obermann or anyone else. Yes, Leah wants to change some things, but not that way. What she would like most of all to change is her husband's brooding, the excess of empty time that lets him worry about everything from too many lemons to what might happen if one of the children, God forbid—. *God forbid.* Leah wishes he would relax. Their life together is a beautiful thing—why can't he see that? *Just relax.* Be happy and act it. Find a way to spend his day that does not include slow-torture chores. She wants to be able to have fun with him again, the Armand she used to know, the man with whom she fell in love; and so does not want to change what needs changing by destroying what exists.

That is what a romance or affair, or whatever we are calling it, would do. Even if it were brief and quickly finished, even if Armand never knew, it would make whatever is wrong between them worse.

*

Max is all smiles. No kiss this time, they just slip into chairs and read the menu. Max has arrived first and a good thing, too, for the converted taproom is packed, every table taken. When Leah was an undergraduate, Asia House was a beery dive notorious for Saturday-night Pick-up and Two o'clock Rush. The Double Jugg. She can hardly believe she ever set foot in the place. During her second B-School year it was closed down for allowing sexual acts to occur on its unsanitary premises. And closed it stayed for three years, Leah has since been told by CU Lifers, until the first in a series of Asian restaurants took up residence. Interludes of Japanese, Tai, and Korean cuisines have separated repeat performances of standard Cantonese, each immigrant family establishing its custom before selling out to the next in an inexhaustible hustle of entrepreneurs-on-the-make. Currently it's Cantonese, serving up corn-starched chow mien and egg drop soup roughly the same in taste and quality as those offered at four other front-room eateries in the Nouveau Asian Ghetto that Collegetown has become.

Red and gold velvet dragons on the walls, red cloths covering the tables. Max, again dressed in spot-stained pants and an Oxford-cloth shirt of dubious freshness, spoons sugar into his tea—absentmindedly, it seems to Leah, because they have discussed it, the need to cut back—while spouting the results of a survey he has devised with three other B-School faculty. It seems they are canvassing the music-downloading habits of a select sample culled from every age group of the generational spectrum. All to the end of effective marketing, which in this case involves not getting people to want the product but convincing them to pay for it.

Unfolding her napkin, a white paper item with *Eat Chinese!* etched in red script, Leah tells him, "I pay for my downloads," thinking, *No kiss.*

"Exactly," says Max. "A person your age, it's more pertinent to say of your generation, invariably pays. Fair and square. Whereas the generation after yours, that is, mine, antes up about half the time. The next generation younger is almost ninety percent likely to download music from illegal free sites."

"Or ninety percent more honest about their dishonesty," Leah says.

Max blinks. "Well, okay. Something like that is possible." The waitress, zipping past, delivers a bowl of wonton soup Leah hasn't known Max to eat before and did not know he has ordered now. It and the egg foo young will make for a salty lunch. He stirs the soup, eyeballing her as if he suspects she is trying to trick him. "Why would oldsters lie on an anonymous questionnaire?"

Oldsters. Is that how he sees her now? What happened to *You are completely charming?* Where did *I love being with you* go? Is there a problem with her today? Hair not brushed within an inch of its life, a fresh wrinkle in her forehead? "Because they are essentially honest," Leah says, "most of them, and so ashamed of stealing music that they compound their guilt by lying."

Max is staring at her. "That's complicated. It sounds far-fetched."

"Well, we over-the-hill types are famous for a tortured conscience."

Max snorts. "More likely your generation isn't savvy to free sites or doesn't trust them. Feels safer buying from established vendors."

That's twice. *Your generation.* Don't they belong to the same generation, each of which, the dictionary tells us, spans thirty years? "Maybe," Leah says, "although you don't have to be a rocket scientist to navigate the Web."

"So you're saying it's not a tech issue or a learning curve. You're saying your generation is intrinsically more honest."

"*I'm* not saying anything. It's your survey. I'm pointing out a design flaw. Your questionnaire can't tell if people who might steal music might also lie about it."

Max shakes his head. His eyes are in his wontons. "You better be wrong. It would ruin our demographic distribution and invalidate some potentially valuable marketing insights."

What passes for knowledge. Well, can you blame him? Max has been taught in spades what she and Armand also learned in B-School. A thing has no value unless someone will buy it. Which means you have to convince people they need it or want it, or both. Of course, very few things, really only essentials like bread and butter, sell themselves. And why should anyone buy your bread, your butter, rather than the bread and butter of your competitors? And so we have marketing. And people like Max Obermann have high-paying professorships to teach it.

"I'm so sorry, dear," Leah says, mock-affectionate. "The bright side is those twenty-somethings are almost certainly telling the truth—unless they're trying to seem edgy by copping to cyberthievery."

Max's face is officially gloomy. "That's silly. The survey is anonymous. There is no audience for anyone's self-dramatization. We're confident they're telling the truth. About stealing music, I mean. They've had the Web at their fingertips twenty-four/seven basically from birth and expect total access at no cost. It's the older generations we want to capture. They have the money. Give a fifty-something Gold Coaster an easy interface and one-hundred-percent secure transactions, there's no limit to the damage she might do."

"I'm forty, Max." Leah feels compelled to point this out. In spite of herself; she does not know why she cares. They're just friends. Right? And determined to stay that way. She is. Especially with this idea he evidently has of her being some kind of borderline old lady, pockets hot with cash. *Gold Coaster.* As if she winters in a 4000-square-foot condo in Sarasota.

Max says, "Oh, I wasn't meaning you." Something in his face almost convinces her that he regrets that crack about oldsters. Almost. "The idea is, we want to know how they prefer to see the merchandise and whether, or under what conditions, there are things they either absolutely will not buy or are reluctant to buy via electronic funds transfer. Also if there are things they prefer to buy online, rather than, you know, driving to the mall and poking through a brick-and-mortar. You would think, or rather I would, that anything a woman would buy through a catalogue she would buy through a Web site." Max's mouth slides sideways. "Turns out it isn't so. Not if she's a Boomer."

Generation X. Generation Y. Generation Z. Just where does Max fit, exactly? He's thirty-two; she's forty. A measly eight years mean nothing. Goddamnit, they are the same generation! His wife, that Rachel, yes, is a bit younger. Fine, more than a bit, twenty-nine is a full eleven years younger than Leah, who by the way looks fantastic and knows it, has been exercising like a madwoman and watching what she eats as if a very tiny and extremely powerful calorie cop lives in her brain and looks out through her eyes at every morsel that appears on her plate or happens to arrive at the table or just sails past on trays. Just let Leah reach for a second fortune cookie or try for pork dumpling instead of the steamed vegetable. That vigilant cop flips the guilt switch, which in Leah is hardwired to a vexed self-image, the latter a gift from Mommy-dearest during Leah's adolescence. The pain food causes her is distressing; Leah likes to eat. So here she is, reinvented at forty through sweat and denial, seldom as well-fed as she would like to feel, with a good complexion, proportional toned figure, not the longest legs in the world but she cannot do anything about that, it is part of the genetic legacy that has given her a sweet tooth whose appetite you would not believe and a tendency to add pounds at her abdomen and hips, and, oh yes, sparkling green eyes and smooth, soft, clear skin, and perfect breasts, Armand has always said, in fact has whispered hotly in her ear and tells her repeatedly even now.

Their entrées arrive, piping-hot and fragrant, steam lifting off shredded chicken and sliced water chestnuts, chopped green onions, bean sprouts, and peas spread over piled white rice. Leah is grateful because, one, she's starving, and two, the food gives them an excuse to stop talking. She mixes moo goo gai pan into the rice and loads her fork. Max, meanwhile, is messing with chopsticks he cannot quite handle, using them more or less to scoop rice and pork straight from plate to mouth while holding the former at his chin. No wonder his pants are stained. Leah tries not to watch or judge. He is brilliant, everyone says, a genius, and we indulge his eccentricities, his social blindspots and moral vagueness. Talking to him is interesting and fun. It lights her up, makes her feel smart and appreciated for being smart, as well as admired for being pretty. Even if she is forty and Max thinks he is oh-so younger because he has a wife who, well, is much younger. And pregnant.

What has she been thinking? What has he been thinking? Are they both out of their minds?

"This slop tastes like shit," Max says. He drops the chopsticks.

"I'm sorry," Leah says. "Mine is delicious."

Never has he complained about the food. Always just shoveled it in. Leah is about to ask what's going on, then realizes that is what he wants. That he wants to complain to her. About something, anything. Even nothing. His lunch, the weather, students who demand re-grades (and of whom he has seen neither hide nor hair for more than two months), the B-School's tenure process, *Rachel's inability to have sex during her final trimester.* And for a month or more after the baby is born, depending on how the delivery goes. His pork fried rice, which is probably just as good as her moo goo, is a pretense to divert them down the Ire Pike, with a longed-for layover at a predictable rest area.

Well, guess what? Leah is not buying. She is not taking that trip, not today, not ever. She is here for lunch and a conversation that is stimulating and pleasant. If Max wants to play Mr. Misery and wants company, let him eat lunch with Rachel. That's what a wife is for. Unless—wait a minute: is it possible it has something to do with her? With Leah? Is he so conceited he thinks she is asking for something? He invited her to lunch, let's not forget—as it turns out, to give himself a better opportunity to run his mouth about this survey he's so proud of co-implementing with a cast of, well, not quite dozens, but still. Always the team project, the collaborative venture. Can't anyone think for himself? For herself?

Leah feels herself losing interest. Not that these things aren't important. Our way of life, its prosperity and security, depend on people like Max to innovate strategies to sell to women significantly older and nowhere near as pretty as Leah whole container stores of stuff they do not need. It is a critical exchange that makes America what it is. Except after so many lunches listening to Max wax, well, not eloquent, exactly, but definitely enthusiastic on the minutia of marketing, Leah feels they are, perhaps not unintentionally, missing the point.

Which is …? Well, it has to be that. Isn't that why they are here, *really* why they are here, despite Max's maybe-useful survey and anything they might say about it? Isn't that why she has come, despite her intentions?

Leah works through her food. She pushes aside peas, adds duck sauce, orders more tea. Max, she notices, manages to choke down half his pork and rice. And he has finished the soup. But she steers clear, talks about her summer workload, Armand's endless house-painting project, Alessandro's obsessive behaviors and loud outbursts. The redemptive sweetness of her daughter. To all of which Max nods and, once each minute, grunts. She has the impression he barely hears her and is not listening at all.

Well all right, then. If it is such a weight on his mind, why doesn't he out with it? None of this is her fault. *He* brought it up. Three weeks ago and counting. *I love to talk to you. I hope we can continue to be ... to be ....* And has been ignoring the issue ever since, they both have, as if it weren't set between them like an oversized centerpiece. Obvious. Vulgar. As prominent as Rachel's butt has maybe become, what with her being almost nine months gone and ready, Leah figures, to pop.

Her cell rings in mid-thought. Max looks aggrieved as she picks up the call.

"This is Leah." She knows before he speaks, by the heartbeat pause she feels him take, who it is and what it is about and how he is going to say it, and why.

"That was some message this morning."

"I could say the same."

Heartbeat.

"Where are you, anyway?"

"I'm eating lunch. Finishing it, actually. Or trying to."

She can feel him checking his watch. "It's almost one-thirty."

"Is it?"

"Are you working really *hard*, Leah?" Armand says. "Is that how you come to spend an hour and a half at lunch? Is your back *hard* against a *wall*?"

"Why are you so angry?" Either he is squeezing the handset too tightly or grinding his teeth across the ether and into her ear. "I eat lunch every day, Armand. Just like you."

"Who with?"

Here we go. She has not done a thing. Thoughts do not count. Especially when more than half of them tell her, No. She would not even call what she has been thinking fantasies. Musings, maybe. What-ifs of a purely speculative kind. And already it's starting, Armand thinking he knows something without knowing what it is. Because what it is, is nothing.

Leah does not miss a beat. "Today I'm having lunch with Max. Tomorrow I'm having lunch with Susan. Thursday's Melissa. Are you going to call me then, too, so I'll know you're angry about it?"

"How nice for you," Armand says. "How pleasant, to have cozy lunch dates from now until the end of time with people who think you are completely wonderful."

"Armand."

"I eat alone. Every day. I'm sure it's unmanly to mention it and of course only a woman is allowed to complain. Then again, I'm off to Wymans with a fucked-up list for groceries, for *marketing*, so of course I'd forget my macho."

"My goodness. Maybe you should take a Valium."

Heartbeat. Heartbeat.

Heartbeat.

She wonders if he will tell her to go fuck herself. He has never said anything quite so nasty but Leah can feel his anger, radiant through the phone. What will she come back with? Not *Fuck you too*. What if she tells him, *I think I'll fuck Max instead?* Not meaning it. Or half-meaning it; because is it possible to say something you intend to be provocative without being half-serious? At least half. But not intending to follow-through, is what she means, just trying to startle Armand out of his craziness over a grocery list she has not had time to perfect. Maybe she can pass it off as a joke. For instance, if, right after he says, "Go fuck yourself," she were to say, "Well, if that's how you feel at least let's do a good deed and give Max a little relief, the poor guy is practically dying for it with his wife out of play." Except that's a mouthful. Also silly. And he would probably cut her off.

He says, "Why don't you take one?" Meaning a pill. And then he's gone.

Poor Armand. He can't do it. He just does not have that facility. The caustic comeback. The quick-cutting wit. Leah almost feels sorry for him, stuck at the house with a catalogue of chores and no opportunities to be smart or needed. But, it is his own fault. He is the one who has gone middle-aged-lazy, not her. She hasn't quit a big job to tend a garden, so-to-speak, even if in Armand's case it is to paint a house. No wonder the man is cracking up.

She closes her cell. Max is watching her with an expression that makes him look half-hopeful and half-annoyed.

"What's up? Big Bad Wolf blow Armand's house down?"

Leah does not want to talk about it. It is none of Max's business, for one thing, and anyway it is all too pat and Max would be too obvious about it in his supercilious way, unless he really has written her off, in which case she will just get angry. Then she could go home and she and Armand could be angry together.

Oldster. She would like to slap him.

She gives their waitress the high sign and gets the check, which they split. Max chatters on, something about consulting gigs that will gross him double his faculty salary, plus open up all kinds of rape-the-poor deductions he can't access as an academic. It is one of his favorite words: access. But Leah is not listening. And ten seconds later Max is not talking. He is staring past her, literally right over her head, with his mouth open.

Leah knows what's up. It is so typical. He is. They are. Men.

Max's head swivels as the girl passes their table, now covered with dirty dishes and a ragged stack of kicked-in cash, and sits by herself at a table Max has to turn around to see. He shifts himself, Max does, actually slides his chair out and angles it so he can look at her without having to turn his head. The girl notices and rolls her eyes. Max is not discouraged. Leah is not surprised. He has done this before in restaurants, and even walking along the sidewalk with her in broad daylight, as if she, Leah, disappeared when one of these vixens strolled into his field of vision. This one is nineteen, maybe twenty, an undergrad in residence for Summer Session and dressed for the season in white shorts and a yellow chemise with spaghetti straps that would not fit so snugly nor seem so skimpy if this young lady—a golden blonde, naturally, with silken hair and a babydoll face, who looks as if she has just stopped in on her way to some non-existent beach—did not possess breasts that make Leah's own seem like small, saggy paps. All of which Leah understands in a flash and despises. Max, meanwhile, looks ready to drool.

Goddamn him. And goddamn him. Goddamn the both of them. Leah stands and begins to walk out. She is not sure what Max is about to do but can feel he isn't following. Can he really be sitting there, ogling that girl, who, Leah has to concede, is really quite something? At the exit she turns and looks back. Sure enough: He is not even trying to be subtle, not for a second feigning that he is studying, say, the unattractively-framed lithograph of a pagoda that hangs on the wall behind the girl. Leah almost believes he is getting set to launch himself full-body at Miss July.

What Leah would very much like to do is march back to the table and haul him out by his ear. If it were Armand that is exactly what she would do. But Max is just a friend. And let's not forget, he is B-School faculty. Tenured or not, he is so far above Leah in the hierarchy that he could probably get her fired, if that were something he really wanted to do.

Leah just leaves. *Forget it.* Forget him, forget them, forget the whole scene. It has been quite a day and it isn't even two o'clock. She walks back to Sage Hall, thinking she will leave early and no one will care. It is Summer Session; everyone kicks back. Except God only knows what her mood will be by the time she gets home, where Armand will be waiting in a mood of his own. Two moods, one house: a dicey proposition.

As she nears the Law School, more than half-way up the slope, Leah understands that Max has not tried to catch her. That he hasn't even faked it.

L ate July morning finds Armand clearing plates while Leah answers email. Julietta and Alessandro are daily campers at Cayuga Nature Center this week and next, practicing catch-and-release on butterflies and salamanders, accumulating mosquito bites that swell like bruises and itch itch itch. With no camp to take him and no one to ping, Armand lingers over eggs and the *Ithaca Journal*, drifts through clean-up, resists the moment he must commit himself to paint. Leah, he thinks, notices. Inside his head, Armand hears her. *No wonder he gets nothing done.* Leah herself has been rattling away to the tune of 120 words per minute. The sound is amazing, as if someone were crinkling sheets of plastic, then smoothing them out and crinkling them again. Over and over without pause. Watching her at it bewilders him—or trying to watch, for his eyes cannot follow her fingers. Leah is not just the quickest typist Armand has ever seen, she is the quickest typist, he's pretty sure, in the world.

He is quick at nothing. Mostly Armand is slow and his slowness knocks him down, makes him late. In doing, in thinking. Understanding. *Retarded* is a fancy word. No one is supposed to use it to describe how someone's mind works, much less to refer to a person afflicted with such a mind. It's like name-calling, like calling someone a bad name. Armand is pretty sure Leah thinks he is retarded. A dimwit; meaning, a retard, in the way he and his brothers and cousins used it when they were kids, growing up on the block. He is thinking of a time almost forty years gone. *God, Armand. You some kind of retard?*

Armand does not believe he is a retard. He admits to plodding, to being a plodder. Armand the Plodder. Two years and counting to paint a house. Well, he doesn't work on it every day, loses half the year to bitter winter, hates it any time. Who on Earth or in Heaven could enjoy such work? Power-sanding sixty-six foot eaves, upper and lower, both sides of the house, while perched on a ladder. Paint dust in his hair, on his face. He wipes down the slats, primes them with syrupy Peel-Stop, brushes Richmond Bisque onto the slats above his head. Drips, runs, smears. Paint flecking into his eyes. Fecking paint flecking. Only goggles save him from blindness. And the stucco. Armand washes it, waits for it to dry; forces high-viscosity block filler into the crevices, waits for it to dry; rolls on Richmond Bisque, loaded, as the block filler was before it, on a shaggy, high-nap roller that he has washed out and, yes, waited on to dry. Attached to one end of a telescoping painter's pole, gooey with latex, the roller feels like lead. Hours each day, all on his own—which for Armand is a point of pride. No one helps him. He has no help and asks for none. He is a man, a true American man. Meaning, self-reliant. He takes care of himself, he takes care of his family. You bet he can. Absolutely.

But he is slow. Slow, slow. Mary Mother of God, is Armand slow. It hurts to realize just how retarded he seems. What would he have done on the prairie? How could he have survived in the wilderness, how suckled a living from the fresh green breast of the New World? The impression he makes is that of a low-energy,

Epsilon-minus semi-moron who *does not know what he is doing*. The effect is unintentional. And yet, it is what people mainly see, Leah included. By all appearances Armand does not have the first clue, has a brain that barely functions, a mind (such as it is) that drifts in a milky fog of wordless limbo. While he has been rinsing dishes and racking flatware in woolly-brained slow-motion, Leah has dispatched a dozen electronic replies. Here she is a solid hour into the day's work and Armand hasn't so much as un-lidded a paint can.

He tries to speed up, maybe rushing a bit, and a glass, one of the remaining eight of the every-day dozen they bought as newlyweds and have been individually breaking over the past decade-plus, slips through his soapy fingers and shatters in the sink. About ten pieces, he figures, reckoning the pattern. Leah says nothing, hasn't heard or doesn't care. As for cursing, Armand doesn't bother. What would be the point? Would another *cunt motherfucker* or *shit goddamn* reassemble the glass? If he barked really hard, say, in boldface type? Would it get Leah's attention? Make him feel better?

Armand digs out a grocery bag, the paper kind he used to insist Wymans hand over to line the flimsy and dysfunctional plastic sacks they were always palming-off before switching to reusable canvas bags that are much better in every way, so long as you remember to bring them. He plucks up the shards one-by-one and drops them in, then carefully rolls the bag and seals it with duct tape, then drops the whole business into the trash just as he realizes, *It's glass. Recycle it.*

Retard. Armand hates being this stupid. As he is lifting the bag of broken glass from the trash, he hears Leah's cell phone. Its ring is a sort-of chortle that makes him think of the word "dulcet" and water—the substance of water, not the word. A dulcet chortle heard through water; water chortling over dulcet stones—not that

Armand thinks stones can really be dulcet. It's the sounds of the words he finds similar to the sound of the cell phone's ring. Armand hears her pick it up, feels her put it to her ear. His wife's indiscreet voice extends, prolongs, and italicizes her hello, which comes out, *"Hiiiiiiiiiiiiiii."* Armand hears her rise from her chair, step into the small bathroom, beautifully tiled, off her home office (itself directly off the kitchen in which he stands), and shut the door.

All right. He is stupid and maybe retarded but she cannot think he is as stupid and retarded as all that. Not to mention deaf and blind. Armand knows what's going on. The goddamn sneaking bitch. The phony lying whore. And she will have the effrontery to lie about it. She will play him for a fool and lie to his face about fucking some local big-shot and pretending all the while she's Ms. Wonderful Who Does Everything, has a career and children, too, and now, no surprise, a schmuck husband who wears the horns.

Armand can hear her through the wall. A murmur, not words, her voice resounding in the tiled space. A gentle murmur he would call tender. Also happy. Pleased. Maybe she is planning to leave him. Maybe she is setting it in motion right now. Making arrangements. Coordinating comings and goings. Synchronizing watches. It must be so. Nothing Armand does inspires her voice to sound as it sounds right now, resonant in a small bathroom that used to be, before they renovated, little better than an outhouse. What Leah is saying, exactly, much less what she is hearing, Armand cannot make out. That's okay. He doesn't want to make it out. He doesn't need to.

Fuck this. He drops the taped bag back into the trash. And *Fuck her.* Except Leah won't let him. And now Armand knows why.

*

Two hours later Armand is painting window trim. Perspiration is running off his head, down his face into the ribbed neck of his tee shirt, which is soaked. His wrists are sweating, slicking his palms, making the paintbrush's laminated handle slippery in his fingers. He lays the brush across the Little Giant's top step, careful that its bristles hang in the air, and descends the Ladder System with tin bucket in hand. He sets it, the bucket, on the concrete and lifts the lid off a gallon can of Green Mountain Green. This is the color Armand is painting the four-inch trim that, well, trims each of the bungalow's forty-three windows, upstairs and down, as well as the doors, front, back, and side. Armand has also painted the ten-inch ledge of the porch railing this same green, ditto the three-inch bead-board below that railing that forms the inside surface of the porch's seat-walls. When he gets around to it, say in a year or two or possibly ten, if that's how he feels, he will paint the cedar shingles that, oh, *shingle* the bungalow's upper half-storey this same rich, deep, Green Mountain Green.

But not now. Now it is just the trim around the antique dining room windows: the two smallish, lead-pane casement-style windows that flank a much larger rectangular fixed window. None of these windows has been improved despite the fact that the large rectangular window ought to be stained glass, or art glass, preferably amber. To filter the light. Soften it. Every book Armand has ever seen on the subject of Arts & Crafts bungalows illustrates this feature in luscious color photographs. Not that there's a law about it, architectural or otherwise. Not that four or five generations of bungalow-builders' and -owners' having used stained and/or art glass in the inevitable rectangular window above the inevitable built-in sideboard-with-mirror, in maybe a million instances of decorative continuity over a hundred years, is any reason you should do it, too. But you might want to consider it. Someone, sometime since they started building this house in 1911, might have taken a moment to give the idea a thought, ha ha. But no. The clear glass has evidently been in place from the start. Budget housing: the substandard 2x6 framing and makeshift floor joists and painted poplar woodwork and originally un-insulated walls have "shoestring" written all over them.

It would be morning light the art glass filtered, if anyone had had the bright idea, ha ha, to spring for it, because the bungalow enjoys a southern frontage (which the maple's canopy cancels) and the dining room windows face east. Which would lave their non-existent halcyon family breakfasts with a warm flood of golden light—amber being like gold, sort-of. Which is why the large rectangular window is a fixed pane. See, you don't want to be opening and closing and in your absent-minded haste or bloody-minded fury possibly slamming a large, leaded, stained or art glass piece of, well, art. The books call it art glass. Armand and Leah have been intending to replace the nothing pane of clear glass with a fabulous piece of art glass designed and fabricated just for them by a local artisan with a studio right in Ithaca, whose name Armand forgets. But they have not gotten around to it. Because what is the point of installing wildly expensive, custom-cut art glass when Armand is still painting exterior trim?

Maybe they will never get around to it. Maybe they are breaking up, on the verge of selling the house they thought they would leave only in the end, feet-first. Armand will be damned if he is going to stand here while some guy moves in and takes everything, takes over, fucks his wife in his bed that he paid for, sits in his chair at his table and eats his food, belches, wipes his lips on the back of his hairy hand or, what's worse, Armand's napkin, then takes Leah up his stairs and back to his bed to fuck her some more.

That is not going to happen. Armand will kill them all first and burn the house to the ground. Painted and unpainted trim, hardwood floors, new walls and old, stucco and shingles, the art glass window they do not have and likely will never get, all of it right down to the clay-tile foundation. Probably not all of it will burn so well, and of course he'll spark it when no one is home. That is not the point. The point is that if Armand is not going to live here, no one is going to live here.

The bitch. The cunt. The lying, phony whore. *Maybe you should take a Valium.* Very funny. Ha ha. He bit his tongue. So many possible replies flooded his mind, nastiest at the forefront. He didn't trust himself to fire back. What he could say, the worst things he imagines, would end their marriage in a minute. Armand does not want even to think it. Lesser-grade insults are harsh enough. Maybe I should take a Valium? All right.

Maybe you should suck my dick.
Spread your legs and I won't need a pill.
Maybe I should break your neck.

Except he does not want to break her neck. He loves her, he does. But anger is toxic. He might say anything. And do who knows what.

A lifetime supply should've come as a wedding gift.
A pill for being bitched-at hasn't been invented yet.
Maybe I should find a coed to suck my dick.

Again, his dick. Why does his rage at all things irritating always lead Armand back to the state of his dick? Is its chronic neglect and the injustice of same really so important?

Lifting the can, about to pour exterior latex at $36 per gallon into the more manageable tin bucket, Armand looks around in a way even he recognizes as weary, as if hoping some itinerant jack-of-all-trades might be passing by, on this little street that leads nowhere, and offer him a hand. No reason: perfectly altruistic.

Meaning, at no charge. Free. Sweetly gratis. But Armand sees no one who fits the description, in fact sees no one on the sidewalk at all, which makes him wonder if so generous a human being exists anywhere in the wide world. A man who would help another man—overwhelmed, melting in the sun, about to be shit-canned by his whore of a wife—paint his house, which soon will not be his, for nothing in return.

Armand pours. Green Mountain Green smoothes from the can and folds itself into the bucket. Armand dips and lifts the rim's leading edge, avoiding the drippy, end-of-pour spill, and sets the can down. Gripping the bucket's wire handle, he looks up and for no reason fixes on the unkempt house next-door. Through a window an old face peers out—at him, Armand would swear—its eyes tightened as if taking aim. Unblinking, lips a hard line. He can't tell if she sees him looking. She does not move.

Armand lets his head turn and his eyes look away. Three heartbeats later, he looks again. The curtain falls and a stooped outline, ghost-like, is visible in retreat.

The old lady is no ordinary shut-in. She is a spy. What does she think she might see, with him doing nothing but home improvement?

Armand climbs his Ladder System, bucket in hand. He dips the brush and lays on a first coat. Actual painting he doesn't mind. It's the prep work that kills him. Scrape and sand for an hour and the wood looks worse than before you started. Paint for ten minutes and it looks like new. Armand feathers the bristles along the grain and draws high-quality Green Mountain Green evenly down 90-year-old oak. The paint covers without streaking or flashing. Even the edges look solid. Armand is almost enjoying it. Maybe not the work but the quick progress and instant results. His eye is sharp today, his hand steady. He is loading the brush just-so every time and applying a uniform coat. His lines are straight and even, almost as if he really knows what he is doing.

He screws up anyway. Doesn't notice a residue of paint that has crept up the brush and oozed onto the tin band that binds the bristles, isn't aware that he is holding the near-vertical angle too long. A thick, swollen drip of Green Mountain Green gobs off the tin and hits the window, smears off and spatters the stucco. The glass is supposed to be clear; the stucco, Richmond Bisque. Now he has to wipe paint off both. Gaffes like this are why he carries a rag in his pocket. To wipe up fuck-ups. A paint-daubed wipe-rag. A fuck-up rag. A fuck rag, to wipe away fucks, a fuck. Fuck.

Fuck.

Armand leaves it, a fuck-up in green. He clambers down the Little Giant, presses the lid onto the open mouth of the gallon can, does not bother to pour the half-inch left in the bucket back into the can before he lids it. He does not bother to clean the brush. Fuck the brush. What does a paintbrush, even one with natural bristles, cost? Fifteen dollars? Twenty, if he is being ripped-off? Fine: He'll buy a new brush. Maybe he'll splurge and buy two, three, what the fuck does it matter, they're rich, they're breaking up, he'll buy a dozen fucking fuck-brushes. Why not, with Leah working hard to make George Juniors four at a time?

He'll show her. Two can play this game. *Maybe you should take a Valium.* Maybe you should walk Toto to Oz. Get yourself a brain. And a heart.

It's okay. Armand knows what it is. He can handle it. He isn't just some nebbish who adores his wife as if she were the only woman in the world.

*

His Subaru's instrument panel says the outside air is 94 degrees. Voices on the radio claim today's heat index is 107. The Wymans lot, jammed with cars and people and grocery carts, is a Rube Goldberg gadget of Minivan Moms and goggle-eyed senior citizens backing-up out of context. Cars idle at a standstill while waiting for a space. Abandoned carts inch, drift, and roll away. Heat-stuck pedestrians walk where walking is not safe. Armand slips the Subaru between a cart-return station and an SUV so massive it makes Armand's car look like a go-kart. All around him, overbuilt vehicles clot ingress and egress: Lincoln Navigators in silver, Ford Expeditions in red, Range Rovers in khaki, Escalades in gold. Armand does not care what people drive, his main ride being a Benz, but he does wonder what they are thinking. Don't they realize it is 2004? That oil is running out? That gasoline prices are set to spike? Average global temperatures have risen 1.8 degrees Fahrenheit over the last 100 years. Already the arctic is melting. A person does not have to be a fanatical environmentalist to see these steel-and-glass behemoths and their single-digit miles-per-gallon as terrorist acts.

He opens all four windows an inch, sets a sun-shade behind the windshield, gets out of the car and locks it. He tries not to breathe as he crosses the parking lot; hot asphalt exudes a petrochemical miasma. Armand enters the solar field of the photoelectric eye and the doors swing open. He grabs a cart and heads toward Market Square.

A blast of super-cooled air turns his sweat-wet shirt clammy in seconds. With a shiver, Armand detours to Seasonal Goods. He grabs a new shirt from the rack, a white-on-red CU classic, and pays for it on Express. Into the Men's Room to change then out again to his cart. It is where he left it, empty, looking un-American, looking retarded. Armand stows his sweated tee on the undercarriage and off he goes, weaving amongst bins and stands, swerving around stalled carts, circumventing aisles backed-up by women kibitzing. Men, too: old-timers and retirees with an afternoon on their hands and cocktail hour in their minds are happy to kill a couple hours in Produce. Not Armand. How people spend the day is none of his business but he does wish they would not block traffic. Move to one side if you want to chat and keep the thoroughfares clear. Old folks shuffle along in Egyptian cotton and cross-trainers that might have served them better sixty years back. Armand might be an old guy himself one day. There won't be any aisles for him to block, no 100,000-square-foot supermarkets with climate-control and imported berries. Farmers will gather in real market squares, authentic ones, and Armand will barter for eggs and beans or pay for same with silver and gold. It is not clear to him what use farmers will have for the precious metals town folk will be happy to exchange for a bag of apples and a loaf of bread, other than to pay private armies to guard their farms.

List-less, also listless, Armand circuits through Produce. He works from memory, a mental fund of food-gathering experience built up over hundreds of runs. Standard green asparagus, non-organic from California, is going for $2.99 a pound. Armand keys the PLU code into one of the electronic scales. The rapid math of this device calculates the Total Price of the 2.37-pound bundle more quickly than Armand could even with a calculator, which he does not have. The scale's accuracy he takes on faith—has no choice, really, if he wants to shop here, and if it is a little off, say by three cents per pound, why, Armand will never know. It occurs to him that Wymans might mis-calibrate its scales just slightly and reap tremendous windfalls by fractionally overcharging on each pound of the hundreds of tons of asparagus and lettuce and tomatoes and so forth it sells every week.

Suspicious man. Ready to believe anything. He has already decided that so-called sale prices are really just true regular prices sellers resort to when goods fail to fly off shelves at their augmented premium prices. The thought arrived the day he almost bought a set of matching soup/salad/dinner/dessert plates for four decorated with Disney World designs, because they were ostensibly price-reduced. He was holding a Fantasyland dinner plate when revelation came: *They are playing you for a fool.* Plus, he did not need plates. They have plates; most people do. Buying what you already have is acquisitive greed. Armand does not want to buy-in to buying-in. It is the impulse that drives the most diabolical of the plots laid against him: the hamster wheel of consumer capitalism. The insults encoded in ordinary items are insidious and deeply nasty. Today, for instance, it's the zucchinis: even the organic are so fat and goddamn long they taunt every man, well, almost every man, who walks past. Armand makes the mistake of looking at them for more than five seconds. It gives a woman standing near him, so she seems to think, a reason to say, "Makes you feel inadequate, doesn't it?" He is not sure he has heard right; she is a ghastly middle-aged witch with ruined skin and hair like steel wool. Nothing like what he has in mind. What Armand has in mind resembles an IC or CU coed in residence for Summer Session, skating through Wymans in a sleeveless undershirt and thin cotton pajama bottoms, open-toe sandals cradling Cinderella feet. He moves along quickly and can feel the spongy weight of the witch smirking after him. What does she know? Is she privy to Leah's secrets? Who is she, anyway, that she can hit him right between the eyes?

Signs and portents abound. Codes are streaming through his skin and mainlining to his brain. Armand picks up a bunch of scallions and shakes off the water before he places it on the scale. He keys in its PLU and the scale asks, "HOW MANY?" So okay, the mist Wymans sprays on its greens does not pad their price. But HOW MANY? How is he supposed to know? Ithaca is a small city; how many can there be? Have been? If she's fucked one, maybe she has fucked them all. Armand has heard-tell of a local whore who had sex with 130 men in a month. Which seems incredible, except it is what a whore does. Now Leah, whatever she is doing, is not a whore. He called her one in his mind but he did not mean it. That was his anger talking. But it doesn't answer the question.

Armand touches "1," meaning one bunch, scallions, and the Total Price appears. He touches PRINT and the scale rolls out a sticker. Scallions, Conven, Bunch. $1.99 per. Armand presses the sticker onto the bag, one of the thinner-than-paper polymer sacks all their fruits and vegetables come in and which, he figures, also will disappear in his lifetime.

After Produce it's easier, the aisles laid out north-south and sporting signage specific to the shelved goods. Armand zips up and down, slowing just enough to pluck boxes of whole-grain cereal and cartons of rice milk from the shelves. Chicken breasts wrapped in plastic come from one refrigerated case; cinnamon waffles, boxed, come from another. Armand loads his cart with cans of organic beans, red, black, and pinto; organic crushed tomatoes, Italian-style; artichoke hearts canned in water, tuna fish packed in canola oil, black olives jarred in brine. Jars of salsa, of sundried tomatoes, of capers, of roasted red peppers in olive oil, of green olives, of sauerkraut, all land in the cart. He doesn't know if they really need these things but they do use them, he's here, the canned and jarred stuff won't spoil and who really knows how much longer it will be available. So he might as well. So: bottles: of ketchup, of olive oil, of canola oil, of salad dressing in three varieties, of wok oil, of cow's milk (in cartons) for the kids, of sparkling water for him and Leah, of pure distilled water for all of them to drink during the approaching apocalypse.

Not really. That's Armand exaggerating. They drink distilled water on a regular basis because it turned out they were being supposedly poisoned by the chlorine dissolved in tap water. From what Armand has read, it is a miracle they haven't already died, that everyone hasn't died due to massive arterial scarring caused by chlorine molecules in the blood. And it isn't even enough not to drink your local municipal chlorinated water because if you shower in it, and who doesn't, you absorb chlorine through your skin. A bath is even worse, and Armand does not understand how anyone who swims in a pool is still alive. How long can it last, this brazen cheating of death?

He finishes up with eggs, toilet paper, maple syrup, a couple loaves of whole-grain bread, and a 6.8-ounce bottle of pharmaceutical-grade fish oil that goes for $27.99 and is supposed to feed his brain at the same time as it wards off the arterial catastrophe caused by all that chlorine. Armand is on his way out, that is, to the shortest checkout line, when he remembers he wants beer. His mental map of Wymans tells him the quickest route to the walk-in cooler is through Candy Cookies Snacks, an aisle he never even glances at, so poisonous are its contents to the human body. Now he swings his cart around, backtracks thirty feet, and turns right. It's a trap, of course. Candy Cookies Snacks is the most popular 100 linear feet in Wymans. Its traffic is practically impassable. Mothers dragged by their kids vie with late-onset borderline diabetics to grab blue-and-white packages of Chips Ahoy, clear bags of Nonpareils, plastic sacks of individually twist-wrapped Tootsie Rolls. Armand tries, honest he does, says, "Excuse me. Excuse me," but no one makes way. A man about Armand's age, riding a Wymans courtesy cart, is waving a cane over his head. As near as Armand can tell, the fellow is trying to knock a box of Butterfingers off the high shelf and into the cart's handlebar basket. The arguments Armand notes as advising against this effort have nothing to do with the perils of falling confectionaries. The fellow is riding the yellow cart because he measures his weight in multiples of one hundred and suffers from what look to be blood clots. In both legs. Which have turned purple and are swollen. His courtesy cart is so-placed that Armand cannot dodge around it, chiefly because an obese woman—possibly the man's sister and conceivably his wife, and in either case too short to reach the treat—stands behind the cart and will not move.

"Leave it," she says. "It's not like you'll starve."

"Goddamn sky-shelf," the man says. "I just want it."

"Let it go," she says. "We got to catch that GADABOUT."

"GADABOUT'll wait, I'm into the driver for twenty bucks. I ain't moving 'til I hook it."

Armand, blocked, ponders the ethics.

He can reverse course, turn left and left again, and scamper up Water Soda Juices, except it is second-most popular and might feature a snarl of its own. He can try "Excuse me" again and bull his way through, although that would be rude, and anyway the aisle is only so wide and these un-nimble people have nowhere to go. Or he can snag those Butterfingers for the man on the cart.

Armand looks at the fellow's legs. Forces himself. The man's thighs are hidden by blue nylon running shorts. Below the knees both legs are so thick and dark they seem to belong to some other, much larger animal. So many blood vessels have broken, the flesh looks like grape skin. Armand is not a doctor and what does he know, but to him this guy looks like an emergency about to happen, unless the double amputation has been scheduled in advance. It is no joke, and if he helps this fellow get those cookies, which every doctor on the planet would order him never to eat, just how guilty will Armand be?

All he wants to do is get by. Literally. Actually. All Armand wants is a Heineken six-pack, wants to nab it from the cooler, cart it, dart back to checkout and send their week's worth of fancy-dress provender over the infrared eye. Then he will pay and finally, FINALLY, get out of Wymans. But no; nothing is simple; he has to parse moral ambiguity. And it is a close call.

What decides him is Rule 1: Do Not Meddle in Other People's Lives. Especially Strangers. And so Armand leaves the crippled diabetic swinging his cane, his fireplug sister/wife shaking her head and saying, "Can you let it be? Can you?" and retreats. At the end of the aisle he makes another U-turn and heads up Water Soda Juices and finds a man wrestling a case of Pepsi-Cola onto his self-propelled courtesy cart. This time, Armand helps. He lifts the case off the floor and sets it in the wide rear basket, the handlebar one being too narrow and anyway already crowded with pretzels, potato chips, nacho chips, cheese puffs. This guy's legs are not purple but he is hopelessly fat. He says, "Thanks a lot," while Armand helps (helps?) him and Armand says, "No problem," as he is walking away.

At the cooler, all the Heineken six-packs are gone. Only twelves are left. Yes, Armand can buy a different beer—but Heineken is his favorite and if you have a favorite then your favorite is what you should have. Something like that. He can buy a twelve but the cart is overloaded already with a lot of things they might not strictly-speaking need, plus the cardboard box the twelve-pack comes in is really too flimsy to hold a dozen bottles of beer and anyway will not fit in the fridge after Armand has stowed milk and eggs and chicken and such. He wonders if he might find someone, a man-boy or greasy-creature who knows stock and will do a little reconnaissance for a five-dollar tip. Odds are, ten pallets of Heinie sixes are waiting in the wings; a five-buck tip shrewdly bestowed might fetch him one. A Heinie six, icy-cold. But no one is around, just other shoppers, as noted mainly women, none of whom are buying beer, and Armand does not know how to find help because generally he does not ask and at present is not inclined to hunt for it because how the fuck long is it supposed to fucking take, anyway, to get groceries?

He hoists a twelve-pack off the shelf and footballs it under his arm, spins the cart with his other hand, elbow raised and canted out for leverage. It is pretty heavy, the cart, being loaded and made of steel, but Armand gets it turned, then leans in and gets it rolling, pushing with one hand clenched on the bar. He isn't too nimble now himself, steering one-handed and unbalanced by the beer, but it is a straight run down Water Soda Juices to the registers and this time Armand's luck is in, the aisle is clear. He slows down before he reaches the end and does a quick-scan of the lanes. He isn't looking for the shortest line. He is looking for Jennifer.

Call it Step One. A modest start, nothing more than a trial run, his flirting with this Wymans staffer. He knows her name only from the plastic tag clipped to her Wymans-issue shirt (white or blue with black pants, uniform of the day) between her left shoulder and the top of her chest. Armand has gone through Jennifer's lane many times, mostly by chance, and now when he finds her he does something he would usually not do, which is form-up behind three other carts each carrying a week's worth. It will cost him time, Jennifer is not the quickest checkout-artist in the store, but for once Armand does not care. He wants to look at this girl, she can't be more than twenty, and see her bright-white smile when he makes some asinine remark about needing a mule, ha ha, to carry all these groceries to his car or, who knows, maybe a quip about being a New Age hunter-gatherer. Or maybe he'll just stick to the weather. It doesn't matter as long as she smiles, which Jennifer seems always ready to do, being beautiful with perfect skin and lovely cheekbones, straight white teeth and large eyes and hair the golden bronze of autumn hickory.

It is a blue shirt today, her better color, and from Armand's distance Jennifer's hair falling against the shirt looks like satin all shimmery and soft. She smiles at a customer and says, "How are you today?" No doubt standard Wymans training but from Jennifer it sounds special. She does not seem to notice Armand standing there behind the others. Why would she? She is young enough to be his daughter.

Foodstuffs nudge along the automatic belt. Carts inch forward. Armand tries not to stare; women find it creepy and he can't blame them. Imagine being Jennifer, twenty years old and beautiful and knowing you are beautiful, and maybe just nineteen, and feeling the grubby, greedy eyes of starving middle-aged men all over your face. As if they want to lick it, and how repulsive is that? Fleshy, saliva-wet, old-guy tongues slicking all over your clean, luminous skin. They ought to be jailed just for thinking it. Armand should be jailed, he should, although he tries not to think such things. It is difficult to resist, seeing her standing there so fresh and lovely and clean. He wants to remove her clothes and press his face into every inch of her gorgeous youth.

Leah. He loves Leah. How can he be thinking of Jennifer in this way?

It's hopeless, by which he means useless, by which he means it is impossible.

Armand slinks from the line and crawls away.

What is left to him? Nothing is left to him.

Crawling toward death. He finds a lane manned by a boy. Plus, the kid has acne, what a relief. Armand can focus on the job at hand. Not just groceries and getting them rung-up and paid-for and bagged, but what matters. The things that are real. As far as Jennifer is concerned, he does not exist.

He might be mistaken, but he believes he does not have to seem that way to everyone.

H ome-at-dawn Luke Robideau drags out of Dad's LeSabre and stands bone-weary regarding the eastern sky. He gazes uphill, away from the house, toward the shopping center someone has helpfully named East Hill Plaza, then north by northeast, in the direction of the Vet School's McConville Barn. Painted red, trim done white, immaculate to look at. Not that Luke can actually see either Barn or Plaza; they are a distance off, *a-ways,* as local folks say, for East Hill continues to rise far past the point on which he stands. He gets groceries at P&C, what does not come gratis from Wymans, and McConville he passes on solo drives to nowhere. Of the Vet School Luke knows nothing except that he probably should have attended it. Forget Arts & Sciences. Eleven cats, without trying. Whoever heard of such a thing? And three dogs. They maybe owe him an honorary to go with the earned one that has, in long run and short, proven worthless.

Birds are singing in the trees. Norwegian maple, paper birch, red oak, black walnut. A redbud, also called the Judas tree. It would be nice, Luke thinks, to awake to birdsong. He would have to quit the night shift. Working four graveyards a week, he is too tired for chirping to wake him. To quit the overnight would mean to change his life. And Luke is all for that.

Shredded clouds high over East Hill give the sky a pink-rose glow. Rain will be falling by noon, at which time Luke hopes to be asleep. Still asleep; he is headed to bed right now. Floor maintenance is like opening a vein, especially when he comes and goes in darkness. At this season it is early light and twilight, which helps his mood. *Luke's moody blues,* Mother calls them. Her boy is solidly on the job while most folks are in bed and returns before they wake.

Change my life. Sure, he would love to. But he is not going to accomplish a damn thing standing on a dirt driveway, staring broken-shoulder-exhausted at the rising sun. He hasn't even shut the car door, on which he is still leaning, meaty forearm laid along the top of the frame. *If you want to change your life,* he tells himself, *you have to make a move.* The world does not care, it will not discover you. You must take initiative, assert your presence, convince it to pay attention, insist it look at *you.* Advertise yourself to persons in positions of power. Persuade these people that you will add to their profits. That their profits are more important to you than your life. That you are a fellow who will put money in their hands.

What a laugh. Luke goes with it, laughs out loud where anyone could hear him, if anyone were here. It feels odd, laughing, for it comes, as near as he can tell, without a smile. That's some trick. To laugh and not smile while you are laughing. Luke has never checked in a mirror but he thinks he remembers what a smile feels like.

He shuts the door and locks it, keeps the keys in his hand. The windbreaker he carries towel-like over one shoulder. Korey and Pavel, out all night, scamper up as he moves toward the house. Luke unlocks the front door and everyone piles inside. From the entry he surveys the living room and mostly what he sees are cats. Cat statuettes, cat figurines, cat faces on plates, embroidered cats, glazed-tile cats, cats in pastel watercolor, as well as the living article in several varieties. Fran and Natasha look up, blank faces a little wary; glass-seeming eyes ask, *Where have you been?* The other cats ignore him. The dogs are asleep. Mother, too, is sleeping, from all indications, or rather lack of them. No breakfast on the stovetop, no radio yammering on the counter, no plates shuffling tableward. The kitchen is dark and shadow, the rooms silent and the curtains drawn, the blinds closed.

This is how it will be when she dies. Luke has had this thought many times. What it will be like at home. When he lives alone with animals. He expects everything to become a mess. Dishes unwashed, clothes unlaundered. Stuff collecting, newspapers, the junk that comes in the mail. A certain amount of it on the floor. Dust everywhere.

He is about to call her. Just to make sure. One day, and maybe when it happens he will know the instant he opens the door, Luke will find her. On the sofa, if she goes while watching television; in Dad's old chair, if that is where she sits when he is away. Most likely he will find her in bed. He will wake up for lunch or breakfast or whatever you want to call it and find no food ready and Mother still asleep.

Mother? Wake up.

Fifteen years ago his father's soul slipped away. Flew up the chimney into an indifferent sky. Now it is Mother who is a matter of time.

Luke drapes his windbreaker on the back of a kitchen chair. He washes his hands and dries them on a dishtowel. She isn't here to see, not awake to hear. He opens the refrigerator and drinks milk from the carton, long cool swallow creamy in his throat, resting that forearm along the open door. Wipes his lips with his fist and replaces the milk, then removes a sealed container from the second shelf, un-lids it, fingers out a strip of broiled meat and folds it into his mouth. Congealed white fat and cold, striated brick-red flesh. Luke, chewing, licks his fingers. Picks out a second as he swallows the first, bundles it into his mouth and chews. Picks out a third as he chews the second, before Mother's sixth sense lights up and she calls down at him to use a fork.

Sit at the table. Eat off a plate.

You are not an animal, Luke reminds himself. He licks his fingers. You have a flatscreen on satellite feed, a computer tapping the Internet via broadband. You know how to spot trends and track stories, keep abreast, touch your finger to the devil's pulse. These are not trivial things. They do not come cheap. They are expenses; you are responsible for the costs. You, Luke Robideau, are a responsible man. Never mind what anyone says, what people think. You are holding up your end. Doing your job, earning your pay, ponying up for bills. You are a solid citizen of this fair and glorious land and you, my son, have rights.

Damn straight. Luke fingers up a fourth beef strip, succulent and toothsome, then re-lids the container and slides it back. Picks up the milk carton, checking first that a fresh one remains, and drinks off what's left in the half-gallon. Turns out it was half-full or half-empty, depending on how you see it. Now it is empty-empty. Luke steps on the pedal and the trashcan doffs its lid. He drops the carton in, lets the lid fall. Closes the refrigerator door. Rubber insulation compresses against the metal, a firm fit. Luke washes his hands again and, still using dish soap, washes his face and beard. Again uses a dishtowel to dry. *So what?* Is Miss America watching via hidden camera? Is he a minute from greeting the Queen?

Removes his shoes and up the stairs he goes, quiet, quiet. If Mother is tired she should sleep. She has earned it, not that sleep is something anyone has to earn. Although it might come to that. Government's always hunting taxes, *revenue streams* they call them, so what could be better than a surcharge on sleep? Completely dependable except they can't charge too much. People have to sleep. How could Mother not be tired? Luke has lived just half as long and he is exhausted. Straight into the bathroom to brush his teeth, then to bed. He strips to tee shirt and boxers, reconsiders, sniffs himself, his skin, its sheen of work-sweat, and decides, yes, a shower is called for, a quick one. He returns to the bathroom. *Good.* It is a good sign, that he is making an effort toward personal maintenance, what is called hygiene and, when you are serious about it, grooming. Like a dog, although Luke cannot imagine grooming a dog, you must be kidding. But for himself, a shower, yes. What it means to be clean. Because after the night shift. Right? Pure sweat of honest work but it stinks up the bed. So, good, he is taking the time, the trouble, he is paying attention, even giving himself credit, in a way, for being worth it. A grown man: he cannot go around smelling like a bear, soiling his own nest, although it is not as bad as that. In fact, it is far from that. Let's not exaggerate. A little authentic b.o. in the sheets. Which, when he reconsiders, Luke figures he can risk. He is worn-out, he sleeps alone. There is no wife or girlfriend to nauseate with his pungent, tacky bulk grinding its stink into the creases. He goes back to his bedroom. What does he care? No one else cares—why should he? It is his bed, what should it smell like but him? He has worked all night cleaning floors, buffed something like forty thousand square feet of commercial linoleum to satin clarity, and, man, he's done. He wants to lie down, wants to shut his eyes and feel his body subside, heavy on the mattress, feel his breathing slow and himself sink through swirls and folds of darkness. Why must he shower just to get some rest?

But it's disgusting. He is. Luke turns around, enters the bathroom, turns on the water. Adjusts the knobs for hot and cold, pulls his tee shirt over his head and steps clear of the shorts. An old-cheese odor hits him, seems to cover his face like a web. Which settles it. Luke hauls himself under the spray.

Afterward, hair towel-dry, deodorant slicked in his armpits, fresh underwear covering his shame, Luke sleeps.

And dreams...

... the next-door woman into his bed and himself between her legs, labial folds slick with passion that gathers him in, smoothes the way of his ardor. Luke sees her face as clearly as a photograph, her breasts round and melting above lace cups of a flipped-down bra, as if he were dreaming a movie of himself having sex with her. Luke watches the movie as he participates in it, watches himself boning the blonde chick with that ass and those tits at the same time as he is doing it. Virtually boning, with the stiffest ramrod he has ever sprouted, the golden cupcake who lives next door with an obvious peasant. It is nearly real, this dreamland fuck. Luke feels his hips moving, *yes that's the way,* except his hard-on is sliding into, alas, nothing. Nowhere. He doesn't, can't, feel it, her, the hot-jelly in-and-out for which no substitute exists. Not even in a dream. And so cannot finish, can only poke air, penis extending through the vent of his boxers like a joke that has gone on too long until it is aching, then numb, and Luke wants to scream.

But does not scream, despite finding himself awake with a dick so hard it could knock down a wall. Morning light is bleeding-in around the edges of the shades. He made it through maybe one REM cycle and here he is with a ridiculous piss-erection that is going to take a couple minutes at least to get rid of. Amazing, at his age, without encouragement. Not that Luke has ideas of himself along those lines. But still. He is a man, nothing better. And Nature insists.

Except right now it is Nature's other call he has to answer. After his confused organ calms down and Luke empties his bladder, he drops into bed again and, it seems, straight into the dream, it is the same every time, that has him showing up late for a class he has never attended, has not even known he is enrolled in, without the term paper he has not known is due. Yellow railroad tiles dull on hallway walls and beige-and-black-flecked linoleum look like grammar school but the feeling is college and Luke seems to be his present age. He does not recognize the other students, who also seem to be adults. A teacher with no face drones about using primary sources, documenting evidence, providing citations in an approved style: long strings of words Luke does not hear so much as absorb like mental telepathy or something he already knows. So it's history class, he figures, and this term paper he knows nothing about is supposed to explain some famous or maybe infamous event or maybe person, and now it turns out it is not due today but next week, which gives Luke hope along with a feeling of sick despair, because the available week means he cannot just take the zero and have done with it; no, he is obliged to try, improve the shining hours and try, goddamnit, *try* to start and finish in seven days what has obviously been designed as a semester's worth of pecking through card catalogues and pulling books from shelves and reading those books and ransacking their indexes for the pages, the paragraphs he needs; and taking notes on 3 x 5 cards and organizing them; and then figuring out what he is supposed to write. Then writing it. And he does not have a topic. At this point he does not know what a topic is. What historical era are they studying? He raises his hand but the teacher does not see him—and how can she, without eyes? If she knows he is there, she ignores him, unless he is invisible, which seems right; it is a dream, after all; he is not really there. Still, he hears a bell ring or seems to hear despite its silence, the bell, or just assumes it rings because everyone packs their notebooks and leaves, all scurrying together down a flight of iron stairs in a dank stairwell then crossing a corridor and climbing a different flight of the same type stairs, steps echoing. The weight that impedes Luke in life is gone, the bulk that makes it difficult to lift his legs slimmed away, his body restored to its youthful litheness, his hair renewed, his beard not grown, then it is, then it isn't. His clothes are neat, new, knees unworn, seat not shiny, topsoil not ground into the fabric. Unfaded, untorn jeans, clean sneakers, fresh shirt. Girls snug in sweaters smile at him; other boys are present yet invisible, their tongues cut out. See, there's one: a pinko-gray four-inch tongue on a window sill and swarmed by ants. There's a six-incher naked on that beige-and-black-flecked linoleum and rolling in the dust. Luke is worried about that term paper and in another way is not. A missed assignment and a big one, a major grade; the zero is going to hammer his GPA and knock him off the Dean's List. Dad will be disappointed. And in another part of his brain: *It doesn't matter. Dad is dead.*

There he is. Dad. Standing on the grass with a newspaper in one hand, a golf club in the other. It looks like a putter. *Smile at the camera, pal.* And he does. Smiles. He seems to want to speak to Luke, seems about to say, but Luke cannot hear the words. Or does not want to. He can imagine. *Are you tired finally of minimum wage? Almost done with numbnuts jobs?* Dad in Luke's dreams does not say these words but Luke knows they are there. What Dad would say if he had the chance. He worked all his life and made a decent living and he does not feel sorry for Luke anymore.

His father's spirit hovers; Luke feels it, wants to think so. He believes his father cares, although he cannot explain how caring is possible for a soul set free. Isn't that the point of dying? To escape this brutal, ruined world and not care? Not have to care, to feel you must or should. Safe in death, we are obligated no more. And isn't it right, as in his dream Luke feels, isn't it fair, fitting and proper that he not trouble Dad's soul?—that he not push obligation on one who has moved beyond it?—that he not insist on a Great Hereafter in which he, Dad, his soul, should continue to sympathize with this man who is still a boy, this son who cannot grow up?

Dad. Luke sees him alive and whole, smiling and hearty. He is washing the LeSabre, then with a soft cloth hand-polishing the smoke-gray paint, still lustrous. Turning the cloth, shaking out polish dust. Always a smile, never a word. In Luke's dreams his dead father, alive again, does not speak. Luke knows why. He believes his father still loves him, despite his failed life. Wherever he is, out among the stars.

He wakes in the silence of an ordinary day. Breathing heavily, his chest wound tight. Maybe he is having a heart attack at last. Three hundred pounds, near enough. This is how it ends. All of a sudden, once and for all. Alone in his bed, no one to hold his hand. He does not hear Mother but assumes she's up. He does not know how long he has slept. No watch, no clock. His face feels cool in the shadowed room. When Luke touches it, his fingers come away wet. But he toweled off after his shower, and anyway it is hours later. Mid-day. He is not perspiring. These must be tears.

He wipes his face with his fingers, wipes his eyes, pig-little in his porky face. It's okay, he knows what he is, how he looks, that it's hopeless. He kicks the sheet off and lies there, waiting to sleep again. Without dreams.

Hunting Old Sammie

*

After a poor second sleep, Luke thanks Mother for a late lunch-breakfast and rises from the table with his mug in his hand. Green tea tastes like boiled grass, as near as he can tell, or rather the water the grass has been boiled in, but it is supposed to be good for him, possibly to the point of warding off that killer coronary. Three hundred pounds. Three-ten. He has to do something, help himself in some way. He takes a stroll, nothing too ambitious, just outside in the warm air, sun blazing in his face, along the sidewalk for a block with pauses to sip the acrid, strangely bland tea, reconnoitering, trying to ignore the heat seeping up from the concrete through his shoes so that his feet feel poached. Luke sizes up his neighbors' grounds, their landscaping, what they have done with what they have, what they've added, what they have tried in desperation and what they have not tried at all, and concludes that these people are lazy or just not paying attention. Patchy groundcover, invasions of weeds, un-thought-out, nugatory plantings that will never challenge his own. Back he walks, having covered barely a block. The sidewalk is cracked, its plates raised, their edges jagged. Just try to lay slate in this climate, he thinks, jealous again of warm-weather places, his siblings in Florida and California who pay landscapers to install gardens with teak trellises and delicate stone borders fussy along slate paths. Just try it here, say from the driveway to the front door, then around back. The ground heaves in winter, floods in spring, in summer goes bone-dry. Just try ornamental stonework, Mr. Landscape Architect, river-rock edging, patio of tumbled brick. After three seasons in the Central Southern Tier, everything looks like shit.

Returning to the house, Luke catches himself muttering. Well, what else can he do? He is a man with grievances, a man who has taken hits and losses and has no one to talk to and so naturally talks to himself. It is better if no one hears. Especially Mother, who would ratchet up her worry. Luke shuts up, clamps down, stands in the front yard and finishes his tea. He is about to go inside, thinking he'll maybe click-on the news for a twenty-minute catch-up, when a deep-throated hum rolls up behind him. A second later, the red car gleams into view. Mr. Johnny-come-lately turns his corner, their corner, the municipal corner they virtually share, and coasts for forty yards down to his driveway, where he almost stops before he steers up it and gently ascends.

Overkill. A car that cruises at a hundred miles an hour, coasting in second gear along local roads. Some people, Luke thinks, just have too much damn money. It is a shame against him, whatever his name is and no matter how rich, to have figured out no better use for $85,000.

Luke goes inside and walks through to the kitchen. Mother is bent over the sink, washing dishes with a sponge fixed to one end of a plastic handle, which itself is hollow and filled with liquid soap the blue of the Adriatic Sea. Luke is guessing, having never seen the Adriatic Sea even on television. But he has read it is especially blue.

"Well now, young man," and even that feels like a gibe. He is not young anymore. "How are you this fine day?"

A sigh rises, a bubble of pure despair. Luke quashes it, pushes it down, back, out. "Thank-you, Mother, I'm perfectly well. As you can see."

"And is the day very fine?"

Why is she so chatty? So happy, almost chummy? His mother. "Yes, Mother, the day is perfectly perfect." He ferrets out a spray bottle from the dim, detergent-smelling cabinet beneath the sink and picks up a dishtowel.

"Get a look at that neighbor lately?"

"Just now. Driving his show-off car." Luke covers the kitchen table, on which he can see grease, with an orange-scented mist.

"I mean the wife." Luke, swabbing Formica veneer, does not look up. "She's wearing her skirts three inches above the knee. Blouses tight across her bazooms, like she wants every fellow to grab 'em. I don't have to tell you, I'm sure."

Has his mother lost her mind? "I haven't noticed," but it isn't true; Luke has noticed, and imagined, and dreamed. But that is not something to say.

"Take a look sometime."

Why does she bait him? What good can she think it will do? "If it makes you happy," he says.

"It isn't too late, you know. A lot of women in the world. Most appreciate a man steady as you."

"Of course it's too late, Mother." He wishes she would stop. "And women, from what I've seen, end up bored with their husbands, whom they try to avoid."

"Oh, what do you know?"

Luke shrugs. What, indeed? Where do these notions sail in from? How can he be sure he knows? "What-say let's change the subject. All right?"

Mother's turn to shrug. She sets herself to finishing the dishes. Luke notices she has replaced the tiny daisies she bunches in jam jars on the sill above the sink. Each spring she clips them as long as they last, well into summer if possible. Another bit of business that goes back years, as if nothing has changed since 1958. It is one of the things Luke counts on, these daisies, green-yellow faces like pebbled rubber looking up from the centers of ruffled collars, and one of the things that make him wish he could leave, she would die, the house burn to the ground.

He leaves his mug in the sink. In the living room he sparks up the flatscreen and sees more reasons to run and hide. A dispatch out of Ramadi reports four U.S. service personnel killed when masked gunmen firing Kalashnikovs ambushed an armored convoy. The attack followed the detonation of an IED that disabled the lead vehicle and wounded its driver. Six insurgents were killed by U.S. Marines in the ensuing firefight, except now we are not calling them insurgents, we are calling them terrorists. Or enemy combatants, Luke guesses, like the hapless bastards penned at Guantánamo. Elsewhere in Iraq, three dozen of these terrorist combatants were killed and dozens wounded when U.S. and Coalition Forces staged simultaneous raids on an undisclosed number of suspected hideouts and safe houses. Reports of civilian casualties are unconfirmed.

Every day. This is the news Luke hears morning, noon, and night. And has been hearing for the past year. And expects to hear for years to come.

Six American Marines died today in an ambush on the streets of Baghdad.

Eight U.S. service personnel were killed in Iraq today when their Apache helicopter crashed after being hit by a rocket-propelled grenade.

Twelve American soldiers died in Iraq today in a series of sneak attacks against unfortified checkpoints.

Simultaneous car bomb attacks took the lives of ten Americans and dozens of Iraqi civilians today in the Sunni Triangle.

It does not let up and it does not change, although some days are worse than others. Today, the U.S. Military has launched an air strike on a suspected terrorist safe house in Fallujah, thought to be the lair of al Qaida kingpin Abu Musab al-Zarqawi. At least ten people have been killed. Zarqawi is not among the corpses and remains at-large.

Mother from the kitchen: "Turn off that nonsense, why don't you, and watch something nice."

He hasn't thought she would hear, what with water running into the sink. Luke lowers the volume. In the relative quiet he realizes the water is not running, after all.

"Luke?"

"Yes, Mother. It's important."

"You do not have to concern yourself. Those awful things have nothing to do with you."

A woman whose world ends at her property line. Old-style thinking for a life that was. Protected by oceans, are we? Nearly self-sufficient in natural resources? Wait. Wait until the first dirty bomb goes off in Boston or D.C. Wait until a clean-cut bioengineer with doe's eyes and a soft-music voice releases an infectious pathogen on the main concourse of LAX. Wait until light sweet crude hits two hundred bucks a barrel and natural gas goes to $50 per thousand cubic feet at the wellhead. Then see what Mother says about that nasty war in a desert 5000 miles away.

Luke stares at the flatscreen. He does not sit because standing, they say, burns calories. It makes sense; look at him, he's getting tired just waiting here, it must be true, unless that weary feeling is boredom, bad news from all over having a drear sameness to it and the talking-head commentary sounding familiar. His mind wanders right out the window and across the narrow yard to the strip of concrete that is his neighbor's front walk. Along which that asshole is drizzling coyote urine straight from a gallon bottle that looks new. Must have found another of Barney's calling cards, unless it was one of the cats. Which makes Luke wonder. Because what, exactly, is the point of spreading coyote urine in quantities and concentration sufficient to ward off cats and dogs, whose piss stinks nowhere as bad? It seems petty, punitive in a spiteful sense, as if this guy wants to keep Luke's animals off his yard just because it is his yard and they are Luke's animals. He ought to piss the concrete himself, if marking turf is what he's after, and save the twenty bucks, which they are all going to need before long to buy a gallon of gasoline. Except there is a law against it, public urination, in Ithaca. Does not apply to dogs, of course. Nor cats.

Luke changes channels, brings up the local weather. Forecast for the Finger Lakes. It is going to rain tonight. Really, he has to laugh. This asshole with his barrel of piss. Come morning, when he steps outside for his *Ithaca Journal* and finds the concrete cleansed and glistening, *then* will he understand the futility? All the neurotic effort to stitch up the world's unraveling. Picturing the look on his neighbor's face, that is, the look it will wear seventeen hours from now, Luke almost smiles. He feels it coming, muscles in his face contracting in an unfamiliar way, trembling a little, long disused. Lips pulling back, teeth showing, *here it is,* even his nose wrinkling a bit. You know, some things are just too good. The prospect of his neighbor discovering that overnight rain has washed away his anti-domestic-pet secret weapon seems to Luke like a thing to see, even if he has to clock-off early from work. If he doesn't head straight to bed and sort-of loiters where he is now, maybe moves closer to the window, he will have a front-row seat. Pretend to glance out, just checking the weather, *checking for rain,* then step back into shadow and take it in.

He tries it. From his window Luke has a sight-line to his neighbor's porch thirty feet away. The asshole isn't there, in fact has vanished with his coyote piss, is maybe laying down a perimeter, thinking he can repel any beast God has invented. Already it isn't working, Luke sees, because there goes Korey at a silver trot through the grass, then sleeking across the walk and up the asshole's porch steps. She leaps onto the wooden ledge, painted green, and settles down for what Luke knows will be a nice long survey of the front yard. She looks elegant lying there, he has to concede, high and supine, silver-gray fur etched against the green, nearly regal and for that reason distinct. From the sidewalk, Luke thinks, you can't miss her.

What happens next is not quite visible. Luke does not understand for half a minute after it ends—after the water stops and Korey bolts off the ledge and tears back across the yard to home, sweet home. What confuses him and has taken Korey by surprise is the water jet that has hit the cat from behind, as if it has come from the house. But as Luke can see, all the windows are shut. And anyway, who keeps a hose in his house? Attached to what in terms of a spigot? So, no—except yes, the water has come from behind and caught Korey solidly along her back and the back of her head. Which must have been shocking, Luke thinks, because so sudden and unexpected. Unlooked-for and unseen. Imagine if it were you, and Luke does, or tries, because he has never been hit in the back of the head by a burst from a fire hose. Which it must have been equivalent to, the asshole using some sort of high-pressure nozzle and Korey being a Korat. A cat.

That bastard. That rotten sonovabitch. Shooting Korey with a hard stream of cold water. Taking dead-aim through the far opening of his three-sided porch and firing at an angle. Lurking. Skulking. For the purpose of blind-siding an innocent creature. What kind of malicious piece of shit does such a thing?

Mother in the kitchen: "Korey! Gracious goodness, what has happened to you?" The cat meanwhile is mewling and wailing. Doesn't that asshole know they hate to get wet? It is basic fact, material every schoolkid understands. So he has done it on purpose, and what Luke is thinking as he returns to the kitchen is that he has done it knowing how bad it would be for the cat. And now for Mother, who is trying to hold Korey still and towel her dry. And for Luke, who is trying to help.

"You naughty kit-cat," Mother says, all affection. "What mischief did you get up to? Making dirty where you aren't allowed?"

Well, yes. There is that. And it is just water. The animal is not bleeding from the neck. Still, a high-pressure blast in the head. And by surprise. Ambushed.

Blindsided.

"Oh you mischief-imp. Oh you kit-cat." Mother seems to enjoy it, holding Korey's paws in her hands as you would a child's and patting them with a dishtowel. Korey seems not to mind, she is drier now and loves the coddling, which she seems to believe she deserves. Luke relaxes. He is not pleased. What if the water hit her in the eye? What if it snapped her neck? Where is that asshole's sense of proportion?

"You pretty pussums," says Mother.

It bothers Luke when Mother speaks to a cat as if it were a baby. Bothers him when people do things without thinking, make mistakes not easily set right.

There is so much that bothers him. So much he hates.

F ive o'clock one August Friday finds Leah Goldman alone in her office, putting the wrap on another week. Her door is shut, the lights dim. Leah herself is drowsy, having lost sleep over Armand, and herself.

She is clicking through her Inbox, responding to what needs a response, forwarding those that need forwarding, deleting all that is unnecessary. It is a discipline and Leah is trying to focus despite burning eyes and a nodding head. She wants to get through this stuff and go home and enjoy the Sabbath. Say the blessings, drink the wine, eat the food. Leah wants to rest.

She has just logged off when someone knocks. Her automatic "Come in," produces Max, looking sheepish with a bouquet of dahlias in his hand.

"Hello, Leah."

She looks him over. Thinning hair, clean-shaven. Sport shirt open at the neck. About three inches taller than Armand. Twenty additional I.Q. points do not show. His pants are washed-up; you would think his wife would buy him a few new clothes, if he can't manage it himself, mind preoccupied by demographic data and what-have-you. Too smart to pay attention. His mouth is crinkled, his eyes are dark. It would be comic if it were not charming in a pathetic way. All he is missing is a bowtie and a haircut. But the flowers are what get her—that, and the idea that he is a genius.

"Hello, Max. Haven't seen you in God knows."

He waves it away. "Hallway fly-bys. Public spaces—these are not conducive..." He seems to remember. "These are for you," stepping forward, hand extended, "obviously."

Leah accepts the dahlias. She looks at their lovely, long, elliptical petals, burning pink and succulent. "Thank-you, Max. These are beautiful."

"It's nothing. A token."

"Dahlias are my favorite." Leah smiles.

"I knew that. I wanted, after last time... you know."

Leah shrugs. "Yes?"

"My behavior was... a bit rough."

Another shrug. "You're free to like what you like. It's none of my business. I'm not married to you."

Max laughs. "How hard would you have hit me, if you were?"

Now Leah is laughing, too. "Mister, I would have knocked your block off."

They laugh together. Max says, "Can you blame me? That girl landed like a bombshell."

"Enough!" Leah is still laughing. "Not another word!"

"There's nothing more to say. She saw me drooling and shot me dead with a glare. I got out fast."

"Funny, I didn't see you walking back here."

"I guess I stood outside a couple minutes. I admit I was stunned. Never saw a girl that beautiful in my life."

Why won't he stop? Is it possible he does not understand how he is insulting her? Leah would like to smack him with the flowers, which she is still holding, and thinks she might do it yet if he does not shut up about the Asia House blonde. She says, "Tell you what, Max. Let's drop the subject forever. It isn't making me your friend." She stands and, dahlias in hand, picks a dusty vase off her bookshelf. Leaving him there, she walks to the restroom. She takes her time, lets the water run, cleans the vase, hums a ditty. All together she is gone maybe three minutes, and when she returns with the dahlias freshly deployed, Max is standing in the same spot—

—and says, "Actually, I don't mind if you're a little jealous."

Leah looks at him as if he has belched with an open mouth.

"I'm not jealous, Max. I would have to be in love with you for that. I'm annoyed. Also offended, but we can let that part go."

Max grins. "Yes, I see."

"Well, I don't think you do."

The silence that follows seems very loud. Now they are irritated with each other. Anyone who happened to hear would assume they were having a spat. That they often spoke in this familiar way. But only they are here. To Leah, the building feels empty. They can say whatever they want, say anything, and no one will hear. She realizes they also can do whatever they like and no one will know.

Now is the time. The thought comes unbidden and she does not trust it. She does not feel romantic, not affectionate, although she is worked up in another way. If she had to describe her feeling, Leah would say she does not want to kiss Max so much as she wants to bite him. Bite and kiss, not bite to hurt but to surprise him, make him pay attention to her, *to her;* then kiss to erase the bite, kiss away the marks teeth make. She moves closer; she cannot quite imagine doing it. She can touch him, however, with her hand on his shoulder, and when she does Max leans in and kisses her on the lips. At first Leah does not respond, then does, then pulls back without breaking the connection, then opens her mouth and presses her lips hard onto his. They feel thin, Max's lips, but his tongue is hot and meaty and when Leah caresses it with her tongue Max kicks the office door shut.

His arms are around her. Leah's hand is on the back of his head. Her other hand she lets fall to touch him through his pants. All in a rage: of course, he has had to keep it shelved. Leah unzips him and reaches inside, wangles him out through the fly.

"Yes," he says.

She caresses his penis, which is long and thin. Different than Armand, who is thicker and not as long. Both are circumcised. She unbuckles his belt, then steps back to push down her panties. Max opens his pants and waits.

Leah perches on the edge of her desk, bracing herself with her arms, legs wavering. "Now, Max. Quickly." He moves into her and the feeling is nice but not as intense as she has expected. His cock is thin; it fills her and it also does not. He moves rapidly, making the most of it, no holding back, and she says, "You can't finish inside me, you have to pull out. Pull out!" His moan is a low rumble in her ear and she is pushing him off, pushing him away. He withdraws just in time. Leah feels the spatter hot on her pudendum. She is not sure if the first spurt happened inside.

Max breaks away, breathing hard. "God, Leah. That was amazing." He fumbles with his underwear, his pants. He seems in a hurry. "You are wonderful, beautiful—thank you."

So. That must be why. To hear him say that. *Acknowledge me. Pay attention.* And to learn again that it is a pleasant thing that does not mean so much to her. Leah enjoys it all right and she is happy Max has enjoyed it, too, and liked her. But she does not need this to feel close to a person. To care about a man—any man.

She slips off the desk and turns her back to him. She reaches for tissues, from a box on her desk. With a clutch of three Leah cleans herself, then wads the mess inside a fourth. She will flush this evidence in the Ladies' on her way home. She does not pick up her panties. They are lying on the flame-retardant carpeting. She hopes Max does not notice. Leah wants him to leave before she retrieves them. She certainly does not want him to watch her put them on. It is bad enough to be standing here naked under her skirt, tissues sodden with his semen in her hand.

Finally he is back together and zipping up. He does not look at her. "It would be unwise to overestimate this," he says, Mr. Suave sweet-talking his paramour. "Not to suggest it wasn't wonderful because it was, for me. And I am grateful to you. I refer, obviously, to our separate situations, each of which makes anything further, anything more ... decisive, or disruptive ... well, impossible. What I mean to say is that whatever we—"

"Stop, Max. Please." Leah turns to face him. "I am not stupid. I know what our situations are—our *respective* situations. And I know our relationship or whatever it is ends on the other side of that door. Really. You don't have to spell it out." She wants to weep. It should not have happened and now that it has happened it should not be like this, with the two of them back-pedaling so fast they each risk breaking a leg. What they have done might be wrong but it was genuine; the feeling was honest. No one would excuse them, almost no one, but some people would understand. Not Armand, of course. Leah knows she cannot expect her husband to be a philosopher in such circumstances. She knows she would not be, were their roles reversed.

"I'm going now, Leah," Max says. "Please don't hate me." He opens the door and steps across the threshold. "Good-bye." A second later he is gone and the door is swinging shut.

"I don't hate you," Leah says, the final words coming as the latch softly clicks.

*

Later that evening, Leah stands with Armand and the children around the table. On it are four place settings of wedding china and inherited silver, two crystal wine glasses, a bottle of Cabernet Franc, a loaf of challah on a ceremonial platter, Shabbat candles in her grandmother's silver candlesticks. Armand strikes a match and together they recite the blessings to celebrate the Sabbath lights, the wine, the bread. Leah reads an ancient blessing for children.

"*Y'simha Elohim k'efra-yim v'hi-mena sheh.* May god bless you, Alessandro, as He blessed Ephraim and Manasseh. *Y'simeyh Elohim k'sara, rivka, rahel, v'leya.* May God bless you, Julietta, as He blessed Sarah, Rebecca, Rachel, and Leah. *Y'va-reh'ha Adonai v'yish-m'reha. Ya-eyr Adonai panav eyle-ha vihu-neka. Yisa Adonai panav eyle-ha v'ya-seym l'ha shalom.* May the Lord bless you and keep you. May the Lord cause His spirit to shine upon you and be gracious unto you. May the Lord turn his spirit unto you and grant you peace."

Together they say, "Amen." Alex and Julietta eat slices of challah. Leah nibbles a piece, thinking her hips are better off without it. She thinks her butt might still be too big, even with all the exercise and walking between work and home. It is a hard thing to know, the exact size of her butt; she cannot ever quite see it full-on. But she thinks it might still be too large for her height and decides that even if it is not too large, it would be better if it were smaller. She watches her children eating bread as Armand, a knot in his brow, dismembers a roasted chicken and serves it onto their plates. She and Julietta have dark meat and the boys share the white. There are oven-roasted butter potatoes with salt, garlic, and parsley; thin asparagus with olive oil and garlic salt; sweet cob-corn with salt and pepper and some butter. Everyone gets a portion that is more than enough.

As they settle in, Alessandro says, "That sniper rifle is fecking awesome."

"How's that?" says Armand.

"The M25. In *Hunting Old Sammie*. It's fecking awesome."

"Alessandro, not at dinner," says Leah.

"What's the matter with dinner?"

"You're weird," says Julietta.

"Shot off a couple turbans, have you?" says Armand.

"Armand," says Leah, and her husband winks at her.

"More than a couple," says Alex. "More than turbans. I blew off their fecking heads."

"Alessandro, really. That's enough."

"Which continued to bleed," says Armand.

"Actually, they exploded."

"Will you two stop it, please?"

"I saw him," says Julietta. "I saw their heads blow up."

"Would you all stop talking about this?"

"Why?"

"Because it is not appropriate dinner conversation, particularly on the Sabbath."

"It's just a game, Mom."

"I don't care if it is just a game. The words are the same. You could be repeating a news report. I do not want to hear it. Not at Sabbath dinner."

"Your mother's right," says Armand, and when Leah looks at him down the long length of the dining room table, he winks at her again. What does it mean, these winks? Armand does not wink, usually; he is not a winker. And he is not clairvoyant, Leah thinks, yet she cannot help thinking that he knows what happened fewer than two hours ago in her office, where she was supposedly working while he prepared their meal. Is it possible? Can he read betrayal in her face? Does he sense Max all over her?

Leah hopes she is not blushing. She doesn't think she is, doesn't feel it, but it, too, is difficult to know. "I would appreciate a change of subject, Alessandro. I know how much you enjoy your game but some topics are not suitable meal-time conversation."

"Ah, Mom, come on. I want to tell Dad about the Special Forces sniper rifle, it's deadly from a thousand yards and in *Hunting Old Sammie—*"

"*Hunting Osama*," Armand says. "The name of the game is *Hunting Osama*. Not *Hunting Old Sammie*, as you've been saying."

"Ugh! Whatever." Alessandro hangs his head and with his finger digs a stray bit of muck from the corner of his eye. He wipes his fingertip on the table, then flicks his fork through the asparagus.

"You are disgusting," Julietta tells him.

"Julietta, please. Don't pile on."

"I'm just eating! Ugh! Why can't you leave me alone?"

"Everybody just eat," Armand says. "Less talking, more chewing."

They eat. Slowly, steadily. The food disappears. Also the wine. Leah relaxes at last. It does not have to mean anything. Armand does not have to know. He does not know now, he couldn't possibly, and why should that change? Not after just one time, and a slam-bang quickie at that. No one was completely naked. Leah thinks she can get away with it. She is sure she will. She just has to be careful not to do it again.

That thought begs a question she is not ready to answer.

*

Come Monday, Leah does not know how she feels. She walks to work expecting to see Max. She will probably have lunch with him, nothing more, and the both of them will likely be thinking, feeling, they need to talk about it. What does she want to say? The part that matters to her does not involve him. The fact that it happened feels less important, upsets her less, than that her family was at home, waiting for her. Her children were waiting, Armand was cooking dinner, it was the Sabbath—and she let Max take her on her desk as if she were an office whore. Fifty years ago it would have been the bad girl in the typing pool with her cap set for a junior executive. That is not Leah; that is the opposite of what Leah is about. But she wonders if Max now thinks of her in just that way.

Passing through Collegtown, she sees him by chance. Just looks up and spies him through a window. She has been thinking about him and, presto! there he is, sitting at a table in a shadow. The woman with him, sitting in the light, is young. Not someone she, Leah, has met. Not Max's wife. Dear Rachel: very pregnant and likely still sleeping in the bed Max has abandoned much earlier than Summer Session demands, purely so he can be seated here at 8:45 this Monday morning. He is listening to the girl, or pretending to listen as she explains something, earnestness visible in every gesture. Leah slows her steps as she approaches, almost stops as she passes, and thinks Max has not noticed her—whether honestly or feigned, she cannot tell—until he looks at her quickly the instant the girl drops her head, and mouths *Not now* extravagantly through the glass.

Leah walks on. She would like to go back but does not. She goes over the gorge, up the stairs, across the quad to Sage Hall. Inside her office she still wants to turn around and walk back, march up to Max and ask him just what he thinks he is doing. Has fucking her impromptu given him carte blanche to make every coed who lets him buy her a cup of coffee?

She more or less falls into her chair. Is that really his game? And if it is, how does it concern Leah? Is it her problem, her business? It is not. Anyway, a public throw-down is the last thing anyone needs. And Leah cannot really confront him, can she, when they are both in the wrong. That also makes her angry; so that now Leah is angry, first, about having done it, about having let herself be used; second, she is angry at Max and how he has acted from the moment he was through with her; and now, third, the fact that she can do nothing about it is making her wild. She cannot even call Rachel, the unknowing Mrs. Obermann, and wake her from babyland dreams with confidential information about her skirt-chasing husband. To betray Max's secret is to reveal her own.

As she sits there staring at a dark screen, swiveling left, then right, Leah realizes it is all Armand's fault. If he weren't so unpleasant most of the time, none of this would have happened. Why is he being such a jerk? Why can't he smile more often, tell a joke now and then? His problems are his own but they affect her, too. If how she responds is not quite right, is she the only one to blame?

Waking her computer at a touch, she finds seventeen messages in her Inbox. The most recent, just arrived, is from Max.

```
That student conference was a bit of a
crisis--why I couldn't break away. Didn't
want you to think I was rude. Lunch today?
```

Leah does not know which to admire more, his prudence or his brashness. She would prefer to admire neither and, ideally, nothing about Max Obermann, and yet the self-assurance of such a person is impossible to deny. The man is willing to offend, no question, and it is impressive, how he manages to not-quite apologize while covering his ass. "A bit of a crisis," indeed—and then to ask her to lunch! Not that she wasn't counting on it, but still. That was before she caught him red-faced with a girl a dozen years too young. No chance will she eat lunch with him now.

Leah clicks Reply, types, *Not today, I'm afraid. I have a date. -L.* No smiley face. And clicks Send.

Maybe he will care and maybe he will not. The thing is, she cares. She wants to make him uncomfortable—make him unsmug, although that is not a word. The "I'm afraid" might have been a bit broad. But all in all Leah feels she has done the right thing, and she smiles.

She picks up the telephone and dials home, listens to it ring. She hopes Armand has not started painting. She hopes he picks up.

Dog-day August morning spies Armand in bed, gathering strength. Leah in the kitchen is putting up coffee. Alex and Julietta are asleep. Armand dreads this day and what he must do. It is the day he will lug his Little Giant through the kitchen and up the stairs to Alex's bedroom. He will open the large window and lift the Ladder System through that window and onto the roof of the front porch, then crawl through the window himself. Standing on sloping asphalt shingles worn nearly smooth, Armand will unfold the collapsed halves and lock the center hinge, set the rubber feet and adjust the telescoping legs. Before he stands on the Little Giant, Armand will rope its bottom rung to the hot-water radiator just inside Alex's window. It is cast-iron, this radiator, and weighs three hundred pounds and looks as if it was last painted during the Coolidge Administration. Armand has been meaning to paint it, he has intended & planned—and has he gotten around to it? He has not. It bothers him but these chores, call them projects, feel like more trouble than they're worth. Oh sure, it would be great if all fourteen radiators were painted to a creamy gloss. But the time! The effort! The larger of two radiators in the living room took three hours first to clean (sawdust had piled-up in all 144 segment apertures), then to double-coat with a slim brush whose long handle was not quite long enough for Armand to touch paint to the inner surfaces. Three hours! He worked steadily, did not daydream or dawdle, which made it all the more discouraging. How could it take three hours? One hundred and eighty minutes. As Armand reckons time, that is too long. Because how much time does he have left?

Leah did not believe him. She did not say, "Liar" to his face but her own face was incredulous. When Armand thinks that all fourteen radiators need painting, he feels his heart sink—actually sink, really sink, not so much toward his feet as deeper into his chest, where it seems to be trying to hide.

But anyway. The Little Giant on the roof. Tying it to the radiator will keep it from slipping down worn shingles while Armand, perched on tip-toe one step from the top no-step, strains to reach the inner peak of the front eave with a screaming random-orbit sander held above his head in one gloved hand. The Little Giant probably would not slip even if not tied down but if Armand is going to wear a respirator and safety goggles and earmuffs and leather gloves and take a face-full of poison lead dust and paint-flake shrapnel every time the 60-grit disk rips into desiccated wood, he is also going to be one-hundred-percent certain he won't be pitched off the roof to break his overextended neck on the concrete walk.

Thinking this way makes him want to stay in bed. Knowing he will fumble for hours through his own ineptitude makes Armand feel heavy and slow. He is not cut out for home renovation. Back in Ossining he had the same feeling of being miscast. The alarm would ring at six a.m. and Armand's waking thought would be *Oh, no.* He would hustle aboard the 6:49 out of Croton-Harmon and stare sleepily at *The Wall Street Journal* during the ride into Grand

Central. Ten minutes on foot to his office, where he spent all day perusing screens dense with information. The difference between feeling not-cut-out to be a petroleum-industry analyst and feeling that way about being an amateur house-painter is less than you might think. Except for the money.

Money: it is the only thing Armand misses about his former life. Big money cancelled ambiguity and promoted forthrightness. No one cared about the label in your suit or the hood ornament on your car, except as these might be signs that you were prospering more quickly than he was. After everything was said and done, no one cared about you, either. All that mattered was the bottom line. If you Earned for the Firm, you were a Winner and a Good Guy. If you Lost for the Boss, you were a Loser, perforce an Asshole. A man could be stupid, nasty, ugly, and mean; if he Earned, he was a Good Guy. Mahatma Gandhi, Martin Luther King, Jesus H. Christ Himself, if they ran in the red, would be Assholes. It was simple and ludicrous and insulting and crass. It was morally blind. It was also honest and effective, practical, evenhanded, and completely fair. Make money = Good Guy. Lose money = Asshole. It was not about being loved or even liked. It was about profit.

Belonging to this culture simplified his relationship with Leah. That bottom line? They had sex regularly. Oh, maybe it's wrong to assume cause and effect, simplistic and reductive and all that, but in Armand's experience a steady income stream is as good as specie ringing on a barrelhead. He never had to wonder, *Will she like me tonight?* Leah seemed to treat it as a given, even to be more than willing. As good as gold. Okay, sure, they did not have sex each and every night. That is not the point. The point, Armand reminds himself for possibly the thousandth time since he quit his job and they moved away, is that they did not have these murderous dry spells. Empty weeks of not the slightest touch. To Armand it feels as if they never have sex at all. He is not sure how Leah feels because he does not talk about it. Complaint always sounds callow; he would come off as a whiner, a boor. To gripe about not enough sex is to guarantee even less. Although he cannot imagine less. Leah has not consented all summer.

He shuts his eyes, lets his right hand slip under the sheet. Inside his boxers, his penis is warm and limp. What if he—? Might do him good. Flush out the pipes. Could set him up just enough to survive another dreadful day. He would be quick; so many weeks of not-tonight-honey have made him as keen as a teenager. Well, almost. Armand gently gets it started and after a minute finds he is not so perky, after all. Feels numb, as a matter of fact, God knows why. Atrophy, maybe. Or it could be he's sleepy. Not really awake. Or tired—*shungot,* the old people used to say, in dialect. His brain is awake but his body is lagging. That happens, especially when he wakes in the heart of night and falls into the silence as if it were a black pool, his body leaden with an impossible exhaustion and his mind racing, spinning, a hundred things crowding in, a thousand, Alessandro and Julietta and Leah, are they happy, will they stay healthy, please God don't let anyone get sick, not seriously sick, not God forbid terminally, he could not stand that, wouldn't make it, would have a breakdown, collapse, grieve forever; he cannot even think about it, it is unbearable; there is so much danger, so many ways to die: a house fire, a car accident, food poisoning, random abduction, falling debris, a madman with a gun; how can he protect his wife and children? He can't; Armand knows he can never do enough to defend their lives. He has trouble doing just ordinary things—house-painting, grocery shopping, even, he realizes, servicing his cars, which he suspects are due for an oil change, particularly his Benz. Because can he remember the last time he had the oil changed in either vehicle? He cannot. Much less recall when the plugs were replaced or the tires rotated; and now, as he mentally sorts his schedule or what passes for one to find time to visit Omar's Foreign Auto behind the scrap metal yard at the wrong end of town, and wait while they do the work because Leah still has not learned to drive and probably never will and so cannot follow him in the Subaru or even pick him up later, his minds skips a grove and comes to rest on the lawn, or rather the mud flat in front of their house that in May briefly masquerades as a lawn, and the other one in back, its ratty grass that dies while dandelions flourish so that Armand has to spread fertilizer with weed-control, although neither so-called lawn is worth the cost of high-tech agronomy, is really no better than a chicken run, you could stand at one edge, say on the concrete walk, and hock up an oyster and spit it clear over the whole expanse, if that is the word, of the front so-called lawn and hit the driveway on the other side; and first-class fertilizer is going for maybe thirty bucks a bag, a small one, which he can pick up at Agway, where he can swing by on his way to Omar's and so combine errands, although strictly speaking Agway is out of the way if Omar's is where he is going, and anyway does he really want to be transporting a bag of fertilizer in his trunk and risk getting stopped by an overzealous Dudley Do-Right of the IPD with nothing better to do than break horns by flagging down a law-abiding citizen for an out brake light and maybe also getting spot-searched by said cop? Then he thinks, *sciocco,* idiot, don't be *kugootz,* it's just one small bag even though it's more expensive that way, and also who turns a MeBe 500SL in clean condition into a bomb, even if said Benz isn't new anymore? Because how can anyone keep a car new and use it at the same time? For starters there is sun damage except not so much in Ithaca, universally known as one of the cloudiest places on earth, and road salt all winter, and dirt and filth and grit kicked up by tractor-trailers and pickup trucks and any number of cars all speeding to God-knows-where so their drivers can do God-knows-what, smoke cigarettes in bars probably, most people are not terribly bright, are not mentally acute or fantastically ambitious and think the best game in town is to sit for hours on a tottering stool in some dank, skanky, low-ceilinged place sour with beer reek and sweat-stench, in which atmosphere they swallow more beer or vodka or mixed sugary concoctions and expect to taste it when really, when you think about it, it's a miracle they can breathe; which brings to mind the asbestos sheathing he himself removed from the old cast-iron pipes in his basement two years ago, when the contractor was renovating the house, and sealed inside two-ply plastic trash bags and left at the curb for City Disposal take away, all perfectly legal if you do it yourself, which of course Armand went ahead and did because professional asbestos abatement would have cost another 10Gs and taken two or three days, during which no one else could have worked on or in the house or even been inside it, because everyone's so panicky about asbestos when the fact is, sure, it's bad if you inhale it but fiberglass is just as bad even if no one seems to realize it or just does not want to say; because what would happen, Sonny Jim, what would happen, Mr. Jack-of-All-Trades, if we had to start ripping all the fiberglass out of hearth and home and insulated attic, which when you think it over is the worst thing you can do, really, with either fiberglass or asbestos, because disturbing the stuff makes it airborne and liable to being inhaled; whereas if you let it lie, if you *just leave it the fuck alone,* as Armand says, chances are it is not going to hurt anyone; but for all that, his contractor told him to get the asbestos off the pipes and out of his basement; and so that's what Armand did: very carefully, very slowly, delicately he means, because the stuff was friable at a touch and now he wonders if the little paper mask was any protection at all or if he inhaled some fibers and if he will develop lung cancer because of said possible trace inhalation and how painful that will be and how scary to know he is going to die at such-and-such a time, probably going to die about then, given the temporal arc of the disease, although everyone is different and who knows? maybe he will get lucky or maybe he did not actually inhale any fibers or so few or so small they won't hurt him and he won't die because of cancer due to asbestos inhalation but because of something else someday except he hopes not soon, his kids are young and it would not be right, it would be kind of a catastrophe for them to lose their father even if he is not the happiest clown in the circus and the financial end at least is squared away not even counting the insurance they will collect if he clocks off before fifty-five, so that is one thing, thank God, about which Armand does not have to worry.

It is a little like madness. What Armand imagines madness might be. Random worry wakes him any average night, sends him skulking bug-eyed through stilled dark to double-check locks and latches and agonize over having forgotten *for yet another day* to install a carbon monoxide detector. The ceiling between the kitchen and dining room, just inside the door that leads down the cellar stairs, would be the best spot. It isn't wrong, this cautious thought, just not useful at three o'clock in the morning.

And now this other thing he is trying to do and failing at also feels like a waste of time. Armand figures he might as well stop. No reason to insist when, obviously, the need is absent. Also, he has a lot to do and morning is stealing away. He ought to get the hell out of bed before Leah comes up to rattle his cage.

Then again, he might pretend to be asleep. Playing possum: a passive-aggressive gambit. Maybe Leah will lie down beside him. Why does he think it might work today when it has never worked before? Not once, in all the seventeen years he has known her. What has changed? Nothing he knows of; and yet, he cannot help hoping Leah will slip her hand in, where his hand is. He will remove it, of course, his hand, the instant he hears her foot on the stairs. To give her a clear shot. Easy access. The kids are sleeping, deep and long. He and Leah can make it if they try. Married a dozen years, they have learned to be quiet. Efficient. Because what, really, are they getting up so early for? Technically, he is retired. What do they have to do, in the sense of an obligation they cannot at least postpone? Well, yes: Leah's job. She takes it seriously, likes getting out of the house and away from the kids, likes to be helpful, collaborate and cooperate, likes being the go-to girl. Go-to for what, Armand is not sure he wants to know. But him. What if he doesn't work on the house today? It's his house. If it is half-painted and half a mess, that's his business. Say he hires a crew to finish in a week what will take him the rest of the summer and into the fall to do. Pay for it: he could. Money is nothing, just inked paper worth only what it can buy. Inherently, it has no value. Except Leah will lose all respect for him if he punts.

He turns onto his side, away from the door. Leah is not coming up. Sounds like she is getting her breakfast or organizing the kids' backpacks, as if a summer day-camp held in a city park were a trek through a Cambodian jungle. On his own; he is. So what does he have to lose?

Trying to concentrate, Armand earnestly fingers it. Actually, he palms it, sort-of brushing it lightly away from his body, inside the boxers, waiting for it to firm-up. The problem is his dry palm, a far, sorry cry from the soft liquid sliding a fellow needs. Also, he hates the mess, a clingy ooze of pure nuisance that quickly goes cold and, if left, crusty, as if a couple tablespoons of egg white have spilled on the sheet. When he thinks of that, Armand isn't sure how far he wants to go—not that his hand has carried him anywhere close. Even if he tissues-up the worst, the sheet will sport a wet spot. Not that it matters; surely Leah knows. How else can he take care of it? No *cumá* for Armand, who faithfully plays his part as a middle-aged married guy, sex-famished, hangdog, woeful. Not too thrilling but there it is.

And there it is. Having found a dancing touch and easy rhythm that just might turn the trick, Armand soldiers on. If he had a squirt of baby oil and a pretty picture to look at or something just naughty enough to read, he would finish in a minute. As it is he still isn't sure because at his age nothing is guaranteed. Anything can break the mood and stop the process dead, especially when memories are all he has to lift him from A to B to C to D and so on up arousal's arc to its apex, where self-consciousness breaks and thinking ceases. A few weightless seconds, five heartbeats, six, then the long slide down to U or V or W or wherever it might be said to end, the final points being mere after-spasms and excruciatingly sensitive repose. Mental images are well and good and sometimes wonderful but Armand has found them as perishable as snowflakes. A favorite memory of a searing summer day sixteen years ago on a white sand beach, never mind exactly where, with the sea air smelling warm and salty, and bikini'd Leah smelling of coconut lotion, and Armand lying on a towel spread on the sand, is liable to shatter and its fragments reform as an ovoid female, 60-something or more with frizzy hair dyed badly red, whom they saw later that same afternoon walking along the tide-line in a gold bikini that showed too much of sponge-cake arms and cellulite. The incongruity between young Leah in her white bikini and the hag in her gold one is complicated further by the fact, both too exciting and disappointing to recall, that Leah, on that immortal day just twenty-four, led him to a hidden place behind the dunes and spread their towels and, after he lay down, dropped her straps and pressed her breasts, one then the other then the first again then the second then the first and so on, into his hot, surprised face; and when Armand pricked out in his bathing suit (sheer purple nylon: he cannot believe he ever wore such a thing), she spread a third towel, a lime-green terrycloth item they were planning to use to dry themselves after a refreshing dip (!) in the cool green sea, to cover him from waist to ankles; and then she, lovely Leah, did the thing Armand had always wished for and imagined and never believed would happen: she ducked under the towel and tugged that purple bathing suit to his knees and took his penis into her mouth and began sucking him as if she meant it and loved it and maybe loved him, her head bobbing under the towel so that anyone who might walk past would have known even if he or she (she!) would not exactly have been able to see what Leah was up to (up to!); and Armand, sun-basked, was smelling the ocean and smelling Leah, her excitement, yes, and would not have cared who saw or knew because Leah was licking him along the shaft to the thrilling head and licking down again, then around and around lapping his balls, then had almost the whole beast in her mouth, which was incredible because Armand had never felt so hard, the breeze had never blown so hot and salty, Leah had never loved it so much, he could tell she wanted him to fill her mouth, why else would she be going at it so steadily, not pausing or coming up for air, just sucking sucking sucking while pressing her bare breasts against his thighs and caressing his balls, tickling them almost, as if to egg him on, spur him to spurt, and Armand was loving it so much he was nearly delirious and wanted it never to end, the act itself and also the thought: that a beautiful twenty-four-year-old blonde put her plump breasts in his face on a sun-struck beach in the heart of a dazzling afternoon, then dove under a happy towel to give him the blow-job of his life.

Except it did end—suddenly, and not as Armand expected.

Leah stopped. She freed her head from the towel. "Whew! It's hot in there!" she said.

Go back, Armand wanted to scream but played it cool. Surely she would resume. Surely she would not just give up. Not after so much, after she had done so much, worked so hard, taken him so far, when he was so close—

"My jaw started hurting," she told him. "Why didn't you come?"

"I was about to," Armand croaked. "I was on the brink—"

"We'll have to finish later," Leah said. "It's too hard to suck and breathe under a towel."

Armand wanted to weep. He still wants to weep all these years later, lying in whitewashed light of an August morning, trying with closed eyes to fool himself that his dry palm and half-curled fingers of his cramping hand are Leah's wet mouth and sliding lips of sixteen summers ago. *The hell with the mess. The hell with what she knows or guesses or figures out.* Maybe she should know. Maybe he should tell her. Maybe he should show her, in case she's wondering and even more so if she isn't. *Show her,* instead of smiling patience in every direction as if one-quickie-per-eight-weeks were even minimally okay. They did not finish that day's pleasure later at the hotel, where Leah complained that the sun had given her a headache; and the day passed, and evening passed, and night; and nothing like that impromptu act of ardent fellatio was resumed. More days passed and the week was gone and led only to other weeks and days that also offered nothing remotely like the ideal conditions of arousal and performance that had finely meshed on that luminous beach; with the result that he and Leah have never completed that lost and unforgettable episode at any moment of the sixteen years they have lived between that gorgeous cocksucking afternoon and this same-old, jerk-off morning.

And so, *Why Not?* If he can finish, that is what he is going to do. Fix his mind on an archived image of his curvy young wife before she was his wife, when she was going at it for all she was worth in broad daylight while wearing half a white bikini; and with every ounce of will try not to remember or even concede the fleeting reality of, first, the hag listing seaward across sloping sands, straw dyed red and a scent of sour milk wafting off her, or so he imagined; or, second, the fact that Leah stopped too soon, at the time a massive disappointment that was also (although Armand had no reason to suspect it might be) the spirit and image of his future frustration.

A frustration he is going to end now. Not permanently end, in any sense of once-and-for-all, but mitigate. Ameliorate. Soon. Almost, almost, almost. Soon. Soo ... Soo ... Nope. Nope, not— no— Lost it. Lost it, lost it, lost it. Goddamnit it, lost it. Try again. Try try try again. Slow. Slow, slow. Don't rush it. Slow. Slow & easy. No force. Don't choke it. Easy, steady, easy, steady, that's it. More ... more ... more ...

"Daddy!"

Armand snaps rigid an inch off the mattress. He removes his hand. Julietta runs into the room and launches herself onto the bed. He hasn't heard her wake up.

"Daddy! Daddy!" She lands in the depression left by Leah and rolls toward Armand, giggling.

His arousal subsides. Armand lays his left hand, always clean outside the sheet, on his daughter's head. Julietta's hair amazes him, its silky thickness and sheen. In summer her hair is dark copper with golden highlights, a variegated richness. Can this beautiful child really belong to him? Julietta's large eyes seem to smile with mischief's own glint. Armand recognizes the wild-child in her and hopes he is wrong even as he is convinced. He knows this look, which Julietta uses to punctuate her replies to everything he tells her: "Why not?" "So what?" "No." Ten or so years from now she will cause him no end of worry, probably some anger, with luck and restraint, no despair. But for today and tomorrow and a few days more she is a six-almost-seven-year-old little girl who loves her father without really knowing him, his flaws and fears and common limits; loves him just-because, the best way and proof of children's wisdom. Armand tells himself to be grateful. To count his blessings.

Julietta. Alessandro. Leah. One day he will lose them. It cannot be helped. Death will force it, will take him from their lives. It is Armand's loneliest thought, the thing he can never say. Whenever it happens he will not want to go. Nothing he can do will change this fate. No amount or kind of goodness, no shriven purity of his dirtied, impossible soul will free him of the obligation finally to disappear.

Armand looks into his daughter's eyes, dark brown irises gilt with amber rims. He feels, he hopes, that Leah still loves him.

Julietta laughs. "Daddy! You lazy head. Time to get up."

Armand smiles; touches her hair; thinks, *Yes. It's time.*

He wakes in a sweat one hot August night, heart weighted with dread. The heat is tremendous. It is a night-presence, almost solid, damp air filled with sound: hum of other people's air-conditioning, tires sizzling along rural asphalt, heavy trucks rolling through the starred dark. An iron rumble is the train that carries coal through downtown and north along the eastern shore of Lake Cayuga, to an electrical plant that churns out power to cool those sleeping homes. Not Luke's. He kicks off the sheet and sits up, thinking he might raid the 'fridge. Cold breast of chicken washed down with iced beer would be a beautiful thing in this night of heat-broken sleep.

He hauls himself off sticky sheets and visits the bathroom. It is not supposed to be this hot, ever, in the Central Southern Tier. We are, remember, just a couple hours from Canada. Not quite in a snow belt; not victims of a snow-apocalypse like those that bury Buffalo. Winter is four months and ninety degrees away. Luke cannot picture it right now, despite having survived it thirty-eight times. When its bone-cold hits, his attic will be frigid. He'll need a parka to do guard duty. Whereas tonight, in the nest, he might suffer heat-stroke.

Taking a long pee, he reconsiders that beer. It will wake him to pee again. Water would do the same. Sleep being difficult, he decides he is not so hungry, after all. On his way back he notices Mother's door is open. Usually she shuts it when she turns in. In fact, she always does. He peeks in; sure enough, a night-light keeps a low glow burning on the bedside table. The doily on which the light stands is a lace circle of shining white. Mother is not in her bed.

His first thought is that she has fallen asleep in front of the flatscreen. Sitting in Dad's chair, too weary to move, nodding at commercials for high-interest credit cards and nothing-down mortgages, her face awash in picture-light. He decides to take a look, just to make sure. Then a knowingness comes to him and he thinks, *Oh, God, no.*

He pads downstairs, crosses the hall, turns into the living room. There she is. Asleep on the sofa. The television is playing, its sound turned low. Something is not right, does not look right, the way Mother is sitting with her head back on the cushion and tilted left. Luke approaches, sees her mouth is open, her eyes closed. He rests his hand on her arm. Mother is cool to his touch.

Like his father, she looks as if she is sleeping. Luke does not shake or call her. He knows. He knows and he cannot believe it and cannot understand why he is surprised. She is old; this is what happens. He knew it must happen sometime, and of course he would be the one to find her. It is his job, you see, one of his domestic duties, to discover his parents at their end.

He shifts her head to a position that looks more comfortable. He realizes he probably should not touch her. Luke is not sure about this. Who is he supposed to call? There is no point calling an ambulance and paying for that. So he should call an undertaker. A funeral home. That is all Mother needs now: someone to take care of her in the right way. In a way that is right and proper. Decorous. There is no need to rush or ring alarms. There is no crisis. All we have is an old lady who has passed in the quiet of her home, on her sofa, in front of her television. Her adult son was asleep in his bedroom upstairs, then not asleep, then noticed she was missing from her bed despite the late hour, then came downstairs and found her. It is straightforward and unremarkable, yet Luke is not sure he is not supposed to call the police.

It seems unnecessary, too dramatic, and it gets him thinking about what happens next. Not just a call to John, then two more to Cindy and Matt, and trying to get through it, the news, the shock and sadness, then the arrangements and the funeral itself, but the aftermath. What will happen to him? It is a selfish thought; Luke acknowledges it as such as he stares at his mother. She is gone and he is sorry. Grief fills his chest like a storm. He begins to weep, little, short sobs he tries to squelch because even though no one is here Luke must be sure no one hears him. He must control himself. He has to think. It is necessary to think clearly. The rest of his life depends on it.

He cannot look at her. That is what upsets him, to look at her as if she is sleeping and know she is gone.

He goes to the kitchen and sits at the table. Little, broken-down sobs he tries to swallow. *Please, God. Please.* He has to think. When they come to take Mother away, will they take him away, too? His brothers and sister might not be interested in supplementing his night-shift salary. Mother's checks will stop, the Social Security and Widow's Benefits that help them live. The mortgage is almost paid. Luke cannot meet taxes and expenses on his own. Without help, without Mother's checks, he is done.

He stands and opens the refrigerator, looks inside. There are green beans and pot roast in plastic tubs, lettuce in plastic wrap, cold breast of chicken in aluminum foil, a new package of hot dogs, no buns. There is a gallon of two-percent milk, almost full. There is a half-gallon of pure green tea in a plastic jug. In the vegetable bin he finds a net bag of yellow onions, a cellophane package of mushrooms, three tomatoes in a plastic bag, a plastic bag of carrots, and one loose yellow squash. Softly he shuts the door, thinking. He inventories the freezer and finds two boxes of pre-formed hamburger patties, eight to a box. He finds a package of chicken thighs and two canisters of frozen concentrated orange juice. No ice cream, no beef. Luke shuts the freezer door. He moves to the pantry and on its shelves finds jars and cans: yellow corn, black beans, small red beans, baked beans, chicken soup, beef and barley soup, vegetable soup. There is a bag of rice and a loaf of Wymans white bread. There is peanut butter, corn oil, sauerkraut, black olives, green pickles. He shifts the bread to the refrigerator to keep off mold. There are two boxes of cereal and a new bag each of pretzels and potato chips. There is a bag of Idaho baking potatoes and two sweet yams.

Plenty of food. He can hole-up for however long it takes. Call in sick and hunker down. Decide what needs to be done. What he must do. He is just beginning to understand. The main thing he is contemplating is awful. It seems crazy; it is certainly wrong. But he has no choice. No true choice, not really. He must hide Mother's death. He cannot call anyone. No undertaker, no police. No one must know. He cannot call Matt or John, cannot even call Cindy. Luke has to take care of Mother himself. He will do it properly, he will be quick and respectful. He will lay her to rest as best he can, in her home that she loved. He will set her to rights, honest to God he will. And in performing that discipline of devotion he will do right by himself.

It is my house now. Luke holds this thought in mind as he swings a pickaxe into the cellar's earthen floor. So many times they talked about pouring concrete. Now it seems lucky the money could never be spared. He is turning their tight budget to account at last, making it pay a kind of dividend. Still, he struggles. Hard-packed, beaten smooth, the floor might almost be concrete. He cracks the surface with six or seven hard blows and tears into the earth. The pickaxe is heavy; after four strikes he has to rest, his arms already rubbery, sweat beading on his forehead and running down his face. He hauls himself up the steps and out to the garage for a shovel but when he tries to dig out broken clods the shovel snags on rocks that will not move. Luke resumes the pickaxe. His arms and hands are wet; the handle slips. He works slowly, steadily, trying to find a rhythm, a pace he can sustain.

Heft. Lift. Swing. Clear.

Heft. Lift. Swing. Clear.

After every four strikes he pauses, heart pounding in his ears. It takes him thirty minutes to rough-out a rectangle to a depth of six inches. He uses the shovel to remove broken earth and rocks, then mounds the excavated material against one wall. At this rate it will take hours to dig a proper grave.

Luke sets the pickaxe on its head and leans on its shaft. He says, "I am digging my mother's grave." Says it to no one, to a night of ordinary sounds, to himself. He thinks of carrying her down here and laying her in the hole. How will he do it? He cannot see her face. He will have to wrap her up. How? Inside what? To the body he will do nothing. He will neither wash nor cleanse, purify nor perfume. He will not change her into a fresh dress. He does not want to touch her more than he has to. What can it matter, her dress? He will wrap Mother in bed sheets, careful not to look at her face as he does it, then duct-tape the sheets around her. Thank God her eyes are closed. That he does not have to close them, does not have to touch her face. He does not want to touch her at all. Her flesh is cold. *As cold as the grave.*

Swinging the pickaxe, Luke weeps. He is digging his mother's grave. All her life she was good to him and now he has to do this thing instead of giving her a decent funeral. *Right and proper.* His brothers and sister would have paid for it. They love Mother. As Luke loves her. But Luke has no money. He can pay for nothing. Is it only his fault? What about the leads that led nowhere, all the people who would not give him a chance? Who would not offer a hand or a smile? He did not set out planning to work the night shift. Something better might have come his way. But still, but still, at the end there is no one to blame, just himself. He does not know what he has done wrong. To this day, this minute, he does not understand. Probably he has done many things wrong but he does not know what they were. Are.

Why are people so unforgiving? Yes, he is a misfit, he knows that. But must he be punished all his life?

Stop thinking, he tells himself. *Just dig.* He tears at the ground. Clumps of earth break free. His arms feel like jelly, his back and shoulders burn. Soon he can do no more. It is too hard. He drops the pickaxe and sits on the mounded dirt. Luke lets his eyes close, his chin fall to his chest. Why must he do this? Why is it necessary? He does not want to bury her. But he has to live. He does not know why he has to live or for what but Luke believes he should go on living. That life still belongs to him. That it is all he has.

*

Resting an hour for each hour he works, Luke finishes the hole at mid-day. It is not six feet deep, it is three-and-a-half-plus, maybe four, but he can go no deeper. As it is he had trouble getting out, almost could not raise his body high enough to roll over the edge onto the cellar floor. He drags up the stairs, bulk of him listing, and lies down dirt-caked and sweaty, and falls asleep. When he wakes six hours later it is just getting dark. He calls-in sick, then sits on the bed's edge and waits for his brain to clear. The job just ahead makes him slow to move. He does not want to do it, and with a small surge of joy he realizes it is not too late to stop. He can still call the undertaker, the police, everyone. He can call Cindy and Matt and John. They can still have a family funeral. He has done nothing wrong, just dug a hole that no one needs to see. He can fill it quickly, a lot more quickly than he has taken to dig it, and then he can do everything that is responsible and right: pick up the telephone and dial the numbers, speak the words, perform the acts and duties. He has nothing to hide. All he needs is a plausible reason to explain the hours he has waited.

Standing, he feels hunger hit him like a wave. The bed is a mess. He has smeared dirt everywhere. The bedroom smells like a stable. He pulls the sheets onto the floor, removes his clothes and drops them with the sheets. He goes into the bathroom and starts the shower and when the water warms steps under the spray. Luke scrubs himself twice from head to toe, then just stands so the water drums on his head. His mind searches for an alternative, and an answer. He realizes he does not trust his brothers and sister. They will vote to sell the house and take their profits. Luke will have nowhere to go. There is no place he wants to go; this is his home, he wants to live here always. Why must he be forced out?

He puts on clean clothes, carries the dirt-caked jeans and shirt and filthy sheets downstairs and stuffs everything into the washing machine, pours in detergent and starts the cycle. Almost faint, he cooks up franks and beans plus a pot of rice and washes it all down with four glasses of iced green tea. Done eating, he sets dishes and pots to soak. He wipes his hands on a dishtowel, returns the jug of green tea to the refrigerator. Then there is nothing left but to go into the living room.

Mother waits on the sofa. Her body is rigid. Luke has forgotten about this. How can he make them believe he has just found her? What can he say? That he was too distraught to call? Will anyone believe him? Or will they look at three hundred pounds of burly, bearded bulk and see a murderer? There is no evidence of any such thing; an autopsy will show Mother has died of heart attack or stroke, or just stopped breathing because her time had come. People will talk about him anyway: how he left her alone, was inattentive, failed to take care of her. His brothers will blame him. Cindy might forgive him eventually but her remorse that someone, even just Luke, was not with Mother when she died, will be unending. They will wonder whether, had he been paying the right kind of attention, she might have been saved.

Gossip will grow; Luke can hear it. The hours he has waited to call will become days. People will whisper terrible things. Abominations. Strangers will drive past the house to get a look at where a dead woman lived with a son so stupid he did not realize she was dead. Fingers pointing, heads shaking. *Can you imagine?* they will say. *Can you believe?* Everywhere he goes. He is too big to blend in, too unusual to hide. Wymans might fire him, not wanting to be associated with a human corpse left for days on a sofa. When it has not been days, only hours. Mother still looks asleep. But Luke knows how people are. That they want to believe the worst.

Unforgiving.

Looking at her, he understands that her body, bent in this way, will conform better to his shoulders than if he had laid her out. In that case her body would be board-straight and difficult to carry, whereas like this, he can hoist her onto his shoulders and use the big muscles in his back and legs to carry her down the stairs. The greater problem is how to wrap her in bed sheets.

Luke uses some old ones fitted to the single beds no one sleeps in unless John or Cindy visits with their kids. He covers Mother in sections: from the waist, up; from waist to knees; from knees to feet. The silver duct tape he tries to tear evenly and lay on straight in lengths roughly equal. He wants a neat, thoughtful appearance. He does not want the look of a body-dump, some kind of horrible killing and hasty disposal. Not that anyone is going to see it. But Luke will know. He will remember what he has done—what he is doing.

It is awkward to move and shift the body, which he does not want to touch. It is tricky to hold the sheet in place while he tries to lay tape on flat and even. He measures the tape out and tears it from the roll beforehand so that he does not have to let go of the sheet every time he needs another piece. The tape does not stick so well to the sheets and after Mother is shrouded he winds tape entirely around her so that it can stick to itself. Satisfied with it, Luke goes to his knees and takes hold of Mother by forearm and shin, and works her onto his shoulders. When he feels she is balanced, he pushes with his legs and stands and lifts. She is much lighter than he has expected.

The hard parts, he thinks, are over. His task is almost done.

In dim lamplight he carries her from living room to kitchen and turns right down the cellar stairs. Bent forward, he takes each step with the greatest care, feels his foot wholly on the tread, feels his weight settle onto that foot. It is the longest descent Luke has ever made and he does it knowing he will not have to do it again. He is breathing hard, is sweating, his sweat is getting on the sheets but there is nothing to be done except to keep going. Finally he is down the stairs and standing on the earthen floor. The cellar feels like a dungeon. Low ceiling of floor joists, dank smell of old wood. Knob-in-tube fixtures, bare bulbs burning with crepuscular light.

He moves toward the hole.

Can he just drop her in? It seems not right, as if the fall will hurt her. It feels disgraceful. Luke goes to his knees, then leans completely to the floor and lets the body roll off his shoulders. Dirt cakes to his shirt. He sets the body next to the hole and, relieved of its meager weight, remains kneeling. He is breathing hard and wiping sweat from his face like tears.

What he is doing is unforgiveable. No one will understand.

For several minutes Luke kneels beside her. He tries to pray; says, *God forgive me* and *Please, welcome her, please have mercy and pity on her soul*. He says, *Please, God, forgive me. Please have mercy on me. This wicked thing is not what I want. I am forced to it. I can't live without money. I am so, so sorry. But I can't. And I don't want to die.*

Sweat-streaked and dirty, Luke sobs. She has had her life and it is over and this is how it ends. Buried in the dank cellar of an old house. Her mortal remains wrapped in bed sheets and set in cold ground. No church. No flowers. No music. No casket. No one to mourn her passing but a fat son who is performing funeral rites, such as they are, alone.

It is more than he can bear. Without further thought, Luke moves the body toward the hole. Lying on his stomach, he tries to take her in his arms and gentle her into the grave. He cannot hold her. She slips from his grasp, falls. Hits bottom with a thud.

Luke stands in panic. He dropped her. He did not mean to drop her but he did. His mother: he dropped his mother into a hole in the ground. A hole he has dug for the purpose of hiding her away. A hole dug in grief and fear, he will tell them. And he dropped her into it, like an old dog into a ditch. What a son he is, what a sad apology of a man, to do such a thing for money.

He is sobbing very hard. It goes on and on.

A long time later, Luke takes several deep, shuddering breaths and shuts his eyes. He tells himself what's done is done. Tells himself it is a bad job, that it is the best he can do. He has not killed her, has not hurt her. She would want him to take care of himself. She would expect him to.

Done, and done. He picks up the shovel and begins filling the grave. He tries to blank-out thought yet cannot help wondering about the next time Cindy calls long-distance and wants to speak to her mother.

Damp stifle of August afternoon has him sweating within an inch of his life. Luke in the attic, in the nest, keeps both eyes peeled for whoever will come in this ungodly swelter. Five nights absent from work, he can feel them thinking. *What has he done with her?* They know. Of course they do. A detail missed. A thing overlooked, something he never knew: a jury summons, a Social Services intake. An official obligation to appear. Could be anything. One false step gives him away. He will not know until a couple black-and-whites roll up and the cops get out, hefting their nightsticks.

Luke can see westward more than halfway down his street; to the south, beyond the park to the state road. His back, facing east, is blind but so is the Cape. No road runs behind it; they would have to come on foot through neighbors' yards to take him. A SWAT team at least. Maybe they radio-in a helicopter with a searchlight, do it up big and dramatic. Luke has his shotgun and deer rifle, plus a .44-caliber revolver with a long barrel. This last, passed along on the sly a decade ago by Uncle Raymond, is not strictly legal. "No need for a permit," Uncle Ray told him. "A gun permit is just an excuse for people to ask questions whose answers are none of their damn business. Don't let on. Put it away. It's a Magnum. Might come in handy."

Luke supposes it might. The .44 is a hand-cannon. One hollow-point Magnum round can blow a man's sternum through his back. Still, he cannot hold them off for long. Cops and SWAT can use whatever they want. Assault rifles, tear gas, a grenade launcher if he really pisses them off, takes out a couple-three uniforms or just wounds them. *By whatever means necessary.* Not that any of it is necessary. He isn't a murderer or backwoods crazyman living off the grid and not paying his taxes, holding children hostage and baying at the moon. He is just a man and now an orphan and he is grieving. He does not want to go to work. He does not want to see people and have to pretend. He wants to stay close to home, safe, contained. He does not care what anyone thinks or says; he knows he is alone, that he will be alone from now on. Cats come and go. Rex and Speckles and Barney eat and sleep and do their business in the park or on the dead lawn next door. Food is running low. His leftover pot roast and green beans, half his hot dogs, most of his bread, a box of frozen hamburger, the green tea, two cans of chili, and all the milk are gone. He can hold out a while longer. But at some point it will have to end.

He stands from his sniper's crouch, shakes blood into his legs. Sweating like a horse. The air is hot and close; an attic in summer is no place to be. Since laying Mother to rest Luke has watched and waited, trying to think as they think, to hear their thoughts so he will be ready. They have figured it out. How could he think it would be possible to hide? Not reporting a death is a crime. Of course they notice—when has he gotten away with anything? He has not been spared failure, not excused from night shifts, not forgiven three hundred pounds of hirsute glumness.

How can he have thought this would be different?

He needs a snack, and a breather. The narrow doorway makes Luke turn sideways. The staircase, too, is narrow, the attic room having been improvised one summer by his father and Uncle Ray. Dad called him Raymo. Uncle Ray figured he could build anything. One look at the Robideau Cape and, "What you need is a room out of that attic," became like an intention fulfilled. Which, eventually, it was. Which made a staircase necessary. There being no good place to install a staircase was a tangible challenge that Uncle Ray grabbed with both fists. He broke through a wall not knowing what was inside it and laid two-by-eights on a guess. It wasn't the first time he had practiced carpentry as if it were aggressive war but before Luke can delve into the family ancient he hears the telephone, which is ringing, ringing, with a sound like forever, as if it has been ringing forever and he has heard it only on his way down the stairs. He has been descending sideways, one arm braced on the wall, and now he stops. He realizes he does not have to answer it. What says he has to? Who? Why should he, when he does not want to speak to anyone? He knows they are on to him. He knows they are biding their time, waiting for what they think is the right moment. Except there is no right moment. Not with Luke camped in the nest, well-armed and leaving his post only on strictest need. They might take him, probably they will, but not without cost.

The telephone rings and rings. No answering machine picks it up because Luke does not have one because he does not need one, does not want one, does not want or need messages. He knows why they are calling but not why they bother. Are they trying to distract him? Have him use his hands so he can't reach as easily for a gun? Occupy his mind so he can't readily pull the trigger? They know he is here; in such circumstances, where would he be but at home? If they are ready to come for him why don't they get it over with?

The ringing stops. Luke does not know what it means. Maybe they are on their way. SWAT and a helicopter, a half-dozen squad cars. A forensics team and a hearse, when they figure out what's in the cellar.

It was ringing, now it isn't. Luke gets himself down the remaining stairs and goes into the kitchen. He slaps together peanut butter and bread and eats it standing at the countertop with a glass of water, wishing he had milk. He chews up the crust and brushes crumbs off his beard. On his way out he grabs the pretzels, maybe twenty left in the bag, twenty-five, broken-up, in pieces. He climbs the stairs. In the nest he has a canteen of water, plus a half-bag of pistachio nuts he found in the back of the pantry. It was unopened and had been in there a while, likely since John last visited because it must have been John who bought it and forgot. Whereas Luke, who would not have spent on this luxury in the first place, would in the second place not have forgotten if he had; and so would have eaten the nuts then, and so would not have them now. A lucky find. He nibbles, trying to make it last.

Back in the nest. He sets the pretzels in reach and picks up his rifle, careful lest its muzzle protrude across the sill. Its barrel, scope and magazine are full-blued, its stock and forestock deep-grained, varnished hardwood. Its leather strap is shiny along its inside. Long walks through autumn woods; incredibly, Luke seldom saw a deer. They live mostly in town now, the local deer, having learned that people's gardens are easy pickings. Tasty, too. Sighting through the scope, he draws the crosshairs over a squirrel stupidly paused in the street. It would be impossible to miss. From his nest, Luke commands the length of his block, although the farthest thirty yards would require shooting through a leaf-canopy of Norway maples and red oaks. That's fine; he isn't gunning for a president in an open car. To lay down some warning fire is maybe as much as he seriously intends. Even that seems like too much, like asking them to hit back, guns blazing, and come for him. Except they are coming for him, anyway.

Flies pass through the open window. Luke leans his rifle on the sandbags and picks up the pretzels. As he munches, he sees his neighbor jog-trotting along one side of his house. The asshole has a garden hose with him, one hand gripping the spray nozzle, the other holding a four, maybe five-foot coil of the hose itself. Only then does Luke see Korey and Pavel darting down the concrete walk and tearing past the lilacs. Going by this glimpse, he thinks neither cat is wet. He does not know if the asshole missed or held his fire or was just bluffing, but judges him lucky. Because Luke would not miss. Not at this range. He could pick that guy off quicker than those cats lit out for home.

Just let me catch him. A man who terrorizes animals is not a man.

He wads-up the empty pretzel bag and stuffs it in his pocket. He drinks from the canteen then screws on the cap, thinking he really needs to show up for work tonight. He does not want to leave Mother—the word he is thinking of is *unguarded*—but he cannot lose his job. Nothing can happen to her but it seems wrong to leave her—as if, in taking care of her as he has, Luke has signed on for permanent duty, a kind of ever-present watchfulness or watching-over that only his own death will end.

His asshole neighbor is hosing down his walk. He works along and works along, and in a minute is standing almost right below where Luke sits. Luke can see that shit is involved. The guy is blasting turds with a hard stream, pushing the shit onto the strip of grass that more or less marks their mutual property line. The shit looks no worse than mud, a runny brown smear that the water rinses away in seconds. It disappears into the grass, as far as Luke can see, and everything is as good as new.

Hunting Old Sammie

He picks up the .44, checks that it is empty. Just for fun, he slips a round into one chamber, gives the cylinder a spin and, while it is spinning, wrists it shut. Luke edges close to the window, shoulders low behind the sandbags, peers between the boxes and over the sill. His neighbor is eyeing the ground as if turds were landmines. A shovel in his hand, which is how Luke knows. Actually, it's a spade, as he sees by the curved flange that tapers to a point, all the more effective for lifting feces. Luke raises the gun and draws a bead. *Just for fun.* A single shot behind the ear will take his head off. Luke will never have to see this asshole again. Which chamber rotated up? The odds are five-to-one in favor of a dry-fire and life-goes-on. The beauty of uncertainty. If the loaded chamber turned up, this guy's luck is done. Maybe if Luke kills him, steals his keys, hides the corpse then hides himself in the asshole's house, he will be able to take the wife by force. Wait until she comes home, grab her, hold her down, fuck her good. Keep her prisoner, belt her to the bed, fuck her repeatedly. Keep her naked, slide his dick all over that smooth, beautiful skin. Luke wants to fuck her breasts. Douse her with baby oil and thrust his penis in-between. When he starts to spurt, stuff his dick in her mouth and cream down her throat. Something he saw in a porno. Big, wicked, fuck-crazy penis cumming like mad. That is what he wants to do. Why not? He is a man; this is how men are made. Maybe it is ugly but it is not his fault. Blame God. And it would serve her right. Parading past his window. Tit-fitting tops. She seems to be asking for it. A wild, well-oiled tit-fuck: she is asking Luke to do it. She wants him to cap her husband.

Luke cocks the .44 and its cylinder rotates. Should he try? It is something that is maybe meant to be. Maybe this asshole deserves to die, deserves really to die for more reasons than even Luke has imagined. Maybe his wife hates him and wants to be rid of him and would be grateful if Luke killed him. Who knows? She might collect life insurance. Might even cut Luke a share: cash payout and a piece of ass. What can he do to make it look like self-defense? Pretty implausible from up here. He cannot snipe the guy even half by accident and claim he was defending himself—although in a larger sense that is exactly how Luke feels. Call this prick an American if you want and talk all day about national interest and a common cause, it means nothing to Luke. As he sees it, his neighbor is as real a threat as any terrorist. Buying the old lady's bungalow over the ask. Flipping shit in his direction as if Luke is a nobody who doesn't count, a moron who doesn't notice. Ambushing cats as if Luke can't see. The guy has two kids and a sexy wife. Very nice. Maybe he also has a bullet with his name on it in a random chamber of an unseen gun.

Thumbing the cocked hammer, Luke holds it off. He pulls the trigger and the cylinder rotates, then he eases the hammer forward until it cozies against the firing pin. *Not today.* Soon, maybe, if nothing changes. But not today. Who knows when the loaded chamber will turn up? Who knows when Luke will squeeze the trigger with his thumb around the stock? It is not exactly close range for a handgun but it is close enough. Or he can scope-in with the rifle and remove doubt from the calculus.

*

During the next week his situation is stable. He returns to work. No one welcomes him back and no one reprimands him. It goes down in the books as five consecutive sick days. His pay will be docked for the last day only, so things could be worse. He does not explain that these are not sick days but days of grief and awe. He cannot tell anyone about it. He cannot say he is going through a death. That he is alone. He speaks little and does his job. As far as he can tell, no one has noticed that anything is out of the ordinary.

Home from work early one morning, he looks at himself on his way to the shower and dislikes more than usual the man in the mirror. He is hairy, fat, mole-mottled, his skin shiny with work-sweat. Bestial. There is no help for skin and fat but he can, Luke thinks, do something about that hair. He digs out Dad's old barber kit, chromed scissors and electric clippers still neat and clean in their original box—left more than twenty years, Luke figures, since his last kid haircut, he being youngest and Cindy anyway keeping clear of Dad's home barbering. The scissors, gleaming, look sharp. Luke has trouble getting a thumb and meaty finger through the loops, and it's tough to lift his arms and reach behind his head at the same time as he tries to turn his wrist so the blades cross his ponytail at a perpendicular. Even for a flexible man, it is an awkward move. This is why we have barbers. But not for Luke; he does not let strangers touch him and anyway does not want a big deal made of a haircut. As if he might be tidying himself for a purpose, grooming with an agenda in mind, when all he wants is to get rid of all that hair.

Holding the ponytail off his neck, Luke sets the scissors in a spot that feels right and squeezes. The blades close, honed edges cut and whisper past each other, *click*. Luke spreads finger and thumb and repeats, and repeats, and repeats, *click, click, click*, cutting away neglect and not-caring, years of just going along. No more. It is time to get serious. He understands. No more fooling, no more fucking around. This counts.

All the marbles. Hairs brown and gray, long strands, fall off his shoulders and drift toward the floor. When he has scissored it short in back, Luke lays into top and sides. He makes quick work of it, knowing Dad's clippers will even it off. He plugs-in the cord, black and twisted, and with the smallest scalp guard in the box shields the sharp-toothed blades. Flicks-on the little black rocker switch, sets the plastic guard against his scalp and draws it along.

Clipped hairs lift off his head and spin to the floor. A haircut. It is simple to do. To make an effort is to accomplish one small thing.

Buzz-cut Luke sweeps up scattered hair, what a lot of it there is, and dustpans it into the trash. After a shower, he checks himself in the mirror. His beard makes him look a wreck. Old and forgotten. A man who sleeps in the woods, propped under a tree. Gray-streaked, scraggly. Might a mouse be hiding in there? Birds building a nest? Setting the trash basket atop the vanity, he stands over it and uses the scissors to restore something like order. Lacking a razor, he buzzes his face with the clippers. The guard leaves hard stubble that matches his head, salt-and-pepper bristle-brush all around. And his skin looks gray.

Seeing himself, Luke cries, "Yiiieeee!"

What has he done? He looks like a lone survivor. Except for the fat he could pass for camp-desperate in 1945.

People will notice. They will look, they will see and wonder. What a stupid thing to do.

He gets dressed as always, old jeans and cotton tee shirt, then rummages through a drawer, then another, and comes up with an old camouflage hat, amoeba-shapes of greens and browns, porkpie style but with a soft, rounded crown. He thinks it belonged to him long ago, then Matt tried to take it. Well, it's Luke's again now. He pulls it down on his head as far as it will go and looks in the mirror.

The effect is not really helpful. It is less startling than full-on buzz-cut head and graystubble face but the cheapie camouflage gives him the look of a back-country loner scouting rural blacktops for roadkill.

That night at Wymans, no one seems to notice. Not that anyone, really, is there. Dave says, "Swift hat," in a way that means he doesn't care.

Days pass. Luke buys food the same as before, returns deposit bottles, recycles plastic, cardboard, paper, and glass. He cuts his grass, tends his garden. He buys a good safety razor and shaves his face to the skin. He is not sure it improves his appearance. Even to himself, he looks like a menace. Every few days, he buzzes his head with the clippers. He wears the camouflage hat to work, then takes to wearing it all the time. *Stay ready. Don't fuck up.* Into the reflecting pool Luke sprinkles copper sulfate to ward off algae. He brooms dust off the white stones, then leans the broom against a maple and takes a seat on the bench. He stares at the water's clean surface and tries to hear its voice and waits for enlightenment to visit his soul.

Mother lies in the cellar, in the cold, hard ground. It is a matter of days, possibly hours, until Cindy calls. He can put her off once or twice, he can try not answering the telephone for a time, but sooner or later he will need something to say.

Mother is traveling, an old friend called out of nowhere, said they should see the West, her treat, yes, that's right, Mother's not paying for a thing, it's a guided tour, some sort of package deal, no it's not charity, no we shouldn't be embarrassed, the woman offered and that's that, oh I don't remember, what does it matter, I mean what's the difference, Evelyn-Something, I think it began with W, well why would I, I don't see how it matters when she's on a guided tour with, you know, a professional tour guide and she's fine, she's fine, I tell you, she's out in Wyoming, yes that's right, Wyoming or maybe it's Idaho, no there aren't any phones, yes I'm sure, they're moving around a lot and I don't have a number, nope, yehup, I'm sure everything's fine, of course they would call if anything happened, of course I'm not worried.

Mother is in the hospital, something to do with her gall bladder, I can't tell you the details because I don't know, why should I, why am I supposed to, the doctor is taking care of it, of her, the nurses, no I'm not worried, no they don't have phones, the noise disturbs the elderly, crackles in their hearing aids, yes that's right it's a special ward, yes, yes, getting the best of care, yes she is, yes, well I suppose you could but the doctor is very busy, all you'll get is his answering service and why pester him is how I think, well if you really feel you have to, I don't have the number at my fingertips, I'll have to call you back, no I'm not kidding, do you think I wear it around my neck or maybe write it on my wrist, because I don't need to know it, it isn't necessary I tell you, she's fine, she is getting the best of care and I don't see any purpose in bugging the doctor, you know how they hate phones and anyway he doesn't know who you are, even if you could get him on the phone, which I doubt, he is not going to give out medical information, what they call divulge, about some elderly woman who might or might not be your—yes I know it's Mother we're talking about but he doesn't know that, the doctor I mean, does not know you are my sister, her daughter, so why don't you take a breath and when she's feeling well enough to come home I'll have her call you, all right?

Mother is sleeping, yes I know she's been sleeping the last six times you've called, no I don't worry about it, she sleeps a lot now, because she's old, is why, yes I think it's that simple, no I don't think anything is seriously wrong, no you don't have to fly in, that's crazy, now you're talking crazy, I'm here and I can take care of her just as well as you, well don't doubt it, just because I'm a man doesn't mean I don't know how to live with an elderly parent, take care of her I mean, yes you say that but I know you don't believe it, well then why don't you trust me, why don't you trust me to take care of her, she's my mother too, well all right then what are you saying, why don't you spell it out if I'm too stupid to understand hints and innuendos, well if that's what you think I don't see how you've let her live here this long, and anyway and anyway and anyway for your information if I'm doing such a bad job why doesn't she complain, has she ever said anything to you about being unhappy or not wanting to live here, no of course she hasn't because we get along fine, of course I'm not forgetting the money you send, no of course not, we couldn't get by without it, just try to understand that I'm doing my best and if Mother is tired it's no wonder, if you were her age and had been through what she's been through you'd be tired, too.

Luke can say he has moved Mother into assisted-living, that it was her choice, at her request—no, at her insistence, and no, she does not have a telephone, and yes, he needs extra money to cover the cost. He can say she is cranky and forgetful and does not want to talk on the phone ever again. He can say she ran away from home and left no forwarding address; that she is hiding under the bed and will not come out, come out; that she has lost the power of speech, the ability to hear; has disappeared in the night; that all of the above are true.

He can say a lot of things. What will they believe?

A maple leaf falls into the pool. It is still green and lies flat and supple on the water. Luke cannot hear the sound it makes: floating, limpid, permeable, so recently alive. He believes there is a sound, a soft, vegetable cry a leaf makes in dying—because it is dying, it began to die the moment it fell; and a sound should mark that passage. A low sound, small and very quiet, a sound like silence that is not silence—a final protest against the indignity of death. Of having to die.

Why does he think this? He has never thought it before. His father died silently and now Mother, too, has passed without a word. Unless, like a leaf's, their cries were too small. Perhaps all of us cry out at the end, too softly for anyone to hear.

He closes his eyes. It is almost over. He cannot get away with it. She is in the cellar, in the ground. He has put her there. When they find out, no one will save him. Cindy will not forgive what he has done. Matt and John will tell her they have always known he was capable of something like it. John will act as if he has always known. They will disown him. The authorities will take over.

He opens his eyes. Leans forward, tries to pluck the leaf off the water. It floats beyond his reach. Luke wants everything neat and clean. Tidy. Tucked-in. When they come, it will all look normal. The business in the cellar will seem like an aberration. An extreme act brought on by grief. A solitary son with no one in the world. A moment of madness. Except that hole took hours to dig. But even there, see, he put her away neatly, tucked her in. Nothing hasty or sloppy about it. *Tidy.* The house overall is in good order. Maybe not completely dust-free, okay, not perfectly spic-and-span, but he is keeping up with the kitchen, using just the upstairs bathroom and cleaning it, washing his clothes, keeping the animals fed. It is a normal house, a situation that is normal. He is a normal man, closely-barbered. True, most days are like a dream. He is not really there, except he is. He feels absent to himself, does not notice his own presence, as if another someone in his body were doing the chores and going to work, eating, washing, staking out street and sidewalk, his neighbor's yard, waiting for the next shoe to drop.

The leaf floats on the water. He cannot stop leaves from falling. Some will fall into the pool. At some point he will rake them out but not now, not just one that has fallen early. As he stares, something pelts it, knocks it under. It floats back to the surface and something pelts it again.

Out of nowhere the sky is raining shit. Turds are dropping into the pool.

Luke is too startled to move. Then he whips around and through a chink in the hedge sees his neighbor stalking off, spade in hand.

A turd has smeared his clean-shaven neck. Luke touches the spot, takes his hand away and sniffs his fingers. That's it: he smells like dogshit. He isn't dogshit but he smells like it. What has he done? He must be a terrible person, to deserve this. Dogshit on his neck, dogshit in his pool. Turds melting at the bottom. Smaller pieces float. The leaf has folded double with a turd in-between and hangs suspended between the surface of the pool and the mess deeper down.

Eat shit. The leaf has. It seems to be what his neighbor expects Luke to do. It is possible he did not know Luke was standing here when he threw dogshit over the hedge. In fact, it's likely he didn't know. But that really isn't the point, is it?

Eat shit. And die. Luke understands. No translation necessary. Doesn't need a picture, doesn't need a map. Wherever he goes, the message is the same. It is the single thing the world is telling him, has been telling him for years, for more years than he can count. Oh, he has always known. He has tried to ignore it—the idea being to answer bad with good, thereby bringing positive energy into the world. The world gives you shit? Don't fling it around, eat it, kick it back, or pass it on. Use it for fertilizer. Nurture something. Make goodness grow.

But not like this. Not when it is dumped on your head, when someone pelts you. There is a time for faith and best intentions, and there is a time for action.

He gets a shovel from his ruined garage and fishes shit from the pool. He stands at the edge for five seconds, then rounds the hedge and crosses the property line. Shovel in hand, shit on its blade. Luke just lets his hand turn over. Doesn't pitch or sling, just lets it fall like a leaf from a tree. Shit plops onto his neighbor's yard. The most natural thing in the world. He hopes his neighbor sees it. He hopes that asshole is watching. Who knows what might happen when he comes raging with his spade to return fire? Luke will be inside the house by then. In the nest. Watching.

F irst cool of September evening tells Leah Goldman a new phase is about to start. On foot toward home, she reminds herself that each season turns a page. She resolves, again, to stop seeing Max. It happened and then it happened again and now it has happened enough. Leah has convinced herself, she has cheated thoroughly and well and more than she intended. She has violated the commandment, her marriage vow, her husband's trust, her own body. Now she is ready to stop.

When she reaches her office and wakes up her screen and finds Max in her Inbox, again, she knows his message, "how about lunch?" is code for spending the hour with her legs spread.

"Not today," Leah types. "Not tomorrow or this week or next. I expect to be busy at home and to have neither time nor desire for lunch." And clicks **Send**.

The day passes as days do. Lunch Leah eats alone, truly eats, not minding that duck with orange and an eggroll are not on-diet. She will skip dinner, she will exercise more, harder, better, she will pretend these calories do not count. Her life is what she makes it. She is what she says she is. Anything she believes she can be, she will become.

Turning a corner and crossing a street, Leah asks herself how she will explain it to Armand. That he was dull and glum while Max was brilliant and interesting? It is most of the truth—is the truth, as far as it goes. And is still true, even if she is finished with Max.

And is that also true? Armand will ask. *How do you know? When did you decide? Why?*

Because it has to end, Leah will tell him, *so our marriage can go on.*

Will it? Only if Armand forgives. And Leah? Why does she want to stay married? Alessandro and Julietta will always be hers, always theirs. So why stay with Armand? Leah asks herself this question in so many words and realizes she has no reason, only a feeling. It is not even a good feeling, particularly, only strong and certain. She guesses it has to do with not wanting to break up their family and start over. Also, she is not ready to concede she was wrong. She continues to believe that Armand will turn himself around. She believes he can get past whatever is troubling him. That he can become again the Armand she loves.

She finds him in the kitchen with two spatulas, flipping shrimp one-by-one. The oven door is open, salads are made and dished. "Hi, honey," he says but his smile seems forced. "How was your day?"

Armand is not wearing an apron but the scene is pure '50's housewife getting hubby's dinner. If she were a drinker Leah expects he would have greeted her with martini in hand. Is this the man she married? She is glad he has fixed dinner, except she does not love shrimp breaded and baked. And the children don't like it, either. So Leah is faced with the fact that Armand has made dinner for himself and whoever is willing to eat one of his favorites. He finishes flipping shrimp and slides the baking dish back, shuts the oven door and sets the spatulas on the counter.

"Glad to see you, honey. Happy you're home."

"How did we decide the menu?" says Leah. "My day was fine, thank-you."

"I just cooked what was here. I'm making linguine with red sauce for Julietta. Alex is getting a hamburger." Leah notices a pot on the stove, steam rising, and a jar of organic tomato sauce with basil standing on the counter. When she moves closer she sees a hamburger inside the countertop broiler, its glass door canted open.

"You're quite the short-order cook."

"The kids don't like shrimp. I thought you wouldn't mind."

"No, I don't mind." She is not going to kiss him. If he tries to kiss her, she won't turn away and she won't invite it. She is not angry and it isn't that she dislikes him. She just is not going to kiss him, that's all. The feeling she has is not the feeling that makes her want anything like a kiss.

She drops her bag, drapes her sweater over a chair. Before Armand can approach her, she moves through the kitchen and into the dining room to check the mail. Finding nothing on the sideboard, Leah peeks out the window and sees catalogues and envelopes and what-all-else lying in the wicker basket on the front porch. When she opens the door, two cats bolt from the Adirondack chairs, startling her. They bound down the porch steps and tear across the yard. Leah is about to mutter, "Goddamn cats," as she steps onto the porch when the sight of a shotgun leaning in one corner makes the words die in her chest. She stares at the gun for fifteen seconds to be sure she is seeing what she thinks she sees. She does not touch it. She picks up the mail and goes inside.

"Armand?" she calls from the dining room. She drops bills and catalogues on the sideboard. "Dear? Why is there a shotgun on our porch?"

She hears him stop what he is doing. He comes into the dining room wiping his hands on a dishtowel, which he then slings over one shoulder. "Dinner's about ready," he says and moves close to her. His hands reach out and Leah lets him, then brushes him off.

"Stop. I asked you a question."

He shrugs. "Nothing. Just fooling around."

"You were fooling around with a shotgun."

"It's not loaded."

"With a shotgun, Armand."

"I'd love to blast those rotten cats."

"You're lucky no one saw you."

"I wasn't stalking. I stayed on the porch. And it isn't loaded."

"I should hope not. I want it put away in any case. Alessandro is already too interested in shooting things."

"That's just video games."

"Nevertheless. Please put it away." As she says this again, it dawns on Leah that Armand has brought a gun into the house without saying a word about it. It isn't that she thinks he needs permission, exactly, but she should have known. It is a real weapon, not a near-toy like the BB-gun on his wall. She says, "Armand, I didn't know you bought a shotgun."

"No, I guess you didn't." He is already moving toward the kitchen.

"Armand?"

"I have to get the shrimp out before they become rubber."

She follows. He has opened the oven door and pulled out the baking dish, which he sets on top of the burners.

"How long have you had it?"

"Weeks and weeks," he says, as if it were a set of tires. "I bought it the day I got Alex his game."

Leah blinks. "You've had a shotgun in the house for almost two months and I am finding out only now?"

"I guess. I mean, if you say you didn't know, then I guess that's right."

"Because you didn't tell me."

"There isn't anything to tell. It's a shotgun." He shrugs. "That's it."

"Maybe I don't want it in the house."

"Oh, don't be such a Nervous Nellie. It's harmless unless it's loaded. There's no ammunition."

"You didn't buy any, you're saying."

Armand nods. He is stirring Julietta's pasta with one hand, the tomato sauce with the other. "Right."

Leah is not sure what to make of this. Can he be lying to her face? "You're sure, Armand. You're not just saying that."

"Of course I'm sure. Look, I know I can't kill those cats. Even the BB-gun would be considered animal abuse. But that day Julietta slipped in shit. Again. *In our yard.* I got pretty worked up."

Leah shuts her eyes, shakes her head. When she looks at him again he is draining linguine through a colander. He waits for the water to stop, then returns the hot pasta to the pot and drizzles olive oil on it. He opens the broiler and slides Alex's hamburger onto a bun, then the bun onto a plate.

"Don't worry about it," he says. "I'm not planning anything crazy. And who knows? It might come in handy."

"Whatever can you mean?"

"As a bluff. If someone tries to fuck with us."

What is he saying? What is he *really* saying? Does he really, truly, honest-to-God *know*? "Armand, who do you think might ... bother us?"

"Oh, I don't know." He forks linguine into three small bowls and dresses the portions with steaming tomato sauce. "No one, most likely. But you hear stories about home invasion. Tattooed thugs force their way into a house and terrorize the people before they rob them. Pretty rare, but you never know. Also, there's the guy next door. Ever notice him? He's pretty strange. Has enough cats to start a pet store. Comes and goes at odd hours. Has a little pond with a bench next to it, where he likes to sit. Doesn't even read a newspaper, just sits there with his eyes closed. Lets his dogs crap our lawn. Of course you see his cats run wild. Pays more attention to shrubs than to people. Likes throwing dogshit into our yard. Never a word or a whistle, unless he's wolf-whistled you, which I'd expect if he didn't seem oblivious to other human beings."

Leah is fairly dazzled. She has not given their neighbor a second thought—hasn't thought of him at all except in terms of his shabby house and domestic menagerie. And here Armand is—what? Keeping tabs? At least noticing. "You obviously know him much better than I do," she says.

He waves this away as he sprinkles grated Parmesan onto Julietta's pasta. "I'm home all day, so I notice. The point is, I don't know him at all. He's a mystery. Could be a serial killer and we wouldn't know a thing about it."

"Of course not. But I wish you wouldn't talk that way. It gives me the creeps."

"That's exactly it! The creeps. It *is* creepy. I tell you, I've been picking up bad vibes for months. Since the beginning of summer, at least. I thought it was those cats, always prowling around and leaving shit everywhere. But no. Something is up."

Leah just looks at him. She can't tell how seriously she should take all this.

"Didn't you say dinner was ready? I think we should eat."

"Fine, fine. You get the kids, I'll get the food."

Leah rousts Alessandro and Julietta from their rooms and herds them downstairs. Armand serves up Julietta's linguine-with-red sauce, Alex's burger on a bun, and shrimp with salad for himself and Leah, pasta on the side. They sit and begin to eat.

For a minute no one speaks. Then Alex says, "It's the hardest flipping game I've ever played."

"What's that?" says Armand.

"*Hunting Old Sammie.* I can't get past level three."

"How many levels are there?"

"Twelve."

"Ouch. That is rough."

"Level Twelve is the parade down Fifth Avenue. You have to secure the route plus all of Manhattan from terrorists disguised as tourists. They try to free Old Sammie by running multiple suicide missions. If they succeed, the game starts over."

"Osama, Alex. His name is Osama."

"O-*sam*-ma, Old Sammie, whatever. I can't get anywhere near Level Twelve. I can't get out of Tora Bora. There are so many caves! And those terrorist assholes—"

"Alex!"

"He said a bad word!" Julietta cries, delighted.

"Sorry, mom. I forgot."

"Never mind," says Armand. "He's not going to do it again."

"I'll try. But it's pretty flipping tough."

Armand chews and swallows. He takes a mouthful of wine and napkins his lips. "It's supposed to be tough," he says. "It gives you some idea of what our troops have been going through in Afghanistan."

"You mean they're still there?" says Alex.

"Yes, they're still there. Al Qaeda is still hiding in the mountains. The Taliban are lurking, the tribes are free agents and not interested in supporting the central government. The national infrastructure is wrecked and the people are impoverished. I read that the farmers are growing opium again."

Alex's stare mixes amazement and horror. "I don't know any of that!" he says.

"Me, either," says Julietta. "I don't understand what daddy is saying!"

"What your father means," says Leah, setting down her fork, "is that real life is much more complicated than any game."

"But not as much fun," says Alex.

"That's right."

"Unless you're very, very lucky," says Armand. "Or unless you're a kid, like you and your sister."

"I want to be very, very lucky, too," says Julietta.

"You already are."

"We all are," says Leah. "We're all very lucky."

"How?"

"We don't live in Afghanistan, for one thing."

"Why would we live there?"

"We wouldn't necessarily live there, or anywhere," Armand says. "That's what I mean. It's possible we could live anywhere or nowhere, so we're lucky to live where we live."

"In Ithaca," says Alessandro.

"In Ithaca, yes. In this house, which pretty much anyone in Afghanistan would consider fit for a rich person, a tribal warlord or top-rank official. Also in this country, which is still one of the best places in the world to live."

"You mean the United States," says Julietta.

"Yes," says Armand. "That is what I mean. The United States of America. And we are lucky to live together—to have each other."

Leah could be mistaken but it sounds as if Armand is choking up. He gets sentimental when he thinks of the children. Despite his griping and foul moods and bad temper, he is a decent man who knows how fortunate he is.

"Where would we live if we didn't live together?" says Alex.

"Well, I don't know. I've never thought of living anywhere except with all of you."

His eyes are welling up, Leah can tell, though he covers it by pretending to laugh and blow his nose. He uses a napkin to wipe away what in another couple seconds would have become tears. The children do not seem to notice; Leah cannot be sure. But she does know she loves him at this moment. She wants to tell him what she has done, what she has been doing, because it has become a burden and she needs to tell someone and Armand, even after all these years, is still her best friend. But he is also her husband. How can she tell him? The children love him; he loves his family. How can she allow him to know about this thing? Their life: they have made it together and lived it and are living it. It is poison, the knowledge Leah feels she must share.

"We are all lucky," she says. "To be alive and live where we do and have each other."

"Yes. That's right. You kids should always remember that."

"We should all always remember it," says Leah. The children are saucer-eyed, staring at their strangely grateful parents. "Rosh Hashanah is coming up," she reminds them, "and we have a lot to be thankful for."

"A thought for the new year." Armand smiles. At last.

They finish their meal. Leah notes that Alessandro and Julietta eat everything on their plates. The table they clear together and

Leah rinses the dishes and racks them in the dishwasher. Armand brushes up the crumbs. The children go upstairs to play in their rooms. Leah says, "Thank-you for cooking," and Armand says, "You're welcome." He comes to her and puts his arms around her and hugs her. It is a big hug and he holds her for long time, and she lets him.

*

Later, Armand retrieves the shotgun. He carries it upstairs and, standing on a chair, puts it in the attic. He reaches this overhead lowspace through a small panel hinged at its top edge and built high into the wall of his office. The shotgun slips easily under the panel's bottom edge. Armand sets it well back, across three ceiling joists. He does not wrap the gun in oily rags or zipper it into a leather case, just lays it to rest above his head. It is not loaded.

Remembrance of a September day. The sky is the same perfect blue ruined three years ago by exploding glass and buckling steel, disintegrating concrete, black smoke and flames. Armand cannot believe three years have passed. Tomorrow is the anniversary. Today, thank God, is just an ordinary Friday. He delivers the children to school, sees Leah off to work with a kiss, finishes his coffee and then, teeth brushed, bowels moved, sets about his chores. He puts out garbage in its barrels, paper, glass and plastic in their bins. He vacuum-cleans carpets and sweeps hardwood floors. Later he might clean the bathrooms, if he is feeling nice, or, if not, leave them and hope Leah takes up sponge and scrub-brush. By mid-morning he is ready to paint. He gathers his gear and goes out determined to finish the house's shady side. He starts the hose and gives the stucco another rinse, having washed it yesterday with a cleanser guaranteed to remove grime. An up-close inspection reveals that forty unwashed years require a second effort. He gets a bucket, cleanser, and brush, and this time only half-dilutes the recommended amount. He applies the solution generously and scrubs, then rinses. While the stucco dries, Armand picks up the spade and makes his rounds.

Luke in his nest is re-reading *The 9/11 Commission Report* and asking himself how it is possible for us to have known about bin Laden, heard his pronouncements, read his words, learned his intentions, and yet to have done so little to kill him. The background is right here, all spelled out by way of creating context for what happened three years ago. Tomorrow is the anniversary; today is A-minus-1. Luke marks the moment by delving into the story again, committing to heart the timing and the moves, flight paths and logistics, failures of security and its near-success, the nightmare of two towers burning in the sky. We knew bin Laden! Knew his name and his purpose, knew his whereabouts, his expulsion from Saudi Arabia and sojourn in Sudan, his refuge in Afghanistan, his safe-caves in the mountains. Luke cannot believe Old Sammie has gotten away. That he survives.

Armand finds shit everywhere. Spade loaded, he turns a corner of the porch and starts up the driveway, where he finds another pile outside a basement window. He spades it up, then walks around back and finds a fourth calling-card not just on the patio but on the flagstones under the table at which they sometimes eat dinner.

It is too much. Too much to see, to smell, to clean up, to know is there. He sets the spade carefully in the grass so as not to spill and goes to the garage for a bucket. He finds a good old one that is perfect for the purpose. Has a hairline crack across its bottom and a handle that works, too. Armand sets it on the grass, lifts the spade and lets the turds tumble in. He scrapes up the shit from under the table and tips it into the bucket. He completes his circuit of the house along its shady side, where the stucco is almost ready for a coat of masonry primer and where he finds yet one more pile of moist, glistening shit, absolutely fresh. He is not surprised, which tells him how far out of hand this situation is.

Armand totes the bucket across the property line into his neighbor's yard. This time he does not fling feces at Jethro's house or lob turds into his pond. Instead, he leaves the whole filthy business right outside the fat bastard's front door, where ol' Jethro cannot fail to find it.

Head sweating under camouflage, Luke sees his neighbor coming at him. He loses sight of him behind a corner of the house but the bucket looked loaded. Is this asshole really about to ring Luke's bell? To ask about shit? Not what it is, everyone knows that, but where it has come from. As if Luke knows—and at the same time, as if the answer weren't obvious.

He starts down the stairs. Luke wants to be sure: hear the bell, see that asshole, watch what he does. It goes without saying he won't open the door. Because what does this guy intend? What is he about to do? It can't be about Mother; he has never seen her, Luke is pretty sure. He might not realize she was living in the Cape. The Robideau Cape: their home all these years. If John and Cindy do not help him, Luke will be priced out. This neighbor came along, paid over the ask, drove up assessments all over the neighborhood. And now, what?—he's knocking on doors to gloat?

When he gets downstairs it isn't the doorbell he hears, it is plastic knocking on concrete. He assumes it's the bucket; that his neighbor has set it on his front stoop. Two seconds later Luke sees him going the other way, walking fast past the windows with his hands in his pockets. If he isn't mistaken, this grown-up so-called man has on purpose and with malice aforethought left shit outside his door.

Luke peeks past Mother's curtains and sure enough. Shit in a beige bucket. The asshole has shit on him.

The stucco having dried, Armand opens a fresh can of primer and pours half a yard into a rolling pan. He dips a deep-nap roller head, loads it up, rolls it even, lifts it clear. The primer goes on thick and white. Armand works it into crevices, presses it in, rolls it out. He loads the roller repeatedly and applies the primer, slowly covering the shady side of the house. The plush roller is heavy with gooey semi-liquid. Craggy stucco resists being covered, seems almost to repel the primer. Armand has played out to its limit the telescoping painter's pole and when he reaches up high the weight of the saturated roller feels to have doubled. His arms and shoulders strain against the dumb desire of the roller head to fall. Armand works for an hour, goes inside for water and returns to work an hour more. He finishes a bit before noon. He lids the can, hoses the roller clean and sets it in the sun to dry. He returns to the house and showers, puts on fresh clothes and heads off to Collegetown for a Chinese-food reward.

Leah at Asia House in a window seat is staring at a plate of moo goo gai pan when a touch comes on her shoulder.

"Mind if I join you?" Max says. He stands there holding a plate of Pork Surprise and twin eggrolls, in his other hand a bowl of egg-drop soup. On his face is a mocking sneer, Leah cannot tell for whom.

"Nice lunch," she says.

"You've done a hell of a job avoiding me."

"Absolutely," she says.

Max takes the chair opposite. "It doesn't have to be this way," he says as if he's quoting from something.

"Yes, it does."

"We can be friends," Max says. "Of course we can."

"No," says Leah. "We can be friendly. That's all. Too much has happened."

They eat for several minutes without speaking. *This is horrible,* Leah thinks. It is worse than being married.

Max finishes quickly, stands, picks up his plate. "All right," he says. "Friendly."

Before Leah can discourage him, he leans down and kisses her on the cheek.

Armand about a block away sees through the window of Asia House some guy kissing his wife. He keeps coming, walking faster, thinking, *All right. I knew. Now I'll kill the fucker.* The guy is out the door, however, before Armand gets there. All that stops him from running the bastard down is the fact that he recognizes him. Max-Something-man: a half-fledged prof whom Leah has introduced a couple times as "My Friend." So, okay, what he saw was not what he thought he saw. Armand knows Leah and Max-Something-man eat lunch together pretty often. Once-a-week, maybe more. Nothing wrong with that. Lunch does not imply something sinister. That little good-bye kiss, which anyway was on the cheek, isn't necessarily some cheap bit of sweet post-coital whatever. Tenderness. A friendly kiss between friends.

On the other hand, maybe a little too familiar. Armand, still walking, thinks about it, and the more he thinks the more he does not like the look of it. Maybe for no reason other than that he himself does not kiss Leah half as often as he once did. She seems not to want him to kiss her. *So who is this Max,* his thought runs on, until he reaches Asia House and goes inside and walks up to the table where Leah is pushing her food around with a fork. With a smile and "Like some company?" unsaid on his lips, Armand is surprised by her surprised eyes looking up to find him before he can speak.

I am not fucking around.
Luke in yellow rubber gloves running halfway up his forearms wonders how large it is, his window of opportunity. He has seen his neighbor walk off in clean clothes. A lunch date will keep him at least half an hour and what Luke plans will take about that long. He brings the dogs—not that Rex or Speckles or Barney is a killer, but they will give hell if his neighbor returns too soon. He crosses the side-yard to the freshly-primed stucco. He reaches his rubber-gloved right hand into the beige bucket and comes up with a turd.

Luke rears back and throws shit hard against his neighbor's house.

He will have this mess in his eyes for a while—this wall faces Luke's windows—but that's okay. Snug in the nest, Luke won't mind watching the progress of air-dried shit, not to mention his neighbor—stiff-necked, fists clenched, incensed—drudge through washing and repainting. He dips into the bucket for a second load, brings up a big one and heaves. It spatters like grease and sticks in chunks. He presses his hand into it, drags it across the stucco, makes sure to work it into nooks and hollows, mixes it with the half-dried primer in an abominable, medium-brown outrage that resembles diarrhea. It occurs to him that his neighbor will know who has done this. That's fine, too. It is nothing but payback. Shit in his pool, assessment driven up. Mother in the cellar. It seems to Luke that he does not have much left to lose.

Methodically, quickly but not rushing, he empties the bucket. Dips, heaves, smears. In twenty minutes, the stucco is atrocious. An atrocity of household defilement. Luke figures it will take a whole day to clean. He will watch from the nest.

Armand and Leah are finishing their food. It has been pleasant and he thinks they ought to do it more often. That's how he is: Armand thinks they ought to do everything more often. He does not know what Leah thinks. In a way he can't quite name, things have felt better between them. Less tense. Friendlier. They still haven't had sex in nearly forever. Armand cannot recall when it last happened but he knows they have broken every terrible record for abstinence by going all summer without. It is always too hot or too late or Leah is too tired, the kids are around, she is not in the mood. Always something, as if it were some kind of experiment in particle physics where each of several thousand variables has to be precisely-just-so right down to the least nano-whatever for the thing to happen.

Maybe it's a joke. Or is it a sign? Just let him find out she is fucking someone. Just let him. Then see what he does. Maybe he'll kill everyone. But Armand does not want to think about that now and maybe does not want to think about it ever.

He says, "How is your friend Max?"

"Max is fine," Leah says, eyes on her plate. "He and his wife recently had a baby."

"Yes, I think I remember knowing that. Boy?"

"Girl. They're calling her Miriam."

"Ah. Nice name. Have you seen her?"

"Of course not. She's an infant, they don't parade her around."

"I meant a picture."

"Oh." Leah looks away as if she has to think about this. "No. Max hasn't shown any. I don't think he carries one."

"What makes you say that?"

Leah shrugs. "He doesn't seem the type."

Luke leaves the bucket. It belongs to his neighbor, right? Like the shit, he has it coming to him. Luke knows he is in for a fight. Are they going to face-off on the side-yard and fling dogshit at each other? Or will they just stand inches apart, get right up in each other's face, and take turns screaming, "Asshole!"? In for a dollar, in for a dime. Luke has guns. He does not think his neighbor is armed.

He herds the dogs inside and locks the door. He gets some quick lunch: a salami stick, a hunk of aged cheddar broken off the brick he has finally splurged on, a bag of kettle-fried potato chips. He refills his canteen and carries everything up to the nest. Careful not to crush the chips or let the salami slip, Luke settles in. He takes a bite of cheddar and chews, then a swallow of water, wiping his lips with his hand, his fingers against his jeans. He figures it's pretty simple from here on out. A little more time will pass; they will know what he has done; they will come for him. He can let himself be taken peaceably or he can resist. He might kill three or four, maybe half-a-dozen before they respect him as a serious shooter.

He pinches the chip bag on opposite sides of its top seam and delicately pulls. The seam opens with a soft *pop*. Luke shovels up a handful. The chips are oil-crisp and salt-crunchy, delicious in his mouth. He plans to polish off the bag. Still chewing, he takes a nice bite of salami. It mixes with the chips, toothsome and succulent, and he follows-up with a bite of cheddar, wondering if it is possible that they won't come for him, after all. Mother did not know anyone anymore. Only Luke knows she is gone. No one else knew she was alive. It might be possible for him to live here some time. Forging her signature. Cashing her checks.

Keep a low profile. Disappear.

Sitting in the nest, salami and cheddar a riot in his mouth, Luke considers. It is worth his while to think closely about what he will say to his neighbor. About what he will do.

Halfway up the front walk, Armand sees it. His first look is not enough to tell him what it is. Even standing in front of the stucco, he is not sure what has happened. It is only when he steps close and smells the odor that stains his days and haunts his nights that Armand understands. He does not have to see the good old bucket, bottom-cracked and lying on its side, to know who has done it. Looks fresh, too: of course Jethro got busy while he was at lunch and seeing something he did not understand. A man kissing his wife. Max. Whom Leah calls a friend; whose own wife has recently given birth to a baby girl. All that is one thing. The thing in front of him, shit-smeared stucco, is something else. It cannot be that one has anything to do with the other. That they are related in any way. It is just the coincidence—the fact that they have occurred at more or less the same time—that gives Armand the feeling that people are laughing at him.

Right? Max-Something-man does not know Jethro, who does not know him. Armand does not know Jethro's true name and is shaky on Max's last name. Like Alex's confusion about bin Laden. *Osama, Old Sammie.* It wasn't Jethro whom Armand saw kissing

Leah. Max hasn't smeared shit onto the freshly-primed stucco of Armand's house. Where he lives with Leah. He doesn't fuck Leah but he does still live with her. Who fucks Leah? Anyone? Why are they throwing shit at him? But it's Jethro—not "they." And the shit hasn't just been thrown, has it? To Armand it looks ground-in, which would require the use of a hand, or hands. Also a certain amount of anger. Armand himself is pretty angry most of the time and all he has done is flip a little shit here and there, at most fling it with a spade. And not so much! The amount of manipulated fecal matter on Armand's house is shocking. Jethro must be in a rage. And why? Well, Armand did leave the bucket outside his door. It is curious that Jethro knew exactly who had done it. Not the least doubt, judging from his right-back-at-you. But it was nothing, just a bucket of dogshit. Which belongs to Jethro, yes? Belongs to Jethro's dogs, for whom the fat man is responsible. Why is he blaming Armand for returning to him what is rightfully his? Shit to which he is entitled. And now Armand has to clean the mess.

He picks up the hose, for once not minding that he has forgotten to turn off the leaky spigot, and shoots a stream at the house. Water explodes against stucco and bounces off, taking bits of shit with it. Armand stands back, he doesn't want crap on his skin or in his hair, and gives the wall a good, long dousing. The shit comes off, for the most part, not having had time to crust-over, but leaves a brown residue that will require scrubbing. When he sees he will have to get the cleanser again, Armand finally gets angry. Oh, he was always annoyed but he was also incredulous and a bit bemused, as if the beshitted stucco were the key scene of a farce he and his neighbor were separately acting. It never quite seemed funny but it did seem absurd. Now, as he contemplates the extra work, Armand realizes how much Jethro hates him. He and his anti-Semitic mother. They hate him and they have him at bay and are creeping in for the kill.

Armand drops the hose, turns off the spigot. He goes into the house and up the stairs to his office, where he stands on a chair to retrieve the shotgun.

Up in the nest, Luke is laughing. He could not see the guy's face but just the way he stood there with his fists on his hips, staring at that fouled wall, was worth the price of admission. He finishes the chips and takes a long drink of water. What's left of the salami and cheddar he saves for later. A snack before dinner. Unless his neighbor stages some sort of action before then. If there's a show, Luke will have to nibble something while he watches. He is a little disappointed about how easily the crap rinsed off. Still, it left a lot of good stains. All in all, he is satisfied. Not that it's over. Not by a long shot.

He should have bought ammo. Couldn't buy it when he bought the gun but he should have gone back sometime for a box of shells. He would be loading the chambers right now instead of holding the shotgun and wondering what to do with it, as if it's his dick. Armand thinks he can bluff them. The mother likely won't stage a frontal assault but Jethro might bull-rush him, mutts barking at his heels. Armand peers from a window at the ramshackle Cape. No sign of life; no malicious intent, manifest or implicit. Maybe he is making it up. Imagining it. Maybe shit on stucco is as far as Jethro goes. No mistaking the message, though, is there? Armand pumps the mechanism, wishing again for a couple rounds. He wouldn't need more than two. That's the beauty of a shotgun: you can't miss.

He steps back, leans into a shadow. He can wait. All in all, he is a patient man. Just waiting for his wife to spread her legs has made him the patron saint of patience. Also forbearance. Never would he have expected such a state of affairs but now it seems like a discipline, a practice that has prepared him for the even more difficult thing he must do.

Watching from the nest, Luke is damned if he doesn't see his neighbor walk out his front door with a shotgun in his hand. Just like that. Holds it as if it were a shovel, muzzle pointed at the ground. What is this asshole up to? He will be lucky if someone doesn't call the police. Not Luke, of course. But someone. Even if he isn't aiming the shotgun, someone is going to get nervous. Out in the woods, hunting pheasants or deer or maybe wild pig, a shotgun is a regular thing. But in a residential neighborhood, well, the law has plenty to say about it. If cops drive up fast and see him before he drops the gun, they might shoot him where he stands, ask questions later. That would really be something. Luke would have a ringside seat. For a thing you don't see every day: a man shot and killed right before your eyes. Or maybe just wounded. Could be the cops would shoot to wound, so long as he didn't point the gun at them.

A citizen shot by police and gravely wounded. An ordinary man fired upon. A neighborhood man shot and killed on his front lawn after threatening police with a shotgun. Better not say "gravely." It's like "grave." *A local man gunned down.* A selfish, unfriendly bastard. A Johnny-come-lately. A cruel, nasty prick known to torment domestic pets and throw shit at his neighbors. His neighbor.

Luke would not be sorry. It would not bother him to see it happen. They only thing that worries him is whether they will want to talk to him afterwards. Say they decide an inquiry is called for; say they want or need to investigate the use of deadly force, especially if the cops killed him. Shot to maim but killed him instead. And now Internal Affairs has questions and needs answers and so wants to talk to Luke. A couple detectives, tall men in suits, can they come in, sit in the parlor, the kitchen, wherever, and talk?

About what?

Ask him a few questions related to what he saw, what it looked like and where he was watching from and so forth and before you know it, before he knows what he is saying, one thing leads to another and God alone knows the things he will tell them.

Outside, Armand is not sure what he is doing. The shotgun is not loaded and although that is important it does not seem to be the point. He walks around his yard, slowly, slowly, as if he is guarding something he can lose. Something everyone wants and anyone can take from him. He does not think he can name it, it isn't anything as simple as his house or his Benz, but he knows it, whatever it is, belongs to him only as long as he can defend it.

Truth is, he feels a little ridiculous out here with a gun, as if Old Sammie were about to invade Cooper Circle with a dagger in his teeth and plastique under his turban. He guesses he would feel even sillier if the gun were loaded. Not that anyone can tell it isn't. Armand thinks about setting it down, maybe leaning it against the maple, but finds he does not want to let it go. It cannot protect him, it is useless unless he swings it like a bat. But no one knows that.

Maybe he is just putting everyone on notice. *It isn't loaded but it can be.* To buy a box of shells is nothing, to load a couple rounds is simple. As easy as that, Armand, finally, would be armed. Potent, as in possessing potential. To do, to act. To bring about the change he wants to see in the world. That he is dangerous goes without saying.

No one would know. From all appearances, he is a normal guy. So maybe he should get back inside before people see him and start wagging their tongues. He would lose his advantage. For what? Is he planning something?

A cat flashes past, a blur from nowhere, as if it is reading his thoughts. Just kidding, Armand raises the shotgun and takes phony aim. *Just kidding.* The gun isn't loaded and anyway the cat is long gone. Armand could not kill it if he wanted to.

In the nest, Luke sees the sonovabitch raise his weapon and draw a bead. *What the hell is that?* As he sets his rifle it crosses his mind that you do not have to aim a shotgun very carefully to hit your target. He scopes-in on this reckless motherfucker and in his crosshairs sees him grinning. The guy's face looks crazy, as if he has gone haywire. Maybe he has had a stroke or is suffering a seizure or has just discovered his wife is screwing some guy, and now he doesn't care where he is or what he is doing. Has the shotgun cocked and shouldered and looks ready to fire.

Shoot to wound. Shoot to kill.

It is happening quickly and Luke cannot think that fast, not with a cruel bastard in his crosshairs about to pull the trigger. In a residential neighborhood firing a gun is murderous: high density of human beings and plenty of soft tissue that low-velocity lead shot will tear and shred. Someone is going to be killed.

No, Luke thinks, *don't do it,* and moves his crosshairs off the guy's head, shifts his aim down and right to that shoulder, and fires.

Armand hears a flat crack the instant his shoulder takes a hammer-blow. The shotgun flies from his hands and spins to the ground. He goes down to his knees, then falls forward as the burn flames up. Armand knows he has been shot but he does not understand how. The shooter must have been in front of him, but where? Hiding where? At what distance? Pain sets in big and hot and he can think only of Leah and the children. Julietta's eyes. The sound of Alessandro's voice. His great, bright smile. Julietta's eyelashes. *Buggy whips.* Leah's face, her fair, soft skin. He cannot feel his arm; it lies lifeless beside him. Armand sees blood spreading on the ground, seeping in.

He lies on his patchwork lawn, sorry he could not get grass to grow. His face rests on a stray tuft but most of his body is in dirt. There is so much he has not done, so many things he has neglected. He does not want to leave Alessandro and Julietta. They are just children. Armand believes they love him. And Leah? Armand loves Leah; he does not want to leave her, either. He does not want her to leave him. Maybe she would be happier if he dies. She would be free, there would be insurance money and she could begin again and he would not be around to hurt her. What has happened between them, he cannot explain. He has wanted only the best and somehow has made wrong choices and spoiled things. But he loves her. Armand thinks of Leah now, feeling blood hot beneath his chest. He tries to see her naked, to remember at last how beautiful she is. So beautiful: a woman's body. *Leah.* She has gone so far away from him and he wants to bring her back. To call her; say, *Here I am. It's still me, Armand.* He tries to call her, to say her name.

Leah. Leah.

He is so tired, his body weak and sleepy. His blood is hot and the ground is warm and he is cold. Legs, chest, everything. So cold, here in the sunlight of a September afternoon.

It is better if he dies. Armand does not want to die but maybe it does not matter. Maybe if he prays, he will not die; or maybe prayer will persuade God to take him quickly, without awful lingering and pain. What prayer can Armand say? "Our Father ..." "Holy Mary ..." No, no. Those prayers mean nothing to him anymore. There is just one prayer, an ancient blessing said for children, the prayer Leah says each Friday night. And the words? Armand is too sleepy to remember, too stupid to know the Hebrew, beautiful Hebrew words that sometimes seem to rhyme or repeat. *Y'simha Elohim ... mena shah. Y'simeyh Elohim ... v'leya. Y'va-reh'ha Adonai ... reha. Ya-eyr Adonai panav ... neka. Yisa Adonai panav ... l'ha shalom.* He doesn't know, can't find it or remember, and it, too, is falling away from him, is retreating, sinking, fading into the past. The lost and gone struggle of his unappreciated life.

He is a stupid man. He has not paid the right kind of attention and now he has nothing to lift him up, bear him on. Armand wants to sob, he wants to cry out, just softly, but has no voice.

The shadow seems deep and as it begins to close around him the words come, the fine English words of the ancient prayer he has heard many times and realizes he loves. He hears the words in Leah's voice.

May the Lord bless you and keep you.

May the Lord cause His spirit to shine upon you and be gracious unto you.

May the Lord turn His spirit unto you and grant you peace.

Come spring, Leah Goldman sits on her porch with a mug of tea and watches men unloading a truck at the house next-door. She tries not to eyeball the proceedings too closely but cannot help looking for hints. Mostly she is keen on signs of children her own children's age: a half-size bicycle, a swing set, bedroom furniture for a young boy or girl. It would be nice to have neighbors who might become friends. She hopes the woman is not too pretty; that the husband, whatever he is or does, turns out to be just interesting enough. Leah does not want complications. God knows she has had enough for a lifetime. She hopes for something normal: ordinary people more or less her age, a husband and wife with two pleasant, reasonably intelligent children and no strange habits. No cats, no pets of any kind unless they live inside a cage or tank. No special interest in ornamental shrubs or Zen meditation. No woe-begotten impulse to bury their mothers in the cellar. The neighborhood is sedate, middle-class, unremarkable. Ordinary people living private lives. No one is looking for excitement.

Leah sips her tea and thinks about chocolate and almond biscotti. They are waiting in her kitchen, whispering her name. The men are bringing in boxes variously labeled "Dining room" and

"Kitchen" and "Bob's first box" in black-ink marker. There are quite a few such boxes, not overly many but quite a few, and near the end Leah notices "Mary's first box" and "Tracy's toys" and feels it is all to the good. When the parade of furniture begins she feels herself losing interest. Her tea gone, she rises from the Adirondack chair and returns to the kitchen to see about those biscotti, sealed in a plastic container and left temptingly on the countertop.

When she pops the lid, Leah finds just four are left. Two almond, two chocolate. She knows she herself has not eaten that many; someone has been at them. Julietta is the likely culprit but if he could find no sweeter treat, Alessandro might have gone for them, too. Not that biscotti are off-limits. They are common property, first come, first served, but because they are Leah's favorites she feels a bit territorial about them. The chocolate, especially, are something of which she likes to have plenty.

The children are at school. She cannot cross-examine them on the subject of who ate what. She can, however, hide the final four and that is what she does: transfers them to a smaller container and slips it into the pantry in a way that is invisible to every eye but her own. Leah wants to eat all four biscotti but first she has to lay-in another pound. Today is not a groceries day, however, so it will have to wait.

It is a strange arrangement, this working-from-home. Taking a tea-break on her porch. Standing in her kitchen in the middle of the morning and thinking about treats. Leah wakes her computer and clicks through email but her heart is not in it, her mind miles away. Everyone is asking about Reunion and although it will be here in six weeks Leah cannot get excited. Her plans are in place; the only thing left for her to worry about is the weather, but as she cannot stop it from raining or being too cool or too hot, she has let that go. What she mostly wants from that weekend in June is no surprises: no lost reservations, lost children, lost keys, misplaced wallets or purses or cell phones, no lost minds. No alums, elderly or otherwise, suffering sudden heart trouble; no outbreaks of flu or food poisoning; no equatorial-scale swarms of mosquitoes. And so on. Because if something goes wrong, she catches the blame.

Leah sleeps her computer and returns to the porch. The men are hauling in a washer-and-dryer combo: front-loading, high-efficiency. Leah is satisfied; they are real people, whoever they are, a real family with plenty of stuff and lives that make sense, and she cannot help thinking, *Thank God.* Not that another recluse with sketchy finances and deadly weapons could have bought the house and renovated it, given what everything costs. Even with a forced sale, the price was fairly high. That was lucky because the house, shabby as it was, turned out to be the only thing worth diddley what's-his-name had. Their former neighbor; the guy Armand called Jethro. That wasn't his real name, just something Armand made up in one of his snider moods. It did not come close to paying the award in full—paid, in fact, much less than half—but the money was consolation after what they had been through. Leah was not about to refuse it.

She wants to wonder about the new people but stops herself. *Let it happen,* she tells herself. *Just let it be. Whatever it is will be better than what was.* It's lucky most of the stuff sails past in boxes. If she could really see what they own, her imagination would run in every direction. As it is, she is embroidering hopes about the little girl, Tracy, along the lines of making her a happy playmate for Julietta. Her daughter needs something, Leah feels, a special friend all her own. Alessandro seems more self-sufficient. As long as he has his video games he seems unaware that other people exist.

Julietta. Alessandro. They love their father. Armand has always been their favorite, usually in spite of himself. It is the genius of children: to forgive so readily, always wanting to trust and believe the best. It is a beautiful thing, this love that is pure and freely given. *Wizards of affection.* It brings Leah's heart into her throat just to think it, to stand on her porch and have the phrase pass through her mind. *My beautiful children,* she wants to say out loud but she hasn't reached the point of talking to herself. How can she tell them how important they are? What words are enough to say how much she loves them? To Leah they are miracles, most of all for showing her, teaching her, a way to love their father.

Armand. He is not the easiest person to live with. Leah looks around, wondering where he has gone. He was here not long ago and now he has wandered off to God knows where. Didn't say a word about where he was going—just vanished. Leah wants him to watch the move-in, dull as it is, and to talk with her about Alessandro and Julietta. She knows he belongs to her in a way no one else can; and that she can love him, no matter how crazy he sometimes seems, if she makes the choice to do so, again and again. Shoveling small-animal excrement onto his neighbor's property; carrying around a shotgun and stalking neighborhood cats. She knows she cannot love Armand as the children do. They have taught her that, as well. But if she lets herself feel it every day, she can recognize the man she first knew when they were young. The man for whom she would have done anything and whom she wishes to love even now—even if he is troubled, and far from perfect.

She wipes away tears. How silly, to be standing here weeping about nothing in full view of whoever might pass by. In the middle of what should be a workday—what by rights is a workday, if she could get her heart in it. Something about being home distracts her. But weeping! On her front porch! Why can't she at least stay in the house? Leah is not one to be sad. She does not mope and sigh. And she is not sad now, she realizes, but grateful. She still has her life. She risked losing part of it, a very great part, then she stopped and the threat passed and she escaped. Survived. Maybe she was lucky. She is content to consider herself just-so. In light of Armand's secret war, which she learned of only after it was too late, her transgressions seem somehow even worse.

Unpunished, Leah feels herself blessed. Oh, it is foolish, a foolish thing, to stand on her porch waxing sentimental in heart and mind! It is not her, it is not what she does. But she is doing it now and seems unable to stop. And anyone can see her! From the sidewalk, from the street, passing in a car, from a window of any house—see her weeping! What might anyone think of so ridiculous a sight? Even as she hopes no one is watching, Leah sees through tears that someone is there. Oh, how embarrassing! She cannot tell if it is a neighbor or someone from off-block walking a dog or just out for a stroll. Tears have turned her vision blurry, have nearly blinded her, and before she can clear her eyes and see it is him, Armand turns up their walk with roses cradled in his arm and calls, "Leah! See what I have for you!"

THE END

About the Author

John Lauricella was born in Brooklyn, New York, and grew up in Scotch Plains, New Jersey, where he attended the public schools. He studied fiction-writing with Frederick Busch at Colgate University, was elected to Phi Beta Kappa, and graduated *magna cum laude*. Later, he earned an M.F.A. in creative writing and a Ph.D. in English at Cornell University. He is the author of *Home Games: Essays on Baseball Fiction* (McFarland & Company, 1999), and has published fiction in *Arts & Letters: Journal of Contemporary Culture*, and in *Stone Canoe: A Journal of Arts, Literature, and Social Commentary*. He has taught fiction-writing, expository writing, and personal essay writing (as well as courses in the American novel, British modernism, and the poetry and prose of Renaissance England) at several colleges and universities. Other episodes of meager gainful employment include stints as a library archivist, golf caddie, commercial freelance writer, proofreader, and copy-editor. He completed the first draft of *Hunting Old Sammie* in January 2010. His second novel, *2094*, is forthcoming from Irving Place Editions. He writes these quixotic fictions in a small room under the eaves of the old bungalow he shares with his wife and children in Ithaca, New York, where they have lived since 2001.

Acknowledgements

Paul Cody read the manuscript and offered encouragement when the author was most in need. I am grateful for his guidance, his patience, and his friendship.

Risa Mish has tolerated the author's quarter-century-long infatuation with a cruel and withholding muse. I cannot say "Thank you" often enough.

For Daniel and Julia: May the Lord bless you and keep you.

Absent members: Augie Grevers; Tony Casesa; John A. Lauricella IV; Grandma Rose and Grandpa Nick; John A. Lauricella III and Martha Caponigri; Emma, Albert, Augie, Emily, Hannah, Georgie, and Salvatore; "Little" Anthony; Betty; Anna.

To enduring family, especially Lucille Lauricella (Rinaldi): You are present to me always.

Made in the USA
Charleston, SC
10 August 2013